FIND
MY
GIRL

BOOKS BY WILLOW ROSE

DETECTIVE BILLIE ANN WILDE SERIES

Don't Let Her Go

Then She's Gone

In Her Grave

EMMA FROST MYTSERIES

Itsy Bitsy Spider

Miss Polly Had a Dolly

Run, Run, as Fast as You Can

Cross Your Heart and Hope to Die

Peek a Boo, I See You

Tweedledum and Tweedledee

Easy as One, Two, Three

There's No Place Like Home

Needles and Pins

Where the Wild Roses Grow

Waltzing Matilda

Drip Drop Dead

Black Frost

FIND MY GIRL

WILLOW ROSE

bookouture

Published by Bookouture in 2024

An imprint of Storyfire Ltd.
Carmelite House
50 Victoria Embankment
London EC4Y 0DZ

www.bookouture.com

The authorised representative in the EEA is Hachette Ireland
8 Castlecourt Centre
Dublin 15 D15 XTP3
Ireland
(email: info@hbgi.ie)

ISBN: 978-1-83618-221-4
eBook ISBN: 978-1-83618-220-7

ONE

MADISON

Madison's feet pounded the spongy earth of the swamplands as she darted past trees cloaked in shadow, whispers of sunlight overhead. The world around was a blur, every second propelling her deeper into the labyrinth of nature's making.

The mangroves loomed large, their limbs twisted and entangling into grotesque shapes that formed an almost impenetrable wall of foliage, their skeletal fingers reaching towards the sky. The air was thick with moisture and the cloying scent of decay that rose from the murky waters. The only sound she could hear as she made her own frantic passage was the water moving, and the occasional splash that felt far too close for comfort.

"Keep moving," she whispered, the words lost to the vastness of the swamps. Her imaginative mind, usually filled with fairy-tale fantasies, now conjured unseen horrors lurking within the crooked embrace of the trees. Madison knew these woods, had explored them with the wide-eyed wonder of a child under her mother's watchful eye. But this was different—this was no game, no adventure. This was survival.

With each stride, she felt the oppressive gaze of the forest upon her, as if it were a living entity, watching, waiting. The trees seemed to lean closer, their branches interlocking to form a tunnel that seemed to stretch into infinity. A shiver traced its way down her spine from the sensation of being hunted.

Her eyes were wide and darting, every sound magnified in her ears. Her heartbeat thundered, deafening her senses. But she couldn't afford to slow down or stumble now. She pressed on, pushing through the dense swampy undergrowth with determination and desperation. One wrong move could mean the end for her. But she couldn't let it be the end. Not here. Not now.

A branch snapped behind her.

Madison froze, her ears straining, but the swamp remained silent, holding its breath along with her.

"You gotta keep moving," she whispered again, urging her body forward.

She knew this land well. It was her land. The knowledge fueled her courage and sharpened her instincts. Left here—there's a sinkhole, hidden beneath foliage. Right—solid ground awaited her. Without hesitation, she veered right.

She skirted a familiar patch of quickmud, expertly avoiding it while being mindful of other traps. She knew this place better than anyone. The swamp whispered secrets to her, revealing paths and pitfalls that only she could hear. And she used them to gain ground on her pursuer.

She ducked into a narrow gap between twisted trunks, branches clawing at her clothes like desperate hands. But Madison knew—they always gave way for her, the daughter of the swampland. She hoped they would trap and confuse her pursuer.

Sweat dripped into her eyes, stinging, as she ducked behind the massive trunk of an ancient cypress tree. Her chest heaved against the rough bark she pressed into, becoming one with the shadows.

"Where'd you go, girl?" A voice, disembodied, drifted through the trees. It was closer now. Too close.

She pressed a hand over her mouth, stifling a desperate gasp. The heat clung to her like a second skin, oppressive, suffocating. She could feel every bead of sweat that rolled down her temple, the way her damp hair stuck to her neck. Insects buzzed angrily in the heavy air, adding to her terror.

Another branch snapped. Madison's heart skipped. She slid lower, her legs folding beneath her as she crouched in the mud, the cool sludge a minor relief against her overheated flesh.

"Come out, come out." The taunt was sing-song, a predator playing with its prey.

Madison didn't hesitate. With a swift glance to ensure she wasn't seen, she slipped into the murky waters beside her, wading with careful steps to avoid ripples. The water was thick, warm, wrapping around her like a living entity. She held her breath, submerged up to her chin, eyes just above the surface, watching.

"Lost her..."

The words from her pursuer were a growl of frustration, drifting across the swamp. They were searching, flitting from shadow to shadow, so close she could hear their labored breathing.

She stayed motionless, a statue, as minutes stretched into eternity. Only when the sounds of pursuit faded into the distance did she allow herself to rise, taking in great lungfuls of the muggy air.

TWO

JOANNE

Joanne glanced at her watch again. The bus stop was a hive of activity, mothers clustered together, chatting about the science fair and soccer practice.

"Did you see the volcano Emily made?" one mother laughed, her eyes bright with pride.

"My kid covered my kitchen in baking soda," another replied, rolling her eyes but unable to hide a smile.

Joanne offered a small grin, nodding along. They all shared this daily ritual, a moment of camaraderie before their children's return.

"Madison's got gymnastics today," she chimed in, while checking her watch once more. "I just hope the bus hurries up."

"Always late, isn't it?" A mother nearby sympathized, her arms crossed as she peered down the road.

"Every day," Joanne sighed. "And we can't be late again, not for the recital."

"Madison will make it," the woman assured her, patting Joanne's arm gently.

"Thanks, Carol," Joanne said, forcing a smile as she tucked

a strand of wavy brown hair behind her ear, though her eyes flickered with concern. "Fingers crossed."

The engine's rumble cut through the chatter. Heads turned, eyes lifted. The yellow giant rounded the corner, its approach stirring a collective breath held in anticipation.

"Here they come," someone murmured.

Joanne edged forward, her fingers entwined tightly. Each child that stepped off was a beat of hope.

"Over here, Jake!" Carol signaled to her son, a whirlwind of energy and flying backpack straps.

"Thank goodness they're finally here," Joanne whispered more to herself than anyone else, scanning heads for a familiar ponytail, a flash of Madison's favorite pink jacket.

"Look at them," another voice joined in, "like bees swarming out."

"Madison?" Joanne called out softly, then louder, "Madison!"

A gap appeared in the stream of kids; no more followed. Her pulse thrummed, a drumbeat of dread. No sign of her daughter.

"Madison?" The name fell from Joanne's lips, each syllable laced with a growing unease. Her gaze darted through the dispersing cluster of children, hoping for a glimpse of her daughter's bright smile or the glint of sunlight off her silky hair.

"Have you seen Madison?" she asked one of the mothers, concerned.

She shook her head. Joanne's breath hitched, a cold knot forming in her stomach.

"Madison!" The call was louder now, edged with urgency. Children scattered to their waiting parents as Joanne's search grew frantic, each face blurring into the next, none belonging to her little girl.

"Excuse me," Joanne said, her approach to the bus driver

almost a sprint. The door was starting to close, the driver preparing to pull away. "Wait!"

"Something wrong?" The bus driver's face, normally so jovial, mirrored Joanne's concern.

"Madison," she panted, "my daughter—she didn't come off the bus."

"Madison, Madison..." The driver tapped his temple, scrolling through mental images of the countless faces he ferried each day. "I don't recall seeing her today. Maybe—"

"No, no, she should've been on this bus." Joanne's words tumbled out in a torrent, her mind reeling. The realization that something was amiss constricted her throat, her friendly and approachable nature dissolving into raw fear.

"Madison," the driver repeated, his round face creasing with genuine worry. "I'm sure she didn't board today. Thought maybe she was getting picked up by car."

"By car?" Joanne's voice cracked. "No, she was supposed to be on the bus. She always goes home on the bus. She is never picked up by car."

She tried to piece together an image of the morning, searching for any deviation from routine that could explain Madison's absence.

"Let me call the school," she said, more to herself than to the bus driver, whose eyes followed her with concern etched deeply into his features.

Joanne fumbled with her phone, her fingers trembling as if they belonged to someone else. Each digit she pressed felt heavy, uncooperative. Finally, the call connected, and she waited for the line to pick up, her chest tight, her breathing shallow.

"Hello, Riverview Elementary, how can I help you?" The receptionist's voice crackled through the phone.

"Madison Harris. She... she didn't get off the bus. I need to know—"

"Just a moment, Mrs. Harris." Papers shuffled on the other end of the line, a keyboard clacked. Silence stretched.

"Mrs. Harris, Madison was marked absent for the entire day."

"Absent?" Joanne's heart skipped, then hammered against her ribs. "That's impossible. She went to school this morning. She—"

"Are you sure?"

"Yes, I'm certain," Joanne said, panic rising. Her mind spun, images of Madison's smiling face that morning blurring with fear.

"Well, she hasn't been to any of her classes today as far as I can see."

Joanne swallowed. The Florida school system would let you know if your kid was absent for one or more periods that day, but not till five o'clock when the automated calls went out.

"Thank you," she whispered and ended the call. The weight of the phone felt like lead in her shaking hand as she called around to the few parents she knew whose children Madison usually hung out with. But no one had seen Madison that day, and the friends said she wasn't in school. No one had seen her all day. Hands trembling, Joanne called John.

"John," she said when he answered, voice barely above a whisper, but sharp, urgent. "It's Joanne. Madison... she wasn't on the bus."

"What do you mean?" His voice was flat, distant.

"What I said. Madison wasn't on the bus, and now the school says she was absent all day."

"Absent? But I..." There was a pause, a hesitation that pricked at Joanne's skin. "I dropped her off this morning."

"Where, John?" Her words were ice, her grip on the phone tightening. "Where did you drop her off?"

"Near the school," he replied, too casually. "She wanted to walk the last block."

"Near the school?" A tremble started deep in her core, spreading to her limbs. "Why would you—"

"Joanne, she doesn't like to be seen with me in front of her friends. You know this."

"Something's wrong, John. Really wrong."

"Okay, okay, let's not jump to conclusions. We'll find her. Try calling some of her friends, maybe she went home with somebody?"

"Near the school isn't *at* the school, John. Why would you do that?" Her voice was sharp, a knife-edge of suspicion cutting through her fear. She was angry and needed to get it out. Now.

"Look, she asked to be dropped off there," John's voice held a hint of irritation. "She wanted to feel grown-up, I guess."

"Feel grown-up?" Madison was careful, not one to take risks. "That doesn't make sense."

"Maybe she just wanted to walk a little," he suggested, but his tone didn't match the words, it lacked conviction.

"Something's not right," Joanne insisted. Her fingertips were numb as they clung to the phone. "I'm calling the police."

"Wait, Joanne—"

But she had already disconnected, her heart thumping against her ribs like a wild thing caged. The air felt too thick to breathe as she dialed 911.

"Police, please, my daughter is missing," she said, the words spilling out in a torrent. "Madison Harris. She's ten years old. She didn't come home from school today."

"Okay, ma'am. Take a deep breath for me. We're here to help," the dispatcher's calm voice instructed. "Can you give me your location?"

Joanne rattled off her address, struggling to keep her voice steady. The world narrowed to the sound of her own ragged breathing and the dispatcher's questions.

"Was anyone else supposed to pick her up?" the dispatcher asked.

"No, no one. She always takes the bus. But today..." Joanne faltered.

"Stay where you are, Mrs. Harris. An officer is on the way. We'll do everything we can to find your daughter."

"Please," Joanne whispered into the phone. "Find my little girl."

Tears brimmed in her eyes, blurring the suburban landscape into a watery tableau. She crushed the phone against her ear, the plastic creaking under the strain of her grip.

"Mrs. Harris, help is on the way," the dispatcher repeated, a lifeline thrown across the chasm of Joanne's despair.

"Thank you," she choked out, barely audible. She ended the call, her hand shaking so violently that the phone clattered to the concrete.

"Joanne?" A concerned mother approached, who had seen the stress on Joanne's face and decided to stay behind, her face etched with worry. "Is everything all right?"

"Madison. She's missing." The confession tore from Joanne's throat raw and ragged.

"Missing?" The word echoed among the few remaining parents, murmurs rising.

"Stay here," one of the mothers instructed. "We'll ask around."

Heads nodded in agreement, but Joanne barely registered the flurry of activity as parents dispersed in different directions talking to their children in hushed tones.

"John said he dropped her off near school," Joanne muttered to herself, piecing together the fragments of her conversation with her husband. Her mind raced through every possible scenario, each more terrifying than the last.

"Did she say anything this morning? Anything that could be a clue to where she's gone?" another mother asked, trying to be helpful. "Maybe she skipped? Was she nervous for some reason? Anxious about going to school?"

"Nothing. Just-just a normal day. I went to work, John dropped her off. Like we always do." Joanne's voice broke as the truth of the situation settled upon her shoulders, a weight too heavy to bear.

She paced back and forth, the bus stop now a cage trapping her in this moment of horror. Her gaze darted to every passing car, every shadow in the distance, searching for any sign of her little girl. A police cruiser stopped and the door opened.

"Mrs. Harris?" A uniformed officer approached, his expression somber.

"Officer, please," Joanne begged, her words tumbling over each other. "My daughter..."

"We're going to start a search immediately," he assured her, his voice firm. "I need you to come with me. We'll need more information."

"Of course," Joanne stammered, following him to the patrol car, her legs numb and unsteady.

As she sat in the backseat, the cruiser's radio crackled with dispatches and updates, a cacophony of urgency. Joanne's world had shrunk to this single, all-consuming quest. Her friendly, approachable demeanor had vanished, replaced by a mother's primal fear.

"Find my girl," she whispered once more, a mantra against the encroaching dread. Each tick of the clock stretched longer than the last. Every second without Madison was an eternity.

THREE

BILLIE ANN

I heaved the last box through the doorway, the cardboard coarse against my palms. It was a typical sweltering day in Florida. The apartment door swung shut with a creak and soft thud, a sound that resonated with the finality of my new reality. I had taken the day off for this, trading the chaos of the department for personal upheaval.

Exhausted, my muscles ached, and an inner weariness was etched into lines of sorrow on my forehead that felt as permanent as the gun I wore on my hip daily. Dropping the box unceremoniously onto the scuffed tile floor, I scanned the space that was now mine alone.

All alone.

The air was stale, tinged with the scent of paint and old memories that didn't belong to me. Exposed walls stared back at me, indifferent to their new occupant. My gaze drifted across the room, landing on the unmade bed in the corner, its mattress bare and unwelcoming.

"Home," I whispered to the emptiness, the word ironic not comforting. "Sweet home. I guess."

I drew in a deep breath, my chest rising and falling with the remembrance of everything that had led me to this moment. My hands, steady when they needed to be behind the trigger or wrapped around a suspect's wrists, now betrayed a tremor as I reached into the box before me. One by one, I pulled out the remnants of a life that once was—spatulas that had flipped pancakes on Sunday mornings, books with dog-eared pages marking late-night reads, notepads filled with scribbled case notes—all finding their new places within these four walls.

It wasn't until my fingers brushed against the cool glass of a frame that my motions stilled, the frame nearly slipping from my grasp. The grinning faces of my three children looked back at me, their smiles preserved in a moment untouched by the turmoil that had since unfolded. Two months—time that felt both like forever and a stolen instant. Two months since those smiles were part of my every day.

"Hey, kiddos," I whispered, tracing a thumb over the glass where their faces beamed up at me.

The judge's words came back to haunt me, cold and final. Joe had been granted full custody. A safe environment for the children—that was what they said I lacked. It was ironic that, as a detective who ensured the safety of others, I couldn't provide it for my own children in the eyes of the court. Of course, Joe and the kids stayed at the house too, which meant I had this empty space to fill and a mountain to climb if I ever wanted to hear their laughter again. I was given two months to find somewhere else to live. And this was it. A small two-bedroom apartment. It was close to the beach, that was the only positive thing I could say about it.

"Stay out of trouble," my lawyer had advised, as if trouble were a stray cat I could shoo from my doorstep. Not crimes I was responsible for investigating. Yet there I was, starting from scratch, every unpacked item a step toward building that so-called suitable environment.

"Trouble's the last thing I need," I told the framed smiles. But trouble, as always, had a knack for finding me.

Gently, I set the framed photograph on a small, second-hand table I had salvaged from a thrift store. The wood was scuffed, bearing the marks of a previous life—much like my own. The kids' grins seemed to brighten the otherwise drab apartment, their joy a stark contrast to the barren walls and unpacked boxes that surrounded me.

"Okay," I said to them, as if they could hear me, "this is it. Our new start." My voice was steady, betraying none of the turmoil inside. I would make this work; I had to. Every decision from here on out was for them—for those smiles to not just be a memory but a future reality in this very space.

I turned away, the image of their faces etched into my mind, and reached for the next box. It was nondescript, save for the label I had scrawled across it in a moment of bitterness: "Divorce Papers." My fingers brushed against the cardboard, and for a moment, I felt the weight of every signed page, every accusation and defense.

"Move forward, Billie Ann," I said, steeling myself with the resolve that had carried me through countless crime scenes and interrogations. With one swift motion, I opened the box, not allowing myself to look at the contents—those were past arguments, past pains.

I lifted the stack of papers, thick and cumbersome, hesitating only briefly as memories flashed—a happier time, a different life, promises made and broken. Then, resolutely, I placed it on the top shelf of an old bookcase. Out of sight, but never entirely out of mind. It was a necessary part of my history, but it wouldn't define my future.

The door cracked open, a gust of stifling Florida heat ushering in my parents. I watched them step into the apartment, their eyes instantly sweeping over the peeling paint, the sagging shelves, and the stained carpet that told tales of tenants past.

"Billie Ann," my father began, concerned, as he ran a hand through his graying hair, "is this really where you're going to live?"

My mother's lips pressed into a thin line, her gaze lingering on the dented refrigerator. "It's so... small," she said, disappointed.

I leaned against the kitchen counter, arms folded. "It's all I need for now," I replied, keeping my tone level.

"Sweetie, your choices..." She trailed off.

"Mom, Dad, we're not doing this again." I cut in quickly, before the familiar lecture could take shape.

"Billie Ann, we don't understand why you had to turn away from the life you built," my father said, the lines in his forehead deepening. "You didn't have to choose this... lifestyle."

"Joe got the house because he has the kids," I reminded them, though it felt like explaining gravity.

"Your sudden change," my mother interjected, "it ruined everything. You put this upon yourself." Her hand found the cross on her necklace, thumb rubbing it as if to draw strength. "Leviticus says—"

"Please, Mom." I was firm, but the sting was there, sharp beneath my ribs. "This is my life. My work is all I have right now."

They looked at me, their kind faces struggling to mask the disapproval etched deep within. In their silence, the distance between us filled with years of disagreement, too wide for any bridge of words or faith.

"Can we just... not do this today?" I asked, the plea evident despite my resolve. I suddenly regretted accepting their help with the move, but they were the ones who had gotten me the apartment through a contact from their church. I wasn't a fan of their church, but I was desperate so I had taken the help I could get. Besides, it was nice to have a few extra hands to carry things. Plus, my dad had a truck so we could bring it all in one load.

My mother nodded slowly, the quoted scripture left unspoken. We stood there, a family divided by belief and love, each of us holding onto our own version of salvation.

My father's gaze met my mother's, a silent conversation passing between them. Their shoulders sagged subtly, the lines of their faces softening into resignation. They had come here with hope, cloaked in the armor of their convictions, but it was clear that the battle had been lost before it even began.

"Billie Ann," my father started, his voice a low rumble of defeat. "We just want what's best for you."

"I know, Dad." My voice echoed in the sparse room. "And I appreciate that. But this is what's best for me right now."

Finally, my mother sighed, a sound that carried the weight of her world.

"All right, honey," she said, her eyes avoiding mine. "We'll leave it be."

The tension in the room lingered, but just as the silence threatened to suffocate us all, the shrill ring of my phone shattered the moment.

"Excuse me," I said, reaching for the device on the counter. The caller ID flashed Chief Harold's name, and instantly, my pulse quickened.

"Chief," I answered, my voice steady despite the storm inside.

"Billie Ann, I'm sorry to call you on your day off," Chief Harold's gravelly tone came through, concerned. "But we've got a situation—a missing child. Ten-year-old girl, Madison Harris. Her mother reported her missing just an hour ago."

"Understood," I replied, the detective in me springing to life, pushing aside personal turmoil. "I can be there—"

"Normally, I would not pull you away on a day like today,"

she interrupted, urgency seeping through. "But it's urgent, Billie Ann. I wouldn't call if it weren't."

"Give me fifteen minutes," I assured her, already mentally cataloging what I would need from my scantily stocked apartment.

"Thanks. And Billie Ann?" There was a pause, and I could almost picture the Chief's stern face softening. "This is the type of thing that will scare everyone in the community, so be as discreet as possible."

"Always am, Chief." I pulled the phone away from my face and looked at my parents, leaving the Chief still on the line.

"Mom, Dad, I have to go," I said, the mantle of my profession settling around my shoulders like a familiar coat.

"Of course, dear," my mother said, though her eyes betrayed her worry.

"Be safe, Billie Ann," my father added, the earlier tension giving way to parental concern.

With a brief nod, I grabbed my gun and badge from the table, leaving their disappointment behind. Today, I had a higher calling, one that transcended personal grievances—a little girl needed me.

"Madison was last seen when her stepdad dropped her off at school," Chief Harold's voice crackled through the line, sharpening my focus, as I put the phone back against my ear. "We need eyes on the ground. Time's not on our side."

"Got it." My grip on the phone tightened, resolve hardening in my veins. I scanned the barren apartment, its emptiness now a distant concern compared to the urgency of a child's life hanging in the balance.

"Get in here and I'll brief you."

"Will do, Chief." I ended the call, my heart thrumming a rapid beat in my chest. There was no time for hesitation, no room for doubt. This was what I did, who I was—a protector, a seeker of truth.

Keys jingled as I snatched them up. I slipped my gun, cool and weighty, into its holster, a familiar presence at my hip. My badge, glinting dully in the sparse light, found its place beside it —an emblem of authority and duty. These were the tools of my trade, extensions of my will to bring order to chaos, to find Madison Harris before it was too late.

"Billie Ann?" My mother's voice was fraught with worry, but I couldn't afford to look back.

"Keep the faith, Mom," I said, already at the door. "I've got work to do."

The click of the door closing behind me severed the last tie to that cramped space. My steps echoed down the hallway, each one a pledge.

The hallway blurred, my stride eating up the distance to the stairwell. Behind me, I left words unsaid, lingering in the air like the stifling Florida heat. The door to the outside world swung open with a push of my shoulder, and sunlight assaulted my senses, a stark contrast to the dimness I'd left behind.

"Madison Harris," I whispered under my breath, her name a silent vow on my lips. My skin prickled, not just from the humidity that enveloped me but from urgency.

Pavement radiated heat as I crossed to where my car sat, an unremarkable chunk of metal.

I yanked the door open, the creaking hinges protesting. The car's interior was an oven, waves of heat rolling out as if challenging my resolve. Ignoring it, I slid inside, my hand already reaching for the ignition.

The engine roared to life, a growl that matched the ferocity of my purpose. In the rearview mirror, I caught a fleeting glimpse of my reflection—short blonde hair plastered to my forehead, eyes fierce with determination.

"Find her," I commanded myself, the steering wheel a firm anchor under my hands. With a smooth motion, I reversed out of the spot, tires eager to bite into the road.

I threw the car into drive, cranking up the AC to high. The station wasn't far, but every second felt like an age when a child's life hung in the balance. My jaw clenched, my grip tightening. Madison Harris needed me, and I wouldn't let her down. Not now, not ever.

I killed the engine and was out, my boots striking the pavement with sharp taps. The glass doors slid open at my approach.

"Detective Wilde," the desk sergeant nodded, noting the tightness in my face.

"Chief Harold?" My question came like a bullet; short, precise.

"In her office, waiting for you." He pointed without another word.

I bypassed the murmurs of the bullpen, the usual clatter of keyboards and phones an inconsequential buzz in my periphery. There was only one voice I needed to hear, one conversation that mattered.

The door to Chief Harold's office stood ajar, her silhouette framed against the blinds. I rapped twice on the metal, announcing myself more out of protocol than necessity.

"Come in, Billie Ann." Her voice was gravel, heavy with responsibility.

I stepped inside, squared my shoulders.

"Sit down." Chief Harold gestured to the chair opposite her desk, but I remained standing, energy coursing through me too restless to contain. "Kid's been gone eight hours," she started, eyes scanning my face for signs of readiness. "Mom's panicked. No one has seen her since she was dropped off by stepdad near the school this morning at 7:45."

"Search parties?"

"Organizing. But we need to lead, Billie Ann. We need your head in the game."

"Of course," I replied without missing a beat. "Is this a kidnapping? Any suspects?"

"Too early to tell." Chief Harold leaned back, her chair creaking under the shift. "She could still just be skipping school. I've seen it before. But time's not our friend."

"Got it."

"Tom and Scott will work with you. Keep me updated."

"Will do."

"Billie Ann," Chief Harold called as I turned to leave. I paused, half-expecting a reprimand, a reminder to keep personal affairs from clouding judgment.

"Bring her home."

"Nothing else matters," I assured, my tone leaving no room for doubt. With that, I strode out, the mission clear, my purpose singular. Find Madison Harris. Bring her home.

FOUR

BILLIE ANN

I left the Chief's office and the familiar buzz of the precinct hit me. I could see countless officers busy with paperwork, on phones and deep in conversation. But I couldn't see Scott and Tom.

"Where are you guys?" I muttered under my breath.

Desks cluttered with paperwork and half-empty coffee cups spanned the room.

Scott's curls bobbed above a monitor, oblivious to the chaos of uniforms and suits around us. They'd be dealing with thefts, road traffic accidents and neighborly disputes. I could hear the hum of less urgent conversations. I picked up the pace, weaving between the islands of activity. His fingers danced over keys, lost in a world of code and data.

"Scott," I called out, but he didn't hear.

Closing in, I reached out and tapped his shoulder. The contact snapped him back to reality, his head jerking up.

"Billie Ann!" He blinked rapidly, pushing his hair from his eyes. "You startled me."

"Sorry," I said, not really sorry. "But we've got work to do." I leaned in so that my words wouldn't drift into the hum of the precinct. "We have a missing child, Madison Harris. She's ten. Vanished on her way to school this morning."

Scott's posture straightened, the playful light in his eyes replaced by sharp focus. "Sounds urgent?"

"Exactly," I confirmed, glancing over my shoulder to ensure confidentiality. "Time's not on our side. I need you to comb through everything on Joanne and John Harris. They're not known to Chief Harold. I can't recall them either. Look into them and their backgrounds. Something might give us a lead or at least a picture of who they are."

"Got it," Scott replied, his fingers already poised above the keyboard.

"Any known associates? Any recent disputes?" His questions came quick and precise, mirroring his keystrokes.

"Check socials, emails, financials—the works," I instructed, watching as the glow from the screen painted his face in a flicker of blues and whites. His curls shook with each rapid movement. "Anything that smells off, I want to know." My gaze fixed on the monitor. The online world was a breadcrumb trail that could lead us to Madison—or nowhere at all.

The aroma of coffee hit me before Tom's looming figure came into view. He handed me a cup, steam curling like whispers into the air.

"Thanks," I said, taking a grateful sip.

The coffee warmed my insides, but did nothing to ease the chill of urgency. I updated him. "I need you on the ground. A team is already at the school, and they'll need coordinating. Talk to people at the school. Kids and teachers. Sweep the perimeter, then the Harris place and neighborhood."

"Got it." Tom's voice was steady, his large hands already reaching for his phone.

"Cover every blade of grass," I added, locking eyes with him. "Playgrounds, parks, alleyways—leave no stone unturned."

"Understood." With a nod, Tom turned away, his strides purposeful as he dialed the first number.

I swiveled back to Scott, who was submerged in a sea of information. "Got something," he announced. I was shocked he'd found something so quickly and leaned in to see what it was. There was the trace of an edge in his voice.

"Spill it," I urged, my pulse ticking up a notch.

"John Harris has an arrest for battery on his record. It happened at a bar three years ago. It's minor stuff, but it's there." His fingers paused, hovering over a revelation.

"Keep digging," I pressed.

"Will do," he affirmed, his focus never wavering from the glow of the monitor.

With Scott on the digital trail and Tom mobilizing the physical search, the wheels of justice were turning, every second propelling us forward in the hunt for Madison.

Chief Harold had told me Joanne Harris was waiting in one of our interview rooms. The police had brought her in after her initial call. She was waiting for news on her daughter; desperate for us to simply tell her Madison had been found at a local park, safe and sound. She wanted us to tell her that her little girl was at a friend's house, that another mother had driven her home, and she was tucked up in bed asleep already. She wanted us to tell her that it would all be okay. But it wasn't that simple. I was about to tell her that she still hadn't been found. And I knew most threats to children came from behind closed doors. I was about to ask Joanne questions she might not want to answer.

FIVE

BILLIE ANN

The door creaked open, and I caught a glimpse of Joanne huddled in the corner. Her trembling form was barely visible in the dim light, all but her disheveled hair and her once perfectly done mascara running down her face. She clutched a crumpled tissue in her hand. As I stepped into the room, I saw her gaze flicker toward me, but she quickly looked away. Her body tensed as I spoke, and I could see the agony etched on her face. Joanne Harris—a broken shell of a woman consumed by fear.

"Joanne Harris?" I tried to make my voice as gentle as possible. "I'm Detective Billie Ann Wilde."

Her eyes met mine, filled with a mixture of pleading and despair. I offered a small smile, knowing words were inadequate in this situation. I had seen in the report she was in her late thirties, and I was surprised to see how much she looked like her daughter, from the picture of Madison she had provided to us.

"Thank you for waiting to speak with me," I said, pulling up a chair beside her with careful movements. "I know Chief Harold mentioned that I'll be leading the search for Madison."

"Anything... anything if it helps find Madison." Joanne's voice trembled.

I flipped open my notepad, pen poised. "I need you to tell me about your daughter. I need to know everything about her. When was the last time you saw her?"

"That would be this morning. Before I left for work. I woke her up with a kiss and told her it was time to get up. John takes her to school because I have to be at work early. But according to the school she never made it this morning. I don't understand how that's possible."

"That's what we will try and find out," I said. "Has she a history of skipping school? Maybe to go and hang out with friends? Does she have older friends? Girls she knows who wouldn't be at school?"

She scoffed. "No. Not my Madison. She gets awarded perfect attendance every month. She never misses a day."

"I see. Any friends who might have talked her into taking off and playing rebel?" I asked.

"Not my Madison. She would never. She's ten years old."

I nodded and wrote a note on my pad. Parents always think their children are angels. They're shocked the first time their daughters break the rules. It didn't mean Madison hadn't skipped school. But it was obvious it made her angry that I would question her daughter's innocence, so I tried another approach.

"What else can you tell me about her?" I asked. "What does she like to do? Favorite places to go. Where should we look for her?"

"Madison." A ghost of a smile touched Joanne's lips. "She's my heart." She looked down at her hands, and I watched a tear escape and drip on the table. "She loves to be outside, and is always looking for adventures in the backyard. She's imaginative... she creates these intricate stories in her mind and is able to play independently for hours all alone."

"Sounds like a bright girl." I scribbled a note, *imaginative, outdoorsy.* "Any changes recently? Anything at all?"

"There was— She's been quieter. Staying home more and not hanging out with her friends as much as she used to. She would often go biking around the neighborhood, and sometimes they would go fishing by the canals, or go to the beach, but not lately." Joanne's fingers twisted the damp tissue. "I thought she was just growing up, you know? But maybe..."

"Sometimes kids go through phases. It's normal." My reassurance felt hollow, even to my ears. But I could sense her blaming herself already. I didn't want her to feel that way. "Her friends at school, any issues there?"

Joanne shook her head, the wavy brown hair falling over her face. "No, she's loved. A gentle soul, feels everything deeply."

Empathetic, I wrote down, my brain already filing it away. Kids who are empathetic are often too trusting.

"Any best friends whose homes she often goes to?"

"She's got one best friend, Anissa, but they haven't been hanging out a lot these past few months. I think they might have had some sort of falling out."

"Last name and address?"

"Watson. She lives on Capri Road, four-seven-zero. But I already called Janell—Anissa's mom—and she said they haven't seen Madison in months and she thought maybe they were not friends anymore."

"It happens, sometimes they just outgrow one another," I said, writing the name down. "But we will still check out her and her home as well, in case Madison went home with Anissa from school or something. I'm sure you already called them but just to be sure. Does Madison have a phone?"

She shook her head. "No, not yet. We were hoping to be able to avoid it till middle school, but some of the kids in her class have one, and I guess it won't be long before she wants one too."

"*We* is you and John, is it?" I asked.

"Yes. My husband John. He's Madison's stepdad—her biological dad left when she was just a baby."

I nodded. "That must have been hard."

She smiled, nodding in agreement with me. "John has been like a father to her since we met eight years ago. I work as a nurse at Health First, the urgent care clinic, and have to be in early in the morning, so he always takes care of her and makes sure she gets to school on time."

"I understand John dropped Madison off this morning."

"Yes. He always does. They get on well. And like I said, I have work in the mornings. But that means I'm home in the afternoon when she gets back on the bus. John is on his way here from work now."

I watched Joanne as she spoke, and I wondered if her words were rehearsed. Was she trying to reassure me? Trying to make sure she had the opportunity to tell me John was a good guy before I even asked?

"It wouldn't be unusual if a young girl and her stepdad didn't get along..." I let my comment linger.

Joanne sighed. "It's not perfect, you know? But they try their best, both of them."

"Do they fight?" I asked quickly.

"Not a lot, but it happens."

"What do they typically fight about if they do fight?" I pushed her.

"Just stupid stuff like her eating food in her room and leaving a plate in there too long so it's hard to clean. Or if she plays computer games and it's too loud. John never had children of his own but I feel like he cares for her, genuinely. He always does his share when it comes to looking after her, and he has been good to her these past eight years we have been together. He's the only father she has known."

"Does she have a favorite spot she might go to when she's upset or needs alone time?" I pressed on, knowing each detail painted a clearer picture of the missing piece in this puzzle. She could have had a fight with the stepdad on the way to school and run off to cry or clear her mind somewhere.

"Under the old oak in our yard. She calls it her 'thinking place.'" Joanne's expression darkened.

"Okay, I assume you've already checked for clues there, but we will go through the entire neighborhood, and your house and yard once more," I assured her, snapping the notepad shut. "We're doing everything we can, Joanne."

"Please," her whisper hung in the air, "just find my baby girl."

"Trust me, we won't stop until we do," I promised, standing up. Her story had given me more than just notes; it gave me a glimpse into Madison's world, and now it was up to us to bring her back to it. I wasn't sure I fully trusted Joanne, and I needed to speak to John.

"Your help means more than you know," I told Joanne, the warmth in my voice belying the steel in my resolve.

"Thank you," she murmured, clutching the crumpled tissue like a lifeline.

"Stay strong, Joanne. We're on it." I touched her shoulder lightly, then turned and walked out of the room, the door closing with a soft click behind me.

* * *

Scott's back was to me when I returned to his desk, his curly hair a wild silhouette against the glow of his computer screen. I pulled up a chair beside him, the legs scraping against the floor.

"Scott, what do we have?" My voice interrupted his concentration.

"Billie," he said without looking up, his fingers pausing mid-stroke. "I found something... about John."

"Hit me," I leaned forward, elbows on knees, ready for the punch.

"More convictions. Old ones," Scott replied, finally locking eyes with mine. "Burglary, assault. Did time in Juvie."

"Anything recent?"

"Clean slate since marrying Joanne. But I dug deeper—"

"Of course you did," I interrupted with a half-smile, pride seeping through the tension.

"Found an alias. Look." He turned the screen toward me, revealing a Facebook profile with John's picture but under a different name. "I did a reversed search for his photo and found several like these across other social media platforms."

"Using an alias," I echoed, mind racing. "Shady. He's hiding stuff."

"Seems so."

"Could be him cheating with other women or chatting them up online. Any ties to Madison's disappearance?"

"None yet. But this guy... he's not clean, Billie. I have this feeling. There's more under the surface."

"Keep digging," I said, standing up. "We need everything."

"Will do."

"Thanks, Scott." I patted his shoulder.

"Next, we talk to the stepdad," I stated, already strategizing our approach. "When he gets here. I was told he was on his way."

"Ready when you are," Scott said.

"Tom, what's the status?" I asked as he strode back into view, a brisk energy in his step.

"Search teams are prepped, Billie. Dogs are sniffing around Madison's school and her home. Choppers are up, scanning from above. Boats are beginning to patrol the waterways," he reported, setting his coffee on the edge of my desk with a thud that suggested urgency.

"Good work." I nodded, telling him about Madison's normal

hiding place and scribbling a note on the pad before me. My hand was steady, but inside, a storm of worry raged. "Keep me posted. Any lead, no matter how small."

"Got it, boss." He flashed a thumbs-up, his expression tight with concern.

"Thanks, Tom." I turned back to Scott, eyes narrowed on the glow of his screen. "We're piecing this together, Scott. Starting with John."

"Right. Stepdad's our next move. When he arrives, we grill him." Scott's gaze didn't waver from his display, but I caught the firm set of his jaw.

I swiveled in my chair, the leather creaking under me. Scott's fingertips danced on the keyboard. The screen flickered with images and text as he sifted through John Harris's digital life.

I stood up, restless energy propelling me across the room. Tom was on the phone, his voice low and urgent. He cupped the receiver, caught my eye.

"I have officers taking statements from Madison's friends at school. We're also talking to the teachers. Unless you want to do any of that yourself?"

"That's fine. I want to focus on John right now."

He nodded returned to the call, coordinating with the precision of a maestro.

Back at my desk, I raked a hand through my pixie cut, willing the tension from my scalp. This case, it wasn't just about Madison. It was a chance for me to prove myself. If I could find her, perhaps I could earn some brownie points with the courts. If I could save a child, then they could hardly say it was too dangerous for my children to be with me. Could they?

The station hummed with action, each officer a cog in a larger machine. I could feel the energy of the hunt, the collective drive. We were all parts of a whole, and every move mattered. My team—Scott with his knack for uncovering secrets hidden in bytes and pixels, Tom with his brute strength and gentle spirit—they were extensions of my own determination.

"The stepdad's here," Tom said, this time coming closer.

"Let's go then." I pushed off the desk, every muscle tensed for the confrontation.

SIX

Then

Sweat trickled down Lucy Everhart's spine as the last chord from Kyle's guitar faded into silence. The audience's applause, warm and appreciative, lingered in the air even as they settled back into their pews. She caught her breath, heart still racing from their performance, when a hush rippled through the audience. This was their fifth gig in just as many weeks, and all had been in churches, but they had been well paying. As they left the stage, they went and sat with the congregation.

"Let us open our hearts to the Lord's messenger," announced a deacon, his voice both grand and solemn.

All eyes turned toward the pulpit where Amelia Hawthorne stood, an aura of serenity framing her silver hair. Her brown eyes seemed to glow with an inner light as she opened the leather-bound Bible with tender reverence.

"Beloved," her voice began, soft yet carrying effortlessly to every corner of the church. "Today we speak of love—the kind that doesn't falter, doesn't judge but embraces all."

Lucy exchanged a glance with Kyle. His eyes mirrored her

wariness. They were used to sermons that spit fire and brimstone, not this gentle invitation.

"Love," Amelia continued, "is the foundation of all scripture." Her words rose and fell like a melody, each syllable a note that resonated within the high-ceilinged sanctuary.

The congregation stirred, a wave of emotion sweeping over them. A stout woman in the front row shot to her feet, arms raised high. "Amen!" she shouted, conviction rich in her voice.

"Preach it!" another echoed.

Lucy felt the floorboards vibrate as one by one, people rose, a forest of uplifted hands swaying like branches in a spiritual wind. Amelia's presence was magnetic, her message seeping into the spaces between doubts and fears.

"Remember," Amelia said, "the Lord's love is unconditional. We are all His children, worthy of grace."

Kyle leaned in close, his voice barely above a whisper. "She's nothing like Pastor Mike, eh?"

"Shh." Lucy nudged him, but her lips curled into a knowing smile. Their shared memories of rigid pews and stern looks were a stark contrast to this celebration of faith.

"Remember when we thought lightning would strike if we laughed in church?" Kyle's low chuckle blended with the amens around them.

"Or if we questioned anything," Lucy added, her smile fading slightly at the recollection. But here, questions seemed not only allowed but welcomed.

"Exactly," Kyle nodded, his gaze fixed on Amelia. The skepticism in his eyes had given way to something softer, more open.

"Love," Amelia's voice crescendoed, filling the space with palpable warmth, "is not about finding fault, but offering a hand to lift each other up."

"Never heard it put quite like that," Lucy murmured, taken aback by the simplicity, the truth of the words.

"Neither have I," Kyle agreed, his hand finding hers, giving it a reassuring squeeze.

As Amelia spoke, the walls seemed to echo with more than just her voice—they reverberated with possibilities, with a faith that was free from the chains of judgment. Lucy and Kyle remained side by side, no longer performers but part of a congregation united by something profoundly different—an unspoken understanding that here, love was the true sermon.

Lucy leaned in, her voice barely above a whisper. "Kyle, it's like she's speaking directly to me."

"Me too," he replied, his gaze still locked on the preacher at the pulpit.

Amelia Hawthorne's hands swept through the air, each gesture an embodiment of the grace and fervor with which she spoke. Her words wove through the congregation, binding them together in shared hope and acceptance.

"Every soul," Amelia proclaimed, "is a vessel of divine love, yearning to be seen, to be understood."

In that moment, Lucy felt as though layers of old fears and doubts were peeling away from her heart.

"Could we have been wrong all these years?" Kyle murmured, more to himself than to Lucy.

"Maybe we were just never told the whole story," Lucy responded, her eyes bright with the reflection of new beginnings.

The final amen echoed, and the congregation began to disperse into clusters of conversation and fellowship. Lucy tugged at Kyle's hand, her decision made without a word. They moved toward Amelia, who stood by the altar, her silver hair catching the light like a halo.

"Pastor Hawthorne," Lucy started, her voice steady despite the fluttering in her chest. "Your message—it's unlike anything we've ever heard."

"Please, call me Amelia." The preacher smiled, her warm

brown eyes inviting them closer. "I'm glad my words resonated with you."

"Resonated? They did more than that," Kyle said seriously, his usual ease overtaken by the depth of this encounter. "They opened something up inside us."

"Many find a new path when they least expect it," Amelia replied, her tone soft yet assured.

"Thank you for showing us a different way to see the Bible, Amelia," Lucy said, feeling the truth of her words vibrate within her.

"Ah, the Good Book is a living thing," Amelia chuckled, a sound as comforting as it was compelling. "It grows with us, if we let it."

"Seems we've got a lot of growing to do," Kyle admitted, and Amelia's laughter rang out again, clear and kind.

"Then you're on the right track," Amelia said, placing a gentle hand on each of their shoulders. "Keep your hearts open, and you'll find your way."

As Amelia continued to speak to people, Lucy felt a sense of belonging envelop her—a feeling foreign and exhilarating. She glanced at Kyle, seeing her own wonder mirrored in his eyes. Here, with this woman's words wrapping around them, it felt like they had stumbled upon a secret garden, hidden away from the world they knew—a place where everything could begin anew.

"Your fire, it's palpable," Amelia addressed them again, her voice a soothing balm that held Lucy's and Kyle's rapt attention. "And you're seeking something more, aren't you?"

Lucy nodded, the warmth from Amelia's hand on her shoulder seeping into her bones.

"We are," she confirmed, feeling the truth of it resonate deep within.

"Then consider this..." Amelia swept her arm in an inviting gesture, her brown eyes alight with possibility. "Join us at the compound. Live among those who have chosen to walk a path of transformation."

Kyle exchanged a look with Lucy, his eyes reflecting a spark of hope. "The compound?" he asked.

Amelia's smile widened. "Yes. A sanctuary for the soul. There, you'll find others like you. The rest of your band, Tyler and Mason, they're already part of our family, sharing their music, living in harmony with the teachings." She paused. "Hundreds of hearts beating together, touched by the divine."

"Sounds... like nothing we've ever known," Lucy murmured, the idea of such unity pulling at her.

"Exactly," Amelia affirmed. "It's a new beginning, should you choose it."

The thought of their empty apartment, that they had just been evicted from, now just a shell of broken dreams, flashed through Lucy's mind. With nothing left to lose, the offer seemed like a lifeline.

"Let's do it," Kyle whispered, the adventure in his eyes matching the leap in Lucy's heart.

"Really?" Lucy breathed out, turning to him.

"Think about it, Luce. Good friends, good music"—Kyle squeezed her hand—"and a roof over our heads. It's perfect."

"Then it's settled," Amelia concluded. "Welcome to your new life."

"Thank you," Lucy said, her voice barely above a whisper, yet laden with gratitude. They were stepping into the unknown, but somehow, with Amelia's guiding presence, it felt exactly like where they were meant to be.

SEVEN

BILLIE ANN

"John, walk me through this morning," I said, my voice even as I slid into the chair across from him. The fluorescent light buzzed overhead, lending a sterile chill to the interrogation room.

"Again?" His fingers drummed on the metal table, betraying his unease. "I told the other officers already. I dropped Madison off early—down the street from the school, about a block away. She wanted to walk the rest of the way. Can I see my wife, please?"

"After this interview," Billie reassured him. Joanne was still in her own interview room awaiting news. "Madison wanted to walk the rest of the way to the school?" I leaned in slightly, studying his face for any sliver of inconsistency.

"Yeah, what's wrong with that?" John's eyes darted to the two-way mirror then back to me, a frown creasing his forehead. "I figured she was meeting her friends or something, and didn't want them to see me."

"Her friends weren't there, John." My words were measured and deliberate. "Did you see them there?"

"No."

"You have a prior, John. Tell me about that," I said.

"I knew you'd bring this up." He sighed. "It was a fight. Some idiot got in my face downtown and I punched him. I was arrested, charged with battery. I did my sixty days and paid the fine. That's all."

"But you do understand how that makes you look in our eyes, right?" I asked.

"Look, Detective." He shifted in his seat, the scrape of chair legs against linoleum breaking the silence. "Why does it matter? What does this have to do with anything?"

"Everything matters when a child is missing, John." I paused and observed him, before continuing. "Tell me about your relationship with Madison."

"Relationship?" he scoffed, folding his arms defensively. "She's my stepdaughter. That's it. What are you implying?"

"Nothing yet," I replied, tapping my pen on my notepad—a slow, rhythmic counterpoint to his nervous beat. I found it interesting that he'd jumped to the conclusion that I was insinuating something. It was a simple question. He was panicked.

"Fine." John exhaled sharply, running a hand through his hair. "But you're barking up the wrong tree."

"Let's hope so, John."

I scribbled a note, then glanced up again. "John, in the past few days, did you and Madison have any disagreements? Anything that might've upset her?"

He bristled at the question, his hands clenching into fists before he forced them flat against the table. "No," he said tersely. "We got along fine."

"Fine?" I echoed, my skepticism clear. "That's a vague term, John. I need specifics—was she acting differently, maybe more withdrawn or agitated than usual?"

"Madison's a quiet kid," he replied with a shrug, avoiding my gaze. "She keeps to herself. We didn't fight, Detective Wilde. There was nothing to fight about."

"Kids often hide their feelings," I pointed out. "Especially from stepparents. Maybe she didn't tell you everything."

"Are you a psychologist now?" His voice had an edge, one that didn't escape me.

"Part of my job is reading people, John." I leaned back, assessing him. "And right now, you're not making this easy. If there's something you know, anything at all, it could be crucial."

"Look, I'm telling you, everything was normal," he insisted, but his eyes shifted too quickly, evading mine.

"Normal," I repeated, jotting down another note, this time underlining the word twice. My gut told me "normal" was the last thing we were dealing with here.

"Is there something you're not saying, John?" I asked, my voice steady despite the frustration simmering just below the surface. "It's important you tell me everything."

"Nothing to tell," he muttered, but his leg began to bounce under the table.

"Because I can't help but notice you seem defensive, John." I tapped my pen against the notepad, each click a reminder of the ticking clock in the search for Madison. "Defensive behavior often implies something's being hidden. Are you hiding something?"

"I'm not—" He cut himself off, took a deep breath, and composed his face into what I assumed was meant to be a look of calm. "I'm not hiding anything. I'm just worried about Madison like everyone else."

"Of course," I said, but the pieces weren't falling into place. His story, his demeanor—they were disjointed, like puzzle pieces from different boxes.

"How's your relationship with Joanne?" I asked.

"It's fine. What do you mean?"

"How did you two meet?" I asked.

"We met online, on a dating site. Like most people do these days. We dated for some time and then I moved in with her and

Madison. I fail to see how this is important. Listen, Joanne needs me right now, I should be with her, can we get this over with?"

"All right, John. For now, you can go. But we might need to talk again soon," I said, standing up, signaling the end of our conversation.

"Fine," he replied, though his tone suggested it was anything but.

As he left, I remained seated, thumbing through the notes I'd taken. The ink on the page was clear, but the truth? That was still smudged with doubt. I needed to find Madison, and every fiber of my being would not rest until I did. John's deflections only fueled my resolve. Something wasn't right, and I intended to uncover it, no matter what stones I had to turn over.

I squared my shoulders as the bus driver approached my desk. I had asked him to come in for a chat to help us out. His round face creased into a smile that soon froze as he remembered why he was there.

"I need to ask you about Madison," I said as he sat down across from me. "Did she get on your bus today?"

He scratched his head, his brow furrowing as he cast his mind back through the dozens of faces he'd greeted at the start and end of the day. "Madison? No, didn't see her this morning or afternoon."

"Are you sure?" The question came out sharper than I intended, but the stakes were too high for pleasantries.

"Pretty sure. She's hard to miss with that big smile and wave she always gives me." He chuckled softly, but the sound didn't reach his eyes.

"Did anyone else mention seeing her around the stop? Maybe talk to her? Maybe she got off with a friend at an earlier stop?"

He shook his head, the laughter gone. "Nope, I would have remembered her if she had been on the bus. We have cameras on the inside, you know. I could ask them to send over the footage?"

"Thanks," I said, ignoring his question while my gut twisted tighter. "I'll let you know if we will need that. And if you remember anything else, anything at all, please give me a call."

"Of course, Detective Wilde. Anything for the kids."

I nodded, turning away from his concerned gaze.

The station was buzzing with the low hum of voices and clicking keyboards as the bus driver left. Scott looked up from his monitor, curls flopping into his eyes. Tom glanced over from a whiteboard covered in timelines and notes, his broad shoulders squared.

"Got anything?" I asked, leaning back in my chair with an urgency that matched my rising frustration.

"Nothing solid," Scott replied, his voice measured but tense. "Social media's quiet on Joanne's end. She has a Facebook profile, but doesn't seem to use it."

"Neighbors didn't see a thing," Tom added, tapping the whiteboard with a marker. "It's like she disappeared into thin air."

"Air leaves traces." I stood up, pacing now. "We need to find where the trail starts."

"Surveillance cameras?" Scott suggested, fingers already poised over the keyboard. "Could be a shop or gas station caught something. Around the school and bus stop. And where John said he dropped her off, perhaps?"

"Who else can we talk to?" I said. "There's got to be something we're missing."

I was eyeing the board plastered with photographs and timelines. Tom's phone rang and he walked out to take the call.

I considered John's guarded demeanor. Every instinct screamed that he knew more than he let on. Sitting down at my desk, I combed through the interview notes again, searching for discrepancies, any thread that might unravel his story.

"Billie Ann?" Chief Harold's voice stopped my focus. She stood in the doorway, her eyes sharp but concerned. "Where are we at?"

"Chief." I stood up, meeting her halfway. "I think we need to keep a closer watch on John Harris. Maybe have him followed? He just left and I want to make sure he actually goes home."

She crossed her arms, considering. "He's the last person to have seen Madison, right?"

"Exactly. And his story's too clean, rehearsed almost." My jaw set firmly. "I can feel it; he's hiding something."

Chief Harold nodded slowly. "All right. I will make sure that happens. You keep digging, but do it by the book. We can't afford slip-ups."

"Understood," I assured her. "We'll bring Madison home."

"Good." A rare glimmer of approval showed in her eyes. "That's what I like to hear."

"That was one of the officers talking to her friends," Tom said. "They mentioned a secret spot she liked. A hidden nook by the creek—"

"Did anyone check it?"

"Search teams are all busy elsewhere. The last spare officer we had is now trailing John."

"That's not good."

"Anything else?"

"Her classmates—they say she seemed worried lately. Distracted. Not her usual self."

"Okay I will go while you hold down the fort," I instructed, already reaching for my jacket. This was what we needed—a crack in the veneer.

"Will do, Billie Ann."

The hunt was on. I grabbed my keys and drove to the creek. If no one else was able to go, then I had to do it by myself.

* * *

Night had fallen when I returned to the precinct, weariness settling into my bones. Chief Harold stood at the window, watching the search lights dance in the distance.

"Teams will keep searching through the night," she stated without turning. "Any luck at the creek?"

"Nothing yet. It's a big area to cover. A search team arrived and took over so I decided to come back." My hands clenched involuntarily.

"You look spent, Wilde. Go home, get some rest."

"Rest won't find Madison."

"All right, then. Couch in my office is yours, if you need it."

"Thanks, Chief." I managed a half-smile.

"Just don't overwork yourself."

"Can't promise that," I replied, gaze returning to the window.

"Suit yourself," she said, the corners of her mouth lifting slightly.

I watched as the search lights continued to probe the darkness, a silent vow forming between the beats of my heart—I would find Madison, no matter what it took.

EIGHT

JOSEPH

Fifteen-year-old Joseph's sneakers dampened with morning dew as he darted across the meadow, his fishing rod clutched like a knight's lance. He glanced back once, ensuring the world of rules and classrooms hadn't followed him. The pale blush of dawn lit his path to freedom.

"Almost there," he whispered to himself, a mischievous grin parting his freckled cheeks. The creek, with its secret nooks and crannies, called to him. It was his sanctuary, a place where textbooks and chalkboards couldn't impose.

He reached the bank, heart thumping with the thrill of playing hooky. Joseph unfurled his gear, movements practiced and sure. He threaded the line, hands steady despite the rush coursing through him. The bobber, red and white, dangled above the water's surface before he swung it into the creek with a flick of his wrist.

"Come on, big catch," he urged under his breath, eyes locked on the gentle ripples spreading from the bobber. His solitude enveloped him, the only sounds his soft breathing and the tender lapping of water against muddy banks.

"Today's the day," Joseph said, a promise to the creek and to himself. He settled in, the rod an extension of his eager anticipation, ready for whatever the day might reel in.

The mist clung to the swamp. Tangled roots gripped the water's edge, and gnarled trees loomed, their branches heavy with Spanish moss that swayed gently in the morning stillness. Joseph felt a chill tickle his spine, not from the cool air, but from the sense that he was being watched by unseen eyes hidden among the dense foliage. This place crawled with wildlife, like snakes and gators.

He grabbed the rod tighter as if it could shield him from the swamp's secrets.

The water's surface broke suddenly—a fish leaping, catching the first rays of sunlight on its scales before diving back into the murky depths. Joseph's heart skipped; excitement surged through him, eager for the dance between predator and prey.

"Any moment now..." he whispered, his voice barely more than a breath.

A memory crept into his mind, unbidden. Last time, just beyond where his bobber floated, an alligator had surfaced, its eyes like two dark marbles studying him. He had frozen, a statue of fear and fascination, until the creature slid away without a sound.

"Keep your distance, and we'll get along just fine," he said aloud, a declaration to the beast wherever it lurked. He imagined the gator giving a nod of agreement from beneath the lily pads, a silent pact between them.

"Come on, fish," Joseph coaxed, scanning for the next jump, the next flash of silver against green. "Don't let me down."

He leaned forward, every muscle taut with anticipation. The creek, with its hidden currents and secrets, held his fate for the day. His adventure rested in the hands of nature, unpredictable and wild, much like the boy who dared to be part of it.

Joseph's grip tightened as the rod went taut, an abrupt yank that nearly pulled him off balance.

"Gotcha!" he exclaimed, a grin spreading across his face.

Adrenaline coursed through his veins as he set the hook with a swift upward jerk. The line whizzed, unreeling with a sound that promised a significant catch. Whatever lurked beneath had heft, had fight.

"Come on," he muttered under his breath, the reel spinning in a blur of motion as he worked to gain ground. "What are you?"

The rod bent in a deep arc, quivering with the force on the other end. Joseph's heart drummed with the thrill and urgency of the struggle. His hands were slick with sweat, and he wiped them hastily on his shorts, seeking a better grip.

"Biggest fish I've ever—"

The resistance was strange, not the erratic tug of a fish but something else—steadier, heavier. Doubt crept into his excitement. He leaned back, planting his feet firmly on the muddy bank, reeling with all his might.

"Come on, show yourself," he coaxed, or perhaps pleaded.

His mind spun wild scenarios; maybe it was a log, a boot, or... no, he dared not think it—the gator. But it wasn't thrashing, wasn't rolling. It was just heavy, so impossibly heavy.

"Can't be," he huffed, his breaths short and sharp. "Just can't."

The creek offered no clues, only the eerie silence broken by the creak of his rod and the relentless churn of the reel. Joseph's arms ached, his fingers cramped around the handle, yet he persisted, drawn by the need to unveil the mystery at the end of his line.

"Almost there," he gasped, squinting to see through the morning mist on the water's surface.

"Please be a fish, please be a fish," he chanted, a mantra to steel his nerves as the silhouette of his catch began to emerge from the depths.

The line went tauter. The reel spinning in stuttered bursts. The silhouette broke the surface tension—an arm, not a fin. His stomach dropped.

"Wha—"

It was fabric, splayed like a waterlogged flower. Pale blue, the cloth clung to something submerged and unmoving. Not a fish. A shirt. Joseph's mouth went dry, his hands suddenly numb on the rod.

"Can't be real," he stammered, voice barely above a whisper.

He yanked again, the creek resisting as if reluctant to reveal its secret. Inch by inch, more of the shirt came into view, snagged by his hook, the edges frayed and dancing with the current.

"Help! Someone!" His eyes darted along the bank, searching for any sign of assistance. No one. Just him and the eerie quiet of the swamp.

"Please, no." His breath hitched, each inhale sharper than the last. As more of his catch surfaced, time slowed—a body, small, lifeless, cradled by the murky waters.

"Mom!" Joseph's voice shattered the silence, panicked. He stumbled back, his reel slipping from slackened fingers, forgotten.

"Help me, please!" He stared, wide-eyed, trembling, as the reality of the lifeless form sank in.

"Come on, come on," Joseph muttered, his voice breaking with urgency. He lunged forward, abandoning the fishing rod as it clattered to the muddy bank. His hands plunged into the cool water, wrapping around the sodden fabric of the shirt and the cold flesh beneath. The creek seemed to tighten its grip, reluctant to release its grim treasure.

"Please, no," he gasped, straining. The small body was a

dead weight in his arms, its limbs swaying limply in the slow-moving current. With a grunt, Joseph heaved, feeling the slippery resistance before the form began to inch toward the shore.

"Gotcha," he panted, his breaths coming fast and ragged. But triumph died quickly, smothered by the stark stillness of the form now half-draped over the muddy bank. Joseph's hands were shaking, his fingers slipping against wet skin and fabric.

"Help!" His cry was a hoarse whisper, barely audible above the chorus of croaking frogs and buzzing insects. He looked down at the face, obscured by strands of dark hair plastered to pale cheeks. No sign of life, just an eerie calm that belied the chaos churning in Joseph's gut.

"Move, please move," he begged, voice cracking as he gently shook the girl's shoulder, hoping for a twitch, a breath—anything. But there was nothing. The cruel finality of it hit him like a wave, knocking the wind from his chest.

Joseph recoiled, stumbling backward as if struck. He landed hard on the bank, mud oozing through his fingers. Tears blurred his vision, stinging his eyes as they traced hot trails down his dirt-streaked face.

"Can't be..." he choked out, the words dissolving into sobs. Fear curled tight in his stomach, a living thing that clawed its way up his throat. Every sound seemed magnified, every shadow a menacing specter lurking just beyond his sight.

"Mom... Please... someone," he whispered, the words spilling from him in a prayer for solace. But the swamp offered no comfort in the relentless press of silence.

"I shouldn't have come here," Joseph murmured to himself, his body racked with tremors. "Why did I... why?"

A lone heron took flight, its wings cutting through the mist with heavy beats—a silent witness to the tragedy unfurling below. Joseph hugged his knees, his gaze locked on the still form beside him, the gravity of his discovery anchoring him to the spot.

"Who are you?" he finally whispered to the girl from the creek, but the only answer was the gentle lap of water against the shore and the distant call of the heron fading into the gray dawn.

Scrambling to his feet, Joseph's breath came in shallow bursts. The world spun, a kaleidoscope of murky water and drab foliage.

"Help!" His voice was a strangled cry, absorbed by the swamp's thick embrace. "I need to get help," he yelped, staggering forward. He tripped over roots hidden beneath layers of fallen leaves, but fear propelled him onward. Each step away from the creek, his mind replaying the ghastly image of the lifeless body tangled in his fishing line.

"Mom! Dad!" he screamed as he burst through the underbrush, the first rays of sunlight cutting weak paths through the trees.

Joseph's house loomed ahead, safety. He hammered on the locked door with fists numb and bruised, the sharp knocks ringing out like gunshots in the quiet morning.

"Mom! Open up!" His voice cracked.

The door swung open, and his mother stood there, her face etched with confusion. "Joseph? What on earth—"

"Down at the creek," he gasped, his words tumbling out in a torrent. "There's a girl—"

"Slow down, honey. Take a deep breath."

He shook his head, unable to slow the racing thoughts. "No time! In the water—"

"Stay here," she commanded, her eyes hardening with resolve as she reached for the phone.

Joseph slumped against the wall, panting. His mother's muffled voice filtered through his fog of shock, talking to the authorities.

"Officers are on their way," she said, turning back to him with a look that mingled worry with something else, something deeper. She wrapped her arms around him, but he felt distant, untethered.

"I shouldn't have skipped school," he mumbled, guilt gnawing at him. "I should've stayed home."

"Shh," she soothed. "It's not your fault."

"Who is she?" Joseph whispered. "Who is that girl?"

"We'll find out. You did the right thing coming to me."

Sirens wailed in the distance, growing louder, drawing nearer. Joseph pictured the flashing lights piercing the swamp's gloom. The image should have comforted him, but it didn't.

"Will they think I—" he started, but couldn't finish.

"Think what?" his mother's brow furrowed.

"Nothing." He shook his head, trying to dislodge the dread that settled there. "Never mind."

"Let's go and sit down in the kitchen," she urged gently.

He nodded, allowing her to guide him back through the house. The warmth of the kitchen felt foreign, as if he'd stepped into another world—a world where boys didn't fish lifeless bodies from creeks.

Joseph sank into a chair, the wood cool against his skin. The room seemed to close in around him, the ticking of the clock loud in his ears. He shivered, despite the heat.

"Police are here," his mother announced, peeking through the curtains.

"Okay." His voice was hollow; it was a struggle to speak.

"Stay here," she instructed before stepping outside to meet the officers.

Images flashed behind his eyelids every time he blinked. He hugged himself, trying to quell the tremors that hadn't ceased since his fingers touched the cold fabric of the shirt in the water.

"Who are you?" he murmured again, this time to the empty room. No answer came, just the lingering unease that drifted around him like the morning fog outside, whispering of questions unanswered and secrets yet to surface.

NINE

BILLIE ANN

I jerked awake, my cheek pressed against the stiff fabric of the station couch. The digital clock on the wall read 7:17 a.m.—barely an hour since my last blurry glance at it. The shrill ring of my phone cut through the silence again, vibrating against the metal side table. I fumbled for it, squinting against the harsh glow of the screen.

"Billie Ann," I grunted, voice thick with sleep.

"Body found at Sykes Creek. I'm en route. You should be too." Chief Harold was all business, a hard edge beneath the static crackle.

"Understood," I said, adrenaline dispersing the fog of sleep. "On my way."

The call ended with a click, and I swung my legs off the couch, feet hitting the cold floor. I stood, my movements automatic as I gathered my jacket, badge, and gun. My mind reeled.

Please don't let it be Madison.

"Stay out of trouble," my lawyer's words echoed, a mantra meant to reunite me with my kids. My nephew had been killed last year, and I suspected that was why the courts didn't trust me with my own children. I needed to prove them wrong. But was I already too late to save Madison?

I brushed down a couple of stray hairs, a futile attempt at order, and headed for the door. The morning air hit me, a humid slap of reality.

All night I'd been turning over the events of yesterday, and I'd woken to scribble down new lines of questioning I had for Madison's mother and John. I wanted to re-interview them and speak again with the officer who'd been instructed to follow him home.

The cruiser's tires crunched over gravel as I pulled onto the uneven path leading to Sykes Creek. I gripped the steering wheel. The image of Madison's bright smile that I had seen in photos flashed before me, stark against the grim slice of reality that waited.

As the creek came into view, bathed in emergency lights, I parked and jumped out. My boots sank slightly into the damp earth, each step heavy with dread.

Chief Harold called my name. She stood near the tape perimeter, her stern face illuminated by the pulsing blue and red lights.

"Chief," I acknowledged, striding toward her. "What have we got?"

"Young girl, multiple stab wounds." Her words were clipped, efficient.

My heart dropped.

"Is it Madison? Show me," I said, steeling myself for the sight.

Chief Harold gestured for me to follow, leading me past the uniformed officers and the buzz of activity. I focused on the sound of our synchronized steps, trying not to let my mind race ahead to the grisly tableau I was about to witness.

"Forensics are already working on it," she continued. "But I wanted you here before they moved her. You've got a knack for seeing the things others miss."

"Let's hope that's enough to catch this bastard," I replied, the edges of anger creeping in.

We approached the body, and despite years on the job, the brutality never failed to shock. I crouched down beside the young girl, taking in the cruel work of violence etched into her once vibrant life. I had to bite back my tears. It was unmistakably Madison. I recognized her from the pictures, but we still needed a positive ID in order to make that conclusion. I had to steady myself before continuing.

Chief Harold walked back to her vehicle, and I began to dissect the scene, piece by painstaking piece. The air had a musky stench, a mix of decay and the swamp's own breath. I trudged through the sludge, my boots sinking into the mire with each step. The twisted mangroves clawed at the gray morning light, their roots snaking across the water's edge like bony fingers grasping for something just out of reach. A shiver crawled up my spine, not from the chill in the air, but from the knowledge that death had visited this desolate place.

"Watch your step," a tech called out as I neared the crime scene tape. I nodded, eyes scanning the ground, taking care not to disturb the silent sentinels of evidence they'd marked with little numbered flags.

"Detective Wilde," greeted Dr. Martinez, our lead forensic analyst. She was hunched over a patch of earth, her tools laid out with surgical precision. "We've got blood samples here, and over there." She pointed without looking up, her focus absolute.

"Anything useful?" I asked, crouching beside her.

"Nothing yet. But we're collecting everything. Blood, hair, fibers. Anything the perp left behind."

"Good." I watched as her assistant plucked a single strand of hair with tweezers, sealing it meticulously in a plastic bag. "And the blood?"

"Already on it," she replied, holding up a vial with a crimson smear. "I'll fast-track it for DNA."

"Appreciate it." My eyes swept the area, noting the precision of the team. Every detail mattered—a partial print, a fiber from a sweater, a droplet of blood—all whispering secrets of the one who had stolen a life.

"Anything out of place?" I asked another tech who was photographing tire tracks a little way off.

"Still piecing it together," he said, his camera clicking methodically. "But it will be hard to find forensic evidence in this sort of setting."

"Keep me updated," I said before standing and stepping back to give them room.

I made my way over to where the body lay close to the murky water, the grotesque stillness of the scene punctuated only by the gentle lapping of the creek against the muddy bank. The mist hovered over the twisted mangroves, and I could taste the damp earth and decaying vegetation in the air.

"Detective Wilde," a uniformed officer acknowledged with a nod as he lifted the yellow tape for me to duck under.

"Thanks," I said, my voice barely above a whisper.

The young girl was on her back, eyes wide open to the indifferent sky. Her once vibrant life reduced to cold flesh, yielding nothing but silence to my questions. The multiple stab wounds on her chest were a shocking contrast to her pale skin, the dark crimson of her blood staining her clothes.

"Jesus." The word escaped my lips before I could stop it.

"Looks personal," remarked the ME, kneeling beside the victim. "These wounds... frenzied."

"Whoever did this..." I trailed off. There was no language harsh enough for such savagery. I agreed, it felt personal to me too.

"Billie Ann?" Scott's voice broke through my thoughts, a touch of concern in his tone.

"Give me a sec," I said, stepping away from the body, feeling the ground sway beneath me.

"Take your time," Scott called after me, but he sounded distant.

I walked to the side, leaning against the rough bark of a mangrove tree, closing my eyes as a wave of dizziness washed over me.

"Damn it," I cursed under my breath, forcing deep breaths into my lungs. And then I took a breath. If I had lost Madison, I was going to make sure I caught her killer.

"Detective?" Tom approached, notebook in hand, ready to dive back into the procedural depths. "We've got some leads to follow up on. A couple of witnesses who saw someone suspicious in this area last night."

"Good," I straightened, steeling myself with a surge of anger that burned through the fog of shock. "Get all the details. Let's get this bastard."

"Already on it," Tom affirmed with a decisive nod, mirroring my resolve.

"Keep me posted on every detail," I instructed, my voice steady now, the dizziness giving way to a laser-focused determination.

"Will do," he confirmed, moving off to coordinate with the team.

A hand landed on my shoulder, firm and grounding. I blinked away the sting in my eyes, the aftermath of my momentary breakdown.

"Here." In the Chief's outstretched hand, a Styrofoam cup steamed quietly against the backdrop of flashing red and blue lights.

"Thanks." I grabbed the coffee, feeling its warmth seep into my palms. She stood beside me. Her gaze lingered on the creek, then back to me, reading the turmoil on my face.

"Rough one, huh?" she said, her voice low enough that it wouldn't carry over to the others.

"Never gets easier." I took a sip, the bitter liquid scalding my tongue, but I welcomed the pain. It was grounding, real. "But I definitely think we're dealing with someone who knew Madison. Someone who had hatred for her. The body, the scene... it screams rage killing to me."

Harold nodded solemnly, and in her eyes I saw the years of scenes just like this one. "We'll get them, Billie Ann. We always do."

I peered up at her, meeting her steady gaze. The lines around her eyes told stories of sleepless nights and battles fought both in the field and behind her desk. But there was an unwavering resolve there too, one that reignited the flame of purpose within me.

"I met Charlene and William the other day in Publix. Did I tell you that? They asked about you," she continued, her voice softening. It was an olive branch, a reminder of what I was fighting for—both in work and life.

"Did they?" A faint smile flickered across my lips. "What did you tell them?"

"That their mom is doing everything she can to make the world a safer place," Harold replied, her stern facade cracking with a rare, genuine smile.

"Even if that means losing sleep and skipping meals?" I quipped, trying to lighten the burden of not being able to see my children.

"Especially then," she chuckled, then her expression sobered. "For what it's worth, I don't think you should have lost custody."

I didn't know what to say, and I felt myself make a joke of it, even though the Chief's words were sincere. "Roger that, Chief." Raising the cup in a small salute, she nodded, and I felt a semblance of control return. Harold's presence, the steadiness of her support, it was a reminder that even in the darkest hours, I wasn't alone in this fight.

"Let's go over what we have so far," she said, turning toward the fray of investigators and the grim scene beyond.

"Lead the way." With each step toward the unfolding mystery, the bond between us strengthened.

I squared my shoulders and stepped back into the scene, the coffee from Chief Harold warming my insides. The early morning mist shrouded Sykes Creek, tendrils of fog caressing the twisted mangroves at the water's edge. My gaze settled on the body again, that poor girl lying among the reeds, her life stolen away.

"Find anything new?" I asked the nearest tech.

"Not yet," he said, eyes never leaving the ground as he swept his brush over a half-buried sneaker print.

The creek whispered secrets as I walked its bank, each step deliberate. A broken branch caught my attention, the jagged splinter pointing accusingly toward the crime scene. I crouched down, examining it closely. Fresh. It told a story of a hasty retreat or a struggle—important details.

"Photograph this," I called out, not looking up from the snapped wood.

"Already on it, Detective Wilde," came the reply from one of the forensic photographers.

The perimeter widened with every passing second as more officers joined the search. We were meticulous, knowing full well that any clue, however seemingly insignificant, could be the key to unlocking this tragedy.

"Billie Ann," Harold's voice broke through the concentration, "check this out."

I strode over, meeting her by a cluster of cattails. She pointed to a piece of fabric, barely visible against the dark soil. I squatted, pulled out a pair of tweezers, and carefully extracted it. "Could match the victim's clothing," I observed.

"Good eye," Harold nodded. "We'll get this to the lab, ASAP."

"Thanks, Chief." I started piecing together the silent testimony of the creek bed—a torn scrap here, a footprint there.

"Let's canvass the area again," I suggested. "Someone might recognize this."

"Agreed," she replied, pulling out her radio to coordinate the effort.

I stood, surveying the land that had become an open-air vault for someone's darkest deed.

The sun hadn't yet risen above the horizon, but the creek was already swarming with activity. I watched as Scott hunched over his laptop. He was cross-referencing local missing persons with the victim's description, in case there was more than one match. There wasn't. Only Madison came up. Tom, meanwhile, directed officers to comb the underbrush on either side of the bank, his voice firm but tinged with urgency.

"Tom, double-check the north end. Look for anything that doesn't belong," I called out, my gaze fixed on the bramble where nature and crime intersected.

"Got it, Billie Ann." His reply was swift, accompanied by the sound of snapping twigs as he moved through the foliage.

"Scott, pull up recent attacks on persons or reports of rape attempts, anything violent in the last month. We might be looking at an escalation here."

"Consider it done," Scott answered without lifting his eyes from the screen.

A shout drew our attention to the water's edge. An officer held a Ziplock bag containing a bloodied rock. "Found downstream," she reported.

"Good work. Bag it, tag it, and log every step from where you found it."

"Will do, Detective Wilde."

I turned away, squinting against the creeping daylight, and

approached the fishing boy and his mother. The boy sat on the
hood of an ambulance, wrapped in a blanket, his eyes wide and
haunted. His mother stood beside him, her arm protectively
around his shoulders.

"Son, can you tell me what you saw?" I asked gently,
crouching to meet his gaze.

"Was just fishin'," he said, voice quivering. "Then I saw
her... in the water. I didn't think she was real at first."

"Did you see anyone else? Hear anything unusual?"

He shook his head, then hesitated. "Maybe a splash? But I
thought it was a fish jumping."

"Thank you. You did the right thing telling us," I reassured
him before turning to his mother. "Ma'am, have you noticed any
strangers around the creek lately?"

"Nothing but the usual joggers and dog walkers on the
trails. It's usually such a peaceful place," she murmured, her
gaze flickering to the crime scene tape fluttering in the breeze. I
showed her a photo of the pale blue fabric we'd found. She
shook her head. She didn't recognize it.

"Okay. If anything comes to mind, here's my card. Call
anytime," I said, handing her a card.

"Of course, Detective," she replied, taking it with a trembling hand.

The scene sprawled before me, a tangle of possibilities and
dead ends. Each interview, each piece of evidence added layers
to the narrative we were slowly uncovering. The truth lay
buried here somewhere, and piece by piece, I would unearth it.

Stepping away from the creek's edge, I squared my shoulders and let out a breath I didn't realize I'd been holding. My
gaze swept the scene: Scott cataloging every print in the mud,
Tom canvassing the perimeter with an intensity that mirrored
my own.

I pulled out my phone, dialed the number that would

connect me to the beginning of someone's nightmare. It rang twice before a tremulous voice answered, "Hello?"

"Mrs. Harris, this is Detective Wilde. We need to talk about Madison."

"Is she...?" The question hung between us.

"Can we meet at your home? I'm on my way."

"Please, just tell me," she begged, and I heard the crack in her plea.

"I'd rather wait..."

"Please."

"Mrs. Harris, I'm so sorry." The words were barely a whisper, but they carried the weight of the world. "We've found a body."

"God, no..." Her voice shattered into sobs, and I fought against the tightness in my throat.

"Ma'am, we don't know for certain that it's Madison yet. I know this is a tough time, but I'm going to need you to meet me at the morgue in a few hours. Do you have someone who can go with you? Your husband? It's important to have someone by your side. We need a positive identification but we do believe it is likely to be Madison. I will send a patrol car to pick you up and meet you there. I'm with you and will help you through all this," I assured her.

"Let's go," I told Scott and Tom, my voice steady, fueled by resolution forged in the fires of too many scenes like this one. "We're not done yet."

TEN

Then

The van's engine chugged its final breath as Kyle turned the key, bringing their old companion to a wheezing halt. Lucy glanced through the dust-smeared windshield at the towering gates of the compound, a silhouette against the waning sun. Her heart hammered with a cocktail of nerves and excitement, a rhythm echoed by the jingle of keys in Kyle's jittery hands.

"Here we go," Kyle said, his voice betraying a mix of trepidation and thrill. "New beginnings."

"Exactly what we need," Lucy affirmed, her eyes reflecting a spark of certainty.

They stepped out, their shoes crunching on gravel. Around them, the world was hushed, save for the rustling leaves whispering of change. With every step toward the front gate, their former life seemed to shed from their shoulders like an old skin.

Lucy's grip tightened around the neck of her guitar case—a talisman of dreams and songs yet to be sung. Beside her, Kyle hoisted their bags, his eyes scanning the massive facade of their new home, searching for signs of welcome.

"Think they'll like my music?" Lucy's voice held vulnerability.

"Lucy, they'll love you," Kyle reassured her, squeezing her hand briefly before they ascended the steps to the large oak gate. "Everyone does. Including me."

It swung open before they could knock. Standing there, bathed in the golden light from within, were two people introducing themselves as Cassie and Ben. Cassie's smile was like a warm blanket, her eyes crinkling at the corners. Ben's stature was imposing, but the gentleness in his gaze softened his rough edges.

"Lucy, Kyle, welcome!" Cassie's voice enveloped them. "We're so glad you're here."

"Let us take those," Ben offered, his deep voice grounding as he reached for the bags that weighed Kyle down.

"Thank you," Kyle said, passing them over with a grateful nod.

"Come in, come in," Cassie beckoned, stepping aside. "There's plenty to show you, but first, let's make you feel at home."

Lucy stepped over the threshold, her senses swimming with the scent of pine and something sweetly floral. It was as if the very walls of the compound breathed a serene welcome. She exchanged a hopeful glance with Kyle, her heart skipping at the thought that maybe, just maybe, they'd found where they belonged.

Lucy and Kyle trailed Cassie and Ben, the gravel crunching under their feet as they weaved through a maze of well-trodden paths. Gardens bloomed on either side, bursts of color from zinnias and marigolds nodding in the gentle breeze. People, clad in an array of soft linens and cottons, tended to the earth with a tender focus, their skin bronzed from hours under the sun. Children of many different ages looked at them with big curious eyes.

"Those are our communal gardens," Cassie said, following Lucy's gaze. "Everyone pitches in."

"Looks amazing," Lucy murmured, her eyes reflecting the vibrant hues.

They passed an open space where children laughed, their voices rising above the thwack of a makeshift ball game. Nearby, an elderly couple sat on a bench, their hands moving in sync as they wove baskets from strips of willow.

"Play areas for the kids, and workshops for crafts," Ben explained, his voice carrying a note of pride.

"Feels like a different world," Kyle added, his blue eyes scanning the scene, absorbing the synchronicity of life here.

"Wait until you see your new home," Cassie promised with a knowing smile.

They turned a bend, and there it appeared—a quaint two-story structure adorned in gentle pastels, its wooden exterior merging perfectly with the surrounding nature. Luscious vines clung to the walls, adding to its charm; and joyous chatter drifted out from the open windows.

"Here we are," Ben announced, pushing open a door with a gentle creak.

The room was modest but inviting, sunlight filtering through the small window that offered a view of the compound's heart. Two beds flanked by simple nightstands promised rest, while a shared wardrobe awaited their belongings.

"Wow," Lucy breathed out, setting down her guitar case beside one of the beds.

"It's perfect," Kyle agreed, running a hand over the quilted bedspread, its pattern a patchwork of community stories.

"Take your time settling in," Cassie said, stepping back into the doorway. "When you're ready, we'll continue the tour."

"Thank you," Lucy replied, grateful and excited.

As Cassie and Ben left, closing the door with a soft click,

Lucy and Kyle exchanged a look of quiet elation. Unpacking their bags felt like unwrapping gifts; each article of clothing, each personal item, a symbol of the life they were weaving here.

"Think this is the start of something good?" Kyle asked, tucking his shirts into a drawer.

"Something great," Lucy affirmed, draping her dresses in the wardrobe. Her fingers brushed against the guitar case, the instrument inside now a harbinger of songs yet to fill these walls.

Together, they stepped back, taking in the room—their new sanctuary. The simplicity of the space belied the richness of the connection they already felt to the world outside their window. Lucy's eyes met Kyle's, the same thought shared between them: they were no longer wanderers. They had arrived.

The soft hum of conversation floated toward them as Cassie poked her head inside. "Dinner's about to start," she said, "it's one of the best times to meet everyone."

Lucy glanced at Kyle, noting the excited flutter in her stomach mirrored in his eyes. They trailed behind Cassie, entering the expansive dining hall where long tables were laden with steaming dishes and vibrant salads.

"Come, sit with us," Ben beckoned from a table near the center, patting two empty seats beside him. The scent of rosemary and baked bread filled the air, comforting and enticing.

"Thank you," Lucy replied, her voice mingling with the clatter of utensils and plates.

"Everyone here contributes to the meal in some way," Cassie explained, passing them bowls of food. "Cooking, setting up, or even growing the ingredients. It ties us together."

"Like a family," Kyle said, accepting a bowl of stew and breaking off a piece of bread.

"Exactly." Cassie smiled, her eyes bright.

As they ate, laughter and stories flowed freely. Lucy found herself relaxed, opening up about their dreams and travels, while community members shared anecdotes of life within the compound.

"Later there's a jam session in the lounge," a woman across from them mentioned, her eyes crinkling with enthusiasm. "You play, don't you?"

Lucy exchanged a look with Kyle. "Yes, we'd love to join."

After dinner, the clinking of dishes being cleared was replaced by the strumming of guitars and the soft patting of drums. In the lounge, a circle had formed, instruments passed around like sacred totems.

"Here," a man said, handing Kyle a guitar with a worn fret-board that told of many songs played.

"Thank you," Kyle murmured, fingers finding familiar chords.

"Got a song for us?" someone asked, looking at Lucy.

"Maybe something to fit the mood?" Kyle suggested, glancing at her.

She nodded, clearing her throat before her voice lifted, pure and haunting, weaving through the chords Kyle laid down. The room hushed, captivated by the melding of her melody with the rhythm of the community's heartbeats.

"Wow," Cassie whispered, once the last note faded into applause.

"Feels like home, doesn't it?" Ben said sincerely.

"More than you know," Lucy replied, her gaze catching Kyle's. She guessed he was feeling the same.

Lucy watched, her heart a thrumming bird in her chest, as Amelia ascended the modest wooden pulpit. The preacher's silver hair gleamed under the soft light, a halo of wisdom that seemed to crown her with ethereal grace.

"Today, we gather not just in worship but in unity," Amelia began, her voice a soothing balm that spread over the congregation. "For it is in our shared faith that we find strength."

Lucy felt Kyle's hand gently squeeze hers, their fingers

interlocking, silently acknowledging the electric charge of belonging that permeated the air.

"Let us open our hearts," Amelia continued, and the room followed suit, a collective inhale and exhale that felt like a single organism breathing.

"Love thy neighbor. This simple phrase embodies our entire ethos." Amelia's interpretation unfolded, a tapestry of ancient words woven with modern meaning. The congregation nodded, murmurs of assent rippling through the room like wind through leaves. "It's as simple as that. We must love one another. That is all that God asks of us. It doesn't have to be complicated. Love. It's all we need."

"Isn't she amazing?" Lucy whispered to Kyle, the resonance of Amelia's words still vibrating within her.

"Never heard anyone speak like that before," he replied, his blue eyes wide with a mixture of awe and reverence.

As the gathering dispersed, Cassie and Ben approached them, their smiles warm and inviting.

"First sermon at the compound. Quite something, isn't it?" Cassie asked, tucking a strand of hair behind her ear.

"Amelia has a way of making the scripture come alive," Ben added, a note of pride in his voice.

"Alive and relevant," Kyle agreed, nodding. "It's like she's speaking directly to you."

"Exactly," Cassie said. "When I first arrived, I was lost. But her words... they gave me direction. A purpose."

"Didn't realize how much I needed this," Lucy confessed, feeling the echo of her own longing in Cassie's admission.

"Many of us didn't," Ben said, his typically serious demeanor softening. "It's the sense of community, of really being part of something greater. That's what makes this place special."

"Feels like we've been searching for this without even

knowing it," Kyle admitted, his voice a low murmur only Lucy could hear.

"Welcome home, then," Cassie said, her eyes twinkling with genuine happiness.

"Home," Lucy repeated, the word settling in her chest with a weightless certainty. It was a new song, one she felt ready to sing with her whole heart.

Lucy's fingers brushed against the spines of well-thumbed books as they wandered into the compound's library. The scent of musty paper and worn leather offered a comforting blanket of knowledge and shared stories.

"Look at this," Kyle whispered, his voice hushed in reverence for the quiet space. He held up an old tome on herbal remedies, its pages yellowed with age.

"Feels like wisdom just waiting to be absorbed," Lucy murmured back, her green eyes scanning the titles before settling on a collection of poetry. She flipped through the pages, absorbing the rhythm of the words.

They continued their exploration, stepping out into the garden where neat rows of vegetables lined the earth and fruit trees offered their bounty. Bees buzzed around blossoms, and the sound of laughter floated from a nearby bench where a few members chatted warmly.

"Even the garden feels like part of the music here," Lucy noted, watching a butterfly dance from one flower to another.

"Harmony in nature, just like chords in a melody," Kyle replied with a smile, plucking a ripe tomato from the vine and weighing it in his hand.

"Exactly," she agreed, taking his hand in hers, feeling the calluses from guitar strings against her skin. "I'm grateful, Kyle. For this place, for us, for a chance to be part of something bigger."

"Me too, Luce. Me too." His voice was low and sincere.

They sat in companionable silence, the hustle of the day melting away into the evening calm.

Later, Lucy and Kyle retreated to their room and let the coziness envelop them.

"Today was..." Kyle began, searching for the right word.

"Perfect," Lucy finished for him, her voice a contented sigh.

They crawled into their separate beds, the day's experiences a comfort.

"Goodnight, Kyle," Lucy murmured, her eyelids heavy.

"Night, Luce," he replied, his voice already fading into sleep.

In the darkness, with the soft rustle of sheets and the steady rhythm of their breaths, Lucy and Kyle drifted off. Their dreams were filled with the melodies of guitars and laughter, until a distant murmur broke the quietude, rousing Lucy from her slumber. Her eyes fluttered open to a moonlit sliver of the room, where shadows danced upon the walls. Disoriented, she listened, waiting for the sound to return. There it was again—a whispered chanting that seemed both within and beyond the compound.

"Kyle," she hissed, her voice barely a breath.

From the neighboring bed, a soft groan, then a rustle of sheets. "Mmm?"

"Did you hear that?" She propped herself up on one elbow, straining her ears against the stillness.

"Hear what?" Kyle mumbled, his words slurred with sleep.

"Chanting... or something." Her heart quickened, the serenity of their arrival now tinged with uncertainty.

"Probably just the wind," he murmured, unconcerned.

Yet the sound persisted, rhythmic and low, pulling her from the warmth of her bed. Bare feet touched cold floorboards as she crept to the window, peering out into the silver-washed night.

Across the compound, a dim light flickered in Pastor Amelia

Hawthorne's quarters, casting long, quivering shadows against the curtains. Figures moved within, their silhouettes merging and parting in a dance of fervor and devotion.

"Kyle, look." Her whisper held an edge of compulsion.

Rubbing his eyes, Kyle joined her side, squinting toward the source of the glow. "What are they doing?"

"Prayer? Worship?" The others had spoken of Amelia's nightly rituals, but witnessing it cast a different spell.

"Intense," he said, a note of reverence creeping into his tone.

"Doesn't it make you wonder... what holds them together so tightly?" Lucy's gaze remained fixed on the spectacle.

"Amelia," Kyle stated, simple and sure. "She's got a way about her."

"An influence..." Lucy mused, her mind grappling with the sight.

"Let's get back to bed," Kyle suggested, tugging at her arm gently. "We'll understand more with time."

They retreated to their beds, the echo of the chant vibrating through the silence. Lucy nestled under the covers, her earlier comfort turned to curiosity now and the faintest twinge of disquiet.

"Goodnight, again," she whispered into the darkness.

"Night," came Kyle's reply, a shadow of concern in his voice.

The chanting continued, and lingered on the edge of their dreams. And as sleep reclaimed her, Lucy couldn't shake the feeling that this sanctuary held secrets yet to be revealed, secrets that hummed beneath the surface of perfect harmony.

ELEVEN
BILLIE ANN

I sat on the cold metal chair, my eyes constantly darting back to the clock above the door of the morgue. The air was thick and sterile, with a faint hint of death lurking beneath the surface. I couldn't help but take deep breaths, trying to replace the smell with memories from my childhood—the sweet blossoms of the tree in our backyard or the smoky scent of barbeques with my family.

"Detective Wilde?" The attendant's voice jolted me out of my thoughts.

"Right here," I replied without moving, my gaze now fixed on the watch strapped to my wrist. It was time.

The door creaked open, and they stepped through. Joanne's face was ashen, and she appeared even smaller than when I'd last seen her yesterday. Her long, wavy hair lay limp over her shoulders. She hadn't showered. The vibrancy in her eyes was replaced by a hollow despair. John came behind her, his own expression one of bleak resignation.

"Mrs. Harris, Mr. Harris," I said, rising. My voice sounded too loud in the hush of the hallway, too certain amidst so much uncertainty. "If you'll follow me, please."

Our shoes clicked against the linoleum as we traversed the
corridor. Echoes bounced off the walls, mocking us with their
normalcy in such an abnormal situation. Joanne's breaths came
in shallow bursts, each one seemingly a struggle to draw. John's
face was a mask, giving nothing away, but there was a tightness
around his eyes that spoke volumes.

We arrived at the door—the final barrier between them and
the undeniable reality of their loss. I hesitated for a fraction of a
second, grappling with what I was about to do. But duty
propelled me forward. The idea that I had already identified
Madison, but that her mother and stepfather were being forced
to do so formally, was horrible. I wished I could have just told
them it was her. This was tortuous and unfair. But I had to
follow the proper procedure.

"Are you ready?" I asked, though no one could ever be
ready for this.

Joanne nodded, a fragile gesture, and I pushed open the
door. The chill inside the room seemed to seep into my bones as
we entered. There she was—Madison. Even in the stillness of
death, her youthful spirit seemed to linger, a painful reminder
of all that had been stolen from us.

John's hand tightened on Joanne's shoulder, as if bracing her
for the impact of the sight before us. She moved as if underwa-
ter, drifting toward the table where Madison lay.

"Take your time," I murmured, standing back, giving them
the privacy of their grief within the shared space of sorrow.

Joanne's hand hovered, a tremor in her fingers as if the air
itself was charged with her dread. Then, with the barest
whisper of contact, she traced the cold, still cheek of her daughter. A single tear breached the dam of her stoic facade, carving a
path down her face.

"Madison," she whispered, the name breaking against the
silence of the room. "My sweet girl."

The words were barely audible, strangled by the knot of

grief in her throat. Each syllable was a testament to a future unfulfilled, to dreams dashed upon the harsh rocks of this cruel reality.

I swallowed hard, my own heart aching. I placed a tentative hand on Joanne's shoulder, the fabric of her blouse damp beneath my palm. She didn't flinch, didn't recoil; she was anchored in her sorrow, moored to the moment of parting.

"I'll give you some time," I said softly.

John, who had remained a silent sentinel until now, placed an arm around Joanne, guiding her away from the table where Madison lay. Seeing John support Joanne made him seem less like a suspect, but was it all an act? I watched him closely. He was in similar clothes to the last time I'd seen him, but he'd shaved.

Their footsteps were leaden, each step a burden they bore together, leaving behind the simple finality of the morgue.

"Come on, Jo," John murmured, his voice low and strained. "We've seen enough."

"Is this really happening?" Joanne's voice cracked, a sliver of denial lingering in her words.

"Unfortunately, yes," I replied.

We walked through the corridor, the quiet punctuated only by the soft shuffle of their feet and the occasional sniffle from Joanne. The distance to the exit stretched impossibly long.

"Detective Wilde," Joanne managed to say, her voice thick. "Thank you for-for being here with us."

"Billie Ann, please," I corrected gently, though formality seemed trivial in the grand scheme of things. "And it's my job, but more than that, it's my responsibility to help you through this."

As we reached the doors leading out, sunlight spilled across the threshold, a stark contrast to the shadows we were leaving behind. But even as the light touched our faces, I knew that for Joanne and John, the darkness wasn't something that could be

left in any room—it was a constant companion that would
follow them, just as I would follow the clues to bring justice for
their lost Madison.

As I entered the precinct, the cold from the morgue still
lingered on my skin. The harsh fluorescent lights illuminated a
bustling scene. Exhausted search teams, having been out all
night, were trickling back in, clutching steaming cups of coffee.
Desks were piled high with hastily scribbled reports and
evidence bags. Detectives huddled in small groups, comparing
notes and theories in hushed tones. The atmosphere held a
mixture of resolve and fatigue as the investigation kicked into
high gear.

"Right this way," I said as I led Joanne and John down a
narrow hallway. We arrived at a small room secluded from the
bustling activity of the main floor. Inside, the walls bore
evidence of Madison's case—photos taken too late, maps with
areas circled in red, and whiteboards scrawled with theories and
timelines. It was a shrine to unanswered questions, a silent
testament to the life that was snatched away.

"Please, have a seat," I offered, and Joanne sank into a chair,
her eyes fixating on a photo of Madison smiling, forever frozen
in time. John took his place beside her, his body rigid, his gaze
flickering erratically across the evidence of his stepdaughter's
last days. I had decided to talk to them together at first, and in
full view of these details, to see John's reaction to it all. He
seemed lost. He didn't seem like he was scanning for evidence
that involved him. Perhaps my original instincts had been
wrong, and he wasn't involved in Madison's disappearance. I
wanted to see the dynamics playing out between them. How
did they interact? What was their relationship like? Did Joanne
suspect it could be John who hurt Madison? Was she afraid
of him?

I pulled out a notepad, poised to capture their words, their memories. Every detail could be the key, every recollection a door to the truth we sought so fervently.

"I know this is going to be harder than before, but I need you to answer some more questions for me," I began, my tone gentle yet firm. "Anything you can tell me about Madison could help us find her killer."

Joanne nodded, but she stayed silent.

I leaned forward, my hands clasped tightly together on the cool metal table. "Joanne, John, we can see from the scene that Madison's death wasn't an accident." I watched their faces closely, bracing for the impact of my next words. "We're treating her death as a homicide."

A sharp intake of breath from Joanne pierced the charged silence that followed. John's jaw clenched tight, and his knuckles whitened around the armrests. Their grief was raw, visceral—a wound reopened as I spoke.

"We won't stop until we find out what happened to your daughter," I assured them, meaning every word. "We'll find the truth and whoever is responsible. We owe Madison that justice."

Joanne's eyes, rimmed red, met mine. A glimmer of gratitude shone through the despair. I nodded at her unspoken thanks and pulled out my notepad, the pages crisp and blank, ready to be filled.

"Can you tell me more about Madison?" My voice softened, coaxing the happier memories from the shadow of their current nightmare.

"Madison... she had this laugh," Joanne began, a sad smile curving her lips. "It could light up a room. She loved hiking, being outside—said it made her feel free."

"Free," I echoed, scribbling down her recollections. The image of a young girl with wild dreams and a thirst for the open air took shape on my page.

"And her friends?" I prompted, remembering that my next job was to track down Anissa Watson. "The girls from gymnastics were the closest ones she had. They were everything to her," Joanne continued, warmth returning to her tone. "They'd have sleepovers, watch movies, or just talk for hours about... everything under the sun."

"Did that include Anissa?" Joanne nodded. "Sounds like they were close."

"Very," she confirmed. "Madison was the glue that held them together. She was always planning their next adventure. You know—planning to go play mini-golf, or go to the springs and go tubing. Stuff like that. Except lately it seems like she wasn't doing that as much as she used to."

"When did they stop being inseparable?"

She sighed and looked briefly at her husband. "I don't know, a year or so ago, I guess?"

I nodded and wrote it down. "Did something happen between them?"

"I don't know," she said. "Madison told me that she just wasn't in the mood to hang out with them. I thought it was just the beginning of the tween years. They say they can be rough."

I noted the names Joanne mentioned: Lisa, Tanya, Chloe... Anissa. I knew we'd already interviewed these girls, but perhaps I'd need to speak to more of them myself.

"Did she have any particular hobbies or dreams for the future?" I asked, already sensing those shattered dreams hanging between us. It was a sidetrack, but I was trying to get Joanne to feel comfortable enough to trust me and tell me things, and as a mom I knew that we all loved talking about our children's dreams and passions. I needed her to let her guard down.

"Animals," Joanne breathed out, her gaze softening. "She wanted to help them, heal them. Dreamed of becoming a vet since she was little."

"Thank you, Joanne," I said quietly. "This helps a lot." Her resilience, her willingness to dig into those precious memories despite the pain—it gave me strength. Strength to press on, to fight for answers, to stand unwavering in the face of whatever darkness we might uncover.

"Of course," she whispered, tears brimming but her spirit unbroken. "Anything for Madison."

"Joanne," I said, shifting slightly closer, "tell me about Madison's gymnastics. Was it a passion of hers?"

She nodded, pulling a tissue from the box I'd placed on the table earlier. "Oh, yes. She was... graceful. Agile. The way she moved... it was like watching poetry in motion." Her voice cracked, but she pushed on. "She loved the balance beam best. Said it made her feel like she was flying."

"Did she compete?" I asked, my pen hovering over the notepad.

"Local competitions mostly," Joanne replied. "But she had talent. Her coach said she could've gone far."

"Coach," I echoed softly and wrote the name down as Joanne gave it to me. Another person in Madison's life that needed to be looked at.

"Thank you, Joanne." I glanced up, catching John's eye for the first time since we'd sat down. He was looking anywhere but at us, his jaw set, his hands clasped tightly together.

"John?" I ventured. "Is there anything you'd like to add? Anything you noticed about Madison's friendships, her routines?"

"No." His answer was clipped, curt. "Joanne covered it. I mostly drove her places."

Joanne placed a hand on John's arm. "John was always so nice to take her to school or to a friend's house or wherever they went. It was a big help for me."

I studied him, the tension in his frame, the way his gaze flicked to the door then back again. A man uncomfortable in his own skin—or perhaps just this room. I scribbled a question mark next to his name on my notepad and decided to press just a bit more.

"Her dream of becoming a vet," I said, turning back to Joanne. "Did she volunteer or work with animals?"

"She used to but not lately. She stopped going there a few months ago. But it used to be every Saturday," Joanne replied, pride seeping through her sorrow. "At the local animal shelter. She-she was so gentle with them."

"Did she ever talk about that with you, John?" I kept my tone casual, non-threatening.

"Sometimes," he said, finally meeting my gaze. It was fleeting, almost defensive. "I would take her there and pick her up. Seemed to me that she cared too much about those dumb animals, got too attached."

"Is that a bad thing?" I probed.

"In this world?" His laugh was hollow. "Yeah, maybe it is."

"Or maybe it's exactly what the world needs," I countered, locking eyes with him until he looked away. I couldn't ignore his discomfort.

"Thank you both." I stood, signaling the end of our talk. "Your insights are invaluable."

As they prepared to leave, Joanne leaning on John for support, I couldn't shake the feeling that John was holding back, that there was a depth to his silence we hadn't yet breached. And I intended to dive deep. Madison deserved that much.

"Thank you, truly." My words were a warm blanket, trying to cover the chill of the sterile room. "We're on this, day and night. Madison matters to us."

Joanne nodded, her eyes glistening with gratitude that fought through her grief. John just stood there, a statue of a man, his face unreadable.

"There's a grief counselor," I added. "They'll reach out soon. Help you through this."

"Thank you, Detective Wilde," Joanne murmured, her voice a whisper of its former strength.

John offered no thanks, no acknowledgment. He remained silent, a ghost beside his wife.

I watched them walk away, her arm linked through his, wondering if she felt the ice in his veins as I did.

Hours later, I sat across from Chief Harold in her office.

"John Harris," I started, leaning forward. "Something's not right."

"How was his behavior today?" Chief's eyebrows lifted, a cue for details.

"At first I thought he seemed normal. Well, normal for a stepdad who had just lost his stepchild. He seemed upset. He was supportive of Joanne. But later, he was defensive. Suggested Madison cared about other people too much."

"Defensive or guilty?" Chief mused, steepling her fingers.

"Could be both." I leaned back, crossing my arms. "But there's more to him. We need to dig."

"Pull his records. Talk to colleagues. Friends, if he has any." She paused, her gaze sharpening. "Just don't spook him."

"I think I already did," I said quietly, regretting how confrontational I'd been. But I was angry and frustrated. I had a lot riding on this. Perhaps I needed to relax. I stood up, feeling Chief Harold's gaze on me as I left.

I sank into the chair at my desk, the metal cool against my skin through the fabric of my shirt. I let out a slow breath, trying to loosen the tightness in my shoulders.

"Long day?" Scott's voice rose above the din.

"Like you wouldn't believe," I replied, eyes fixed on the file in front of me—Madison's file.

"Anything I can do?"

"Keep an ear to the ground. Or in your case the computer."

I flipped open the folder, scanning the pages for the hundredth time. "I can't stop thinking of John. There's something there."

I pictured Madison's face, so full of life in the photos, now turned into silent witnesses of what had been. My fingers brushed over the images.

Tom approached us. I straightened, tucking away the swell of emotion.

"What's up?"

"The Harrises just left. They formally identified Madison." I leaned back, eyes on the ceiling tiles, seeing beyond them. Madison's case sprawled out in my mind like a roadmap, each path a lead to explore, every dead end a frustration to overcome.

I knew the road would twist, turn, and maybe double back on itself. But somewhere down that convoluted path lay the truth, and I'd follow it to the ends of the earth if I had to.

TWELVE

BILLIE ANN

We gathered around the cluttered table, elbows knocking against case files and coffee cups. The overhead light buzzed like a trapped fly, adding to the tension that already filled the cramped room. I glanced at Tom, then Scott. Their faces were drawn, eyes shadowed with the same urgency in my gut.

"Where are we?" I asked, voice low.

"Pressure's mounting," Scott added. He didn't have to say it; I felt the weight of expectation heavy on my shoulders. My mind flashed to the courtroom, the judge's steely gaze as he read the verdict that had destroyed my life. Stay out of trouble. Get your life together. And now, more than ever, I needed that win to tilt the balance back home.

"Let's go over John's alibi again," I suggested, pushing aside personal thoughts. This was about Madison. About justice.

"His shift at the store checks out," Tom said, but his brow creased. "Where he said he went after dropping off Madison."

"Camera footage?" I pressed.

"Timestamped. Clear as day," Scott chimed in, handing over the prints.

I riffled through them, checking the angles, the time codes.

John behind the counter, a steady stream of customers. But something gnawed at me—an inconsistency I couldn't immediately place. A feeling, maybe, or a detail just out of reach.

"Any gaps?"

"Nothing significant," Tom answered. "It takes about twenty minutes for him to get to the store from the school, and that fits with the time frame. Still, no one has come back and said they saw him actually drop the kid off. No neighbors living in the area, or people walking in the street."

"Convenient," I said, studying John's face frozen in pixels. Average, forgettable. Yet something lurked behind those glasses that didn't sit right. "What about earlier that morning?"

"Claims he was home," Scott said, "he drove Madison to school at eight fifteen, according to his testimony but no one to verify."

"Joanne was already at work at Health First urgent care," I mused, tapping a finger against the photo. "I checked her alibi myself. She always works morning shifts, so she can be home in the afternoon. That's why John usually took Madison in the mornings. Did we check neighbors?"

"Interviews all came up clean," Tom responded, but he knew me well enough to understand the unspoken question. Double-check. "No one saw them leave that morning."

"Clean alibi. Cooperative. Doesn't scream guilty," Scott concluded, leaning back in his chair.

"Except..." I trailed off, my gaze locked on the image of John, the way his eyes seemed to follow something just out of frame. "There's a coldness. I notice it when he talks about Madison."

"Maybe that's just his way," Tom offered, but I shook my head.

"Intuition's nagging me," I admitted. "He's too composed. Detached."

"Could be shock, grief," Scott countered, but he was

watching me closely, reading the doubt etched in every line of my face.

"Or it could be guilt," I stated flatly, setting the photos down with a decisive snap. "A mask for something darker."

"Enough to bring him in again?" Tom asked, eyebrows raised.

"I've already interviewed him twice," I conceded. "But we're going to find out what John Harris is hiding. And we're going to do it fast."

Tom showed me a map of the swamps, and pointed to red marks he had placed on it. All places where they had found trace evidence.

"We believe Madison tried to evade her attacker through the swamps, as we have found many small pieces of her clothing ripped off on branches, and rocks with her blood on them, where she might have fallen, trying to escape," Tom said.

The very thought made my stomach hurt. This little girl running for her life. It was unbearable. My phone rang and I picked it up. It was the forensic department.

"We got something," Dr. Martinez said. "We confiscated John's car since it was the last place Madison had been according to him. And we found something. Fresh blood found in John Harris's car matched that of Madison's."

I hung up my heart hammering in my chest. Then I rose to my feet. "I'll get a warrant for his arrest."

My team and I met an hour later, warrant in my hand. The patrol car following John had told us he was at home. He had been cooperative so far, but I was worried for Joanne's well-being if he knew we were coming for him. We had to be careful. We gathered around the iPad showing a map of the house. Tom was circling exit points for the house. We wanted to be sure we could corner him if he tried to run.

"Coordination with our PD?" I asked.

"Check. They're on standby for crowd control and perimeter security. In case he runs or something else unexpected occurs."

"Good." I glanced up, meeting the eyes of my team. "Check equipment," I ordered, and we moved as one, checking vests, radios, and firearms. My own vest was comforting—a solid reminder of the line between us and chaos.

"Radio check," I heard through my earpiece, a whisper against the backdrop of adrenaline.

"Clear," I responded in the thick silence that had settled over us.

"Five minutes out," came the driver's voice, jolting us into action.

"Let's move," I commanded, and we piled into the unmarked vehicles, engines growling softly under the cover of darkness.

The convoy slipped through the city like a shadow, and Madison's face hovered in my mind.

"Go time," I whispered as we approached John's street, the vehicles pulling to a stealthy stop.

"Go, go, go!" I barked, bursting from the vehicle. My boots hit the pavement hard.

We knocked on the door yelling, "Police," but there was no answer.

"Breaching!" Tom called out, and the front door shattered under the force of the ram.

"Clear!" Scott's voice echoed from the back.

Room by room, we swept through the house, a whispering tide of dark figures. Professional, precise. Every corner checked, every shadow investigated.

"Living room clear!"

"Kitchen secure!"

"Upstairs moving!"

"Bedroom, go!"

"Clear!"

"Clear!"

"Clear!"

"Police! Hands in the air!" Tom's command was a thunder-clap in the stillness. It made us rush for the back. He had caught John just as he was reaching for the back door, a rabbit poised to bolt at the first sign of the hounds.

"John Harris, you are under arrest," I declared, stepping forward, cuffs in hand. His reaction was immediate—panic etched across his ordinary face, glasses askew. He lunged clumsily for the door, his desperation palpable.

Tom was faster. A mountain of muscle, he blocked John's path. Scott flanked him, wiry and quick, darting in to grasp one of John's flailing arms. I moved in tandem, securing the other.

"Stay down!" Tom was firm but controlled as we wrestled John to the ground. The struggle was brief; our training prevailed against his frantic thrashing.

"Got him." My voice was steady, but adrenaline surged through my veins like wildfire. I snapped the cuffs on with a finality that echoed off the walls.

"Clear!" Scott confirmed, his long hair falling into his eyes as he scanned the room.

"Secure him," I commanded, catching my breath.

"Copy that," Tom grunted, hauling John to his feet, his sweet-natured goofiness nowhere in sight amidst the operation.

"Detective Wilde," John said, his voice desperate. "You've got the... I never—"

"Save it for the interrogation room," I cut him off, pushing him forward. It was done, or at least, this part was. The real work would come after, but for now, we allowed ourselves a moment of grim satisfaction. Two officers led him to a patrol car and took him away.

"Team, secure the scene," I instructed, watching as they

began to comb through the house with the meticulousness that had become our trademark. Each piece of evidence, another step toward justice.

"Good work, everyone," I said, though the words felt hollow against the gravity of what lay ahead. We had a tiny piece of evidence against John, though the fact that he had tried to flee the house didn't exactly make him look innocent.

Gloves snapped against wrists. Eyes scanned, methodical and sharp. The house loomed, now a crime scene, silent but for our measured movements. The car we had taken in when her body was found. The house was searched earlier, but now it was time to expand the search for evidence. I led the way, my team fanning out behind me.

"Start with the office," I directed, my voice steady despite the adrenaline that still coursed through my veins. "Check every file, every drawer."

"Got it," Scott affirmed, heading toward the small room that reeked of stale cigarettes and secrets.

"Tom, bedrooms. Anything that looks off, I want to know immediately."

"Copy that," he responded, his tall frame disappearing up the stairwell.

The search was rustling papers and soft thuds of furniture moved just enough to reveal what lay beneath. Drawers slid open with precision; contents were photographed, lifted, bagged. We had searched the house before, but only briefly when Madison went missing. This time we left no stone unturned, no crevice unchecked.

"Billie, you should see this." Scott's voice cut through the silence, pulling me toward John's makeshift office. My gaze fell on an array of flash drives scattered across the desk—too many for casual use.

"Bag them all," I instructed, a knot forming in my stomach.

"Already on it," he replied, his own expression grim.

I turned to the computer, its screen dark and waiting. I powered it up, ready to sift through the digital maze for any clue, any thread that could lead us closer to justice for Madison.

The desktop flickered to life, icons aligning like soldiers ready for inspection. I navigated to the video folder, each click a step deeper into John's private world.

And then I saw it—thumbnails of videos, each displaying images that made my blood run cold. Children. My hands trembled as I opened the first file, the moving pictures more horrific than the stills suggested.

"Jesus Christ," I whispered, my heart pounding with a mix of fury and disgust. The air tainted by the evil that had unfolded within these walls.

"Billie?" Scott was concerned, hovering at the edge of my peripheral vision.

"Look at this," I managed, gesturing to the screen.

His curse was soft but laden with revulsion. "We need to get forensics on this ASAP."

"Get them here now," I said, tearing my eyes away from the screen. Each image seared into my memory, fueling a fire that no amount of darkness could extinguish.

"Will do," Scott replied, already dialing the number.

With John detained, the meticulous documentation began. Every step, every action was recorded—the securing of the scene, the systematic collection of evidence, and the unwavering observance of protocol. I watched as Scott donned gloves, carefully bagging the computer hard drive, tagging it with precise detail.

I watched as Scott passed the bag to another officer who logged it immediately.

"Everything's by the book," Scott responded, his eyes serious behind the screen of his hair.

"Good. Let's keep it that way."

"Forensics will have a field day with this," Tom mused, eyeing the evidence bags.

"Let's hope they find what we need to put this guy away for good," I said, Madison's memory pressing on my shoulders, as I felt more certain that he had something to do with what happened to her. Could he have been abusing her? I had to consider this; the websites on John's computer indicated he may have been.

"Billie Ann, we're ready to transport," an officer called out from the front door.

"Coming," I replied, tucking my notepad into my jacket pocket.

"Let's move out," I ordered, and we filed out of the house, leaving behind the silent crime scene soon to be dissected by the meticulous eyes of forensic experts.

The squad car's engine hummed a low dirge as we rolled away from John's house, the rearview mirror reflecting the flickering blues and reds of our retreating parade. I leaned back into the headrest, feeling the vibrations of the road beneath us, letting them massage the tension in my neck. The evidence bags in the trunk, with their terrible secrets, seemed to pulse with urgency.

"Billie Ann, you all right?" Tom's voice penetrated the haze of my thoughts, his brow wrinkled with concern.

"Fine," I lied, looking out the window at the blur of passing streetlights. "Just thinking about what's next."

"His computer was a jackpot," Scott chimed in from the passenger seat, eyes fixed on the laptop where he was reviewing case notes.

"It won't bring Madison back," I said, clenching my fists on my knees. "Or even link him to her murder."

"True," Tom agreed softly, "but it could save others. Plus, we have the blood in his car. We're getting there, Billie Ann."

"Are we?" The question escaped with an edge, sharp

enough to slice the silence. In the darkness of the car, my mind replayed the image of John's home. Had we missed anything?

"Without a doubt," Scott affirmed, his reflection in the rearview meeting mine. "You could tell something was off with him from the very beginning, and you were right. Relentless in uncovering this..."

Relentless... A mantra that had kept me afloat in the murky waters of divorce court, the whispered promise to my kids each night that I'd be there soon. But I hadn't been relentless enough. I hadn't saved Madison. I hadn't proved that I should have my own children back. Perhaps the courts were right.

"Hey." Tom's hand rested briefly on my shoulder, grounding me. "Take a breath. We're in this together."

"Thanks," I said, managing a half-smile.

The car ride ended, depositing us back at the precinct where the fluorescent lights buzzed like an interrogation of their own. I stepped out into the warm night air, drawing in a deep lungful, trying to expel the darkness that clung to my insides.

Back inside, I claimed my desk, the surface cold under my touch. The evidence would be processed, analyzed, scrutinized for the clues that tied John to Madison's death, and possibly to more unseen horrors. No matter the personal cost, I promised myself, I wouldn't stop until justice was served for every lost soul who crossed my desk.

"All right, team," I called out, my voice steady. "Let's get to work."

* * *

Evidence bags lined the table, each one tagged and sealed. Madison's face flashed in my mind, her bright eyes dull in the unforgiving light of tragedy. I pushed the image away. Focus.

"Forensics is en route for pickup," I informed them.

"Already? That was fast," Scott noted, surprise lifting his brow.

"Pressure from above. They want this wrapped tight," I said, thinking of Chief Harold's stern warning.

"Understandable," Tom chimed in, his posture rigid with readiness.

"Detective Wilde?" A uniformed officer approached, snapping me back to the present.

"Report," I said without preamble.

"John Harris is being processed. No statement yet."

"Got it."

I glanced at the clock again. Midnight loomed.

"Get some rest," I advised Scott and Tom. Their nods were weary but determined.

"Same to you, Detective Wilde," Scott added, a knowing look in his eyes.

"Rest is for the innocent," I quipped, though fatigue pressed down on me.

I stepped out of the precinct into the night air. The moon hung low, casting long shadows across the pavement.

THIRTEEN

Then

Lucy Everhart wove through the throng of community members. Her anticipation for Pastor Amelia Hawthorne's sermon hummed within her like a well-tuned string. Months at the compound had shaped her. She had realized she didn't need a big stage or audience clapping. This community was enough, this place was where she got everything she required.

She slid into a pew, hands clasping together as if ready to receive the melody of Amelia's words. The pastor's sermons were often crescendos of hope and acceptance, notes that resonated deeply with Lucy's own song of life. A long line of children walked past in the back, going to their separate sermons at kids' church.

Amelia ascended with an air of grace that hushed the congregation. Silver hair glinted under the soft light, her warm brown eyes sweeping over her flock, and Lucy felt that gaze draw her in, a silent invitation to listen, learn, and be inspired.

"Beloved," Amelia began, her voice a clear bell in the silence, "today I share a revelation, a truth bestowed upon me."

Lucy leaned forward, attentive. The others mirrored her, a sea of rapt faces.

"I stand before you not only as your shepherd but as the Chosen." Amelia's pause was deliberate, weighty. "I am God's daughter."

The words crashed into Lucy like dissonant chords. Around her, the room remained still, breaths seemingly caught in collective chests.

God's daughter?

The phrase tangled in Lucy's mind, a knot she couldn't unravel.

Chosen echoed off the walls, rebounding in Lucy's ears. She searched Amelia's face for a sign of metaphor, an allegory perhaps, but found none. Amelia stood firm, conviction etched into every line of her elegant visage.

This was not the sermon she had envisioned, not the harmony she sought. But around her, heads nodded slowly, acceptance blooming on their features. Was she the only one questioning what Amelia was saying?

"God told me this Himself. He came to me in a vision," Amelia continued.

Lucy's hands clenched the wooden pew tightly.

Amelia's voice rose, a clear bell in the hushed hall. "It is not only through words that we spread divine love," she intoned, her gaze sweeping over the congregation like a beacon, "but through life itself."

Lucy felt the murmurs around her, a low hum of intrigue. Amelia stepped down from the pulpit, her silver hair catching the dim light as she moved among them, a shepherd mingling with her flock.

"Brothers and sisters," Amelia continued, her warm brown eyes alight with fervor, "the time has come to embrace a new covenant. I am to bear children with the men of our community." She paused, letting the gravity of meaning sink in. "These children will be holy, for they will be born of God's lineage through me. Through them we will create a new and better world."

A murmur of assent rippled through the room. Lucy turned slightly, catching glimpses of faces lit with awe. No one raised a voice in dissent—not even Kyle, whose eyes shone with a fervor she had never seen before.

"Such a beautiful vision!" someone exclaimed, and others quickly agreed, their voices a chorus of affirmation.

"Imagine, children of God among us," another whispered reverently.

"Divinely blessed from birth," a third added, hands clasped together in veneration.

Lucy's heart pounded. The wooden pew felt hard against her back as she sat frozen, the world tilting on its axis. This meant—did it mean Amelia would lie with Kyle? *Her* Kyle?

Was this truly a message from above, or was it something else entirely, something... profane?

"Each union will be sacred," Amelia declared, certain. "Chosen by God, through me, to propagate His divine essence on Earth. A new dawn is coming."

Union? Union, a euphemism so gentle for an act that now seemed anything but.

"Kyle," she mouthed, a plea lost amidst the rising tide of adulation. She cast a furtive glance at him, but his profile was already etched with reverence and awe. He was already a believer, a disciple of this new gospel. His loyalty to Amelia was clear, unshakable.

Lucy's stomach churned. A fissure was opening between them, between her beliefs and this reality unfolding before her eyes. Amelia's intentions tangled around Lucy's thoughts like thorny vines, threatening to choke her reason.

"Is this faith?" she wondered. "Or is it madness?"

Doubt crept in, cold and slithering. Had she been blind to

who Amelia truly was? To what this community stood for? Lucy searched within herself for clarity, for some vestige of understanding, but found none—only a growing unease and a fear of what was yet to come.

Lucy clasped her hands together until her knuckles whitened, her fingernails digging into the flesh of her palms in a silent act of self-discipline. She stood motionless among the congregation, her eyes fixed on the wooden grain of the floor beneath her feet—anything to avoid being noticed. She was certain her concern would be obvious if anyone looked at her face.

"Each of you has been chosen," Amelia continued, her voice weaving through the silence, "to be part of something greater than ourselves."

The air was charged with an electric current that buzzed against Lucy's skin. Shadows seemed to hold a little too tightly to the corners of the room, whispering secrets that only added to the suffocating atmosphere.

"Isn't it beautiful?" a woman beside Lucy murmured with awe.

"Truly," Lucy replied, the word brittle on her tongue, a shard of glass swallowed whole. Her smile was a masterful lie, a curve of the lips devoid of warmth.

The candles onstage flickered as if caught in a breeze, casting a dance of light and dark upon Amelia's silver hair. The subtle play of shadows seemed to momentarily distort her features—a visual trick, or a revelation of something more sinister beneath?

"Let us embrace this gift," Amelia said, her arms outstretched as if to gather the very souls of those present.

Lucy's throat tightened as applause broke out across the room. A man to Lucy's left blinked rapidly, his Adam's apple bobbing in a silent swallow. An elderly woman clasped her hands together, lips moving in what looked like fervent prayer.

A young couple exchanged glances, their brows furrowing before smoothing into smiles of acceptance. Someone fell to her knees, arms stretched up as if overwhelmed by something divine. A woman next to her started rolling across the floor, crying manically.

"God's will be done," a man on her other side whispered, nodding to his partner.

"God's will," she echoed, a touch of hesitancy in her voice that quickly gave way to conviction.

"Amelia speaks the truth," someone said from the back, and it was met with murmurs of agreement.

"Her words are blessings," another added, the sentiment rippling through the congregation like waves lapping at the shore.

Lucy felt something cold and heavy settle in her stomach as she observed the scene. Her mind recoiled from the memory of the woman she'd met months ago—the one whose wisdom had appeared as deep and boundless as the night sky. That Amelia had radiated a gentle strength, a beacon that had guided Lucy here.

But this... this was a stranger wearing Amelia's skin.

Betrayal curdled within her. The Amelia standing before them now was a sculptor, and they were clay in her hands— willingly malleable, eagerly shaped by her every decree.

"Kyle..." Lucy whispered. But when she found him, he was not the refuge she sought. His face was alight with an unsettling zeal.

"Lucy," he said, his voice firm, "Amelia is our leader. We must trust in her guidance. It's what we came here for."

The words stung, a slap of realization that the gulf between them had grown wider than she had feared. She gazed into his eyes, searching for a flicker of the man who had questioned, who had challenged, who had loved. But all she saw was a reflection of the blind devotion that filled the room.

"Kyle," she tried again, her voice barely audible above the swell of conversation, "don't you see—"

"Shh," he hushed her gently, but with a finality that cut her off completely. "We have to obey her, Lucy. She knows the way. Isn't it wonderful?" Kyle's eyes lit up, reflecting a fervor that Lucy didn't recognize. "She's bringing new life, it's—"

"Is it? Wonderful?" Lucy interrupted, the question sharp. "Have you thought about what that means for us?"

"Us?" Kyle echoed, confusion creasing his forehead. "We're part of something bigger now, Lucy. You know that."

"Part of... But doesn't it feel wrong to you? That she wants—"

"Amelia's our leader, Lucy," he cut in, the gentle tone of his voice belying the firmness of his words. "We have to trust her vision. We have to obey."

"Obey," she repeated, tasting the word, a bitter pill. Her hand fell to her side, the connection broken.

"Trust me, this is right," Kyle assured her, reaching for her hand, but she withdrew, the gulf widening between them.

"Right," she murmured, turning away.

Lucy walked aimlessly through the compound. The once-comforting walls closing in.

FOURTEEN
REBECCA

Rebecca Travers' double shift had ended in the kind of exhaustion that seeped into her bones. She trudged home, the sun dipping low and painting the sky in orange and pink. Her shoulders ached, and she was desperate to reach her cozy home.

"Almost home," she whispered to herself.

Passing through the gate, the familiar sights of the trailer park helped her to relax. Rebecca's mind turned to Kayla, her granddaughter, and the special dinner planned—a secret chicken casserole recipe, the one with extra cheese that always brought a smile to the girl's face. She imagined Kayla's delight, heard her laughter, the sound more rejuvenating than any night's sleep. She fumbled with her keys, desperate to see Kayla's face.

"Surprise is the best spice," she often said, and tonight she'd serve it up in spades. It wasn't often she cooked, but Kayla loved it when she did.

The door creaked, a slow groan of hinges begging for oil as Rebecca stepped into the gloom. Dim light from the fading day filtered through the dusty blinds, laying uneven stripes across the cramped space of the living room. Shadows like cobwebs in the corners were thick and almost tangible in the silence that pressed down on her.

"Kayla?" Her voice seemed too loud, an intrusion on the stillness, dissipating slowly into the hush of the trailer. She reached for the switch, flicking it up and down. The bulb above sputtered, a weak protest before dying completely, leaving Rebecca in the half-light.

"Kayla, honey, are you here?" she called again, louder this time. The words bounced off the walls, hollow echoes with no answer. Silence gnawed at the edges of her anticipation, turning it sour.

"Kayla, it's Nana," she tried once more, each syllable fraying with a creeping unease. Her hand found the back of a dining chair, gripping it as though to anchor herself in this suddenly alien terrain. Her gaze darted from one shadow to the next, seeking out the reassuring outline of her granddaughter, but finding none.

Rebecca's hand trembled as she withdrew it from the empty chair. A shiver ran through her. "Must be out with friends," she said, the words a feeble shield against worry's sharp edge.

She shuffled to the kitchenette, the linoleum cold and unwelcoming underfoot. Pots clanged as she pulled them from the cupboard, the noise a temporary distraction. She set water to boil, measured pasta with a practiced eye. "I'll make a side of mac and cheese," she whispered, "her favorite."

"Kayla's going to love this," she said aloud, trying to believe it. The hum of the refrigerator joined her solitary conversation, a steady drone that filled some of the silence.

Dusk crept in unnoticed until Rebecca glanced up, the window now a dark mirror reflecting her furrowed brow. The trailer seemed to exhale, a long sigh that ruffled the curtains and toyed with the frayed edges of her nerves.

"Things settling for the night," she told herself, but the creaks that followed spoke of age and secrets, not peace. Wood groaned softly, making the hairs on Rebecca's neck stand on end.

"Stop it," she scolded the empty room. But the whispering shadows mocked her bravado, creeping closer as if to listen. She stirred the pot more vigorously, the spoon hitting the sides with sharp taps.

"Kayla will be home any minute," she assured the gathering darkness, each word a plea. The trailer responded with another creak, longer, more plaintive, as if lamenting the deepening night. With every passing moment, the safety of daylight seemed like a distant memory, leaving Rebecca alone with her simmering pot and her simmering fears.

Rebecca set the wooden spoon aside, wiping her hands on a dishtowel as she reached for her phone. The screen lit up—a bright square in the dim kitchen—void of notifications. She thumbed through her contacts and pressed Kayla's name, the ringing tone a stark contrast to the quiet creaks around her.

No answer.

"Kayla, this isn't funny," she whispered, tapping the "end call" button with more force than necessary. Her thumb hovered, then jabbed at the message icon, her eyes scanning for any sign of recent activity. Nothing.

"Okay, okay," she mumbled, scrolling now through her contacts. Names of Kayla's friends emerged. She called Jenna first.

"Hey, Rebecca," came the chipper voice on the other end.

"Hi, Jenna. Have you seen Kayla tonight?" Rebecca's voice betrayed a note of urgency.

"Um, no. Not since school." The line crackled with Jenna's confusion.

"All right. Thanks, hon."

She hung up, her fingers stiffening before dialing the next number. "Mia? It's Rebecca. Is Kayla with you?"

"Sorry, Mrs. Travers. I haven't seen her," Mia replied with a hint of concern.

"Okay, thanks." Rebecca's hand shook slightly as she ended the call.

The room seemed to shrink as she continued down the list. Each call, each negative response, twisted the knot in her stomach tighter.

"Kayla!" she shouted out of the window of the trailer, her voice cracking. No reply came, only the buzzing hum of the refrigerator and the distant bark of a neighbor's dog. She wrung her hands, the skin dry and stretched tight.

"Stop it, Rebecca. Stop it," she admonished herself, but the thoughts wouldn't relent. They swarmed her, each scenario more horrific than the last. Was Kayla hurt? Had someone taken her? The possibilities clawed at her, savage and unyielding.

"God, no." Her breaths came sharp and shallow. Reaching for the phone again, she dialed with quaking fingers, the numbers blurring before her eyes.

"Come on, come on," she urged the silent device. No ringing, just a vast void waiting to swallow her whole.

"Pick up," she hissed into the receiver, her plea dissolving into the growing dusk outside. Her chest tightened, a vice of fear squeezing the air from her lungs.

"Please, please, let her be safe," Rebecca whispered to the emptiness, her words a fragile prayer in the gathering gloom.

Rebecca flung open the trailer door, a gust of stale air clashing with the night's warmth. She stepped out, the metal stairs unyielding beneath her feet. Her eyes darted left, then right, piercing the darkness that had settled over the park like a suffocating blanket.

"Kayla!" Her voice shattered the silence, each shout growing more desperate. "Kayla, are you here?"

The trailer lights threw her shadow long and distorted across the gravel, an ominous sign that seemed to mock her fear.

Rebecca squinted, searching for any glimmer of her grand-daughter—a tossed backpack, a stray shoe, anything.

"Kayla!" she called again.

She trudged forward, her heart a heavy drum in her chest. The surrounding trailers stood silent, their windows dark. A dog barked somewhere in the distance, a lonesome sound that echoed Rebecca's dread.

Then, movement.

A figure, small and slender, emerged from the shadows near the community mailbox. Rebecca's breath caught, hope surging like a wave.

"Kayla?" Her voice trembled, laced with tentative relief.

The figure drew closer, and Rebecca's pulse quickened. But as it moved into the light, the cruel truth sank its teeth into her. Not Kayla. Not her bright-eyed girl.

"Sorry, ma'am," said the boy from down the road, his fishing pole slung over his shoulder. "Haven't seen her."

"Think, Rebecca, think," she scolded herself, pacing the cramped space. "Where would she go?"

Images assaulted her—dark alleys, strangers with ill intentions, Kayla's face twisted in fear. She shook her head, trying to dispel the visions. "No, not my Kayla."

She grabbed her phone from the counter, the screen a cold glow in her palm. No messages. No missed calls. Her thumb hovered over the keypad.

"Call someone. Anyone." Her whisper was lost beneath the hum of the refrigerator.

"Josie." She dialed. Waited. Two rings. Three. "Pick up, please..."

"Becca? What's wrong?" Josie's voice came through, tinged with sleep.

"Kayla's gone. Not home. Not with friends. I don't know where—" The words tumbled out, a mess of fear and confusion.

"Okay, okay... calm down," Josie soothed. "Have you called the police?"

"No. Not yet. Should I?" Rebecca's gaze darted around the room, as if answers might materialize on the floral wallpaper.

"Becca, yes. Call them now."

"Okay." Rebecca's breath hitched. "I'm scared, Jo."

"I know. I'm coming over. Call them. Now."

The line went dead. Rebecca's finger hovered, then pressed. Three numbers that felt like a lifeline.

"Police, please help me. It's my granddaughter, Kayla. She's missing."

The words echoed in the hollow space, filling it with a tangible dread. Her hands clenched the phone like a vice, waiting for a response. Fear consumed her, dark and ravenous, as she whispered a silent prayer into the night.

FIFTEEN

BILLIE ANN

The fluorescent lights hummed above me as I tidied up the scattered papers. My eyes were tired from spending countless hours poring over John Harris's statements. He was an enigma, his emotions as bland as the off-white walls of the interrogation room where I would confront him once again. But somewhere within those words, I was certain there was a contradiction that could unravel his story about Madison's death. We had gone through all the evidence gathered so far, hoping to find something that would point to John's involvement, but everything we found only seemed to strengthen his alibi. The fabric samples taken from the crime scene did not match any of the materials in his wardrobe, leaving us at a dead end.

"Detective Wilde," my own voice echoed back at me, practicing the questions I'd drill him with the following day when I tried again. "Can you explain the blood in the car, Mr. Harris?"

I imagined his face, impassive behind those glasses, but this time I'd make him admit to something. I had to. I was worried our one piece of evidence against him wouldn't hold up in court. We had Madison's blood in his car, but what if he had an excuse for that? The videos found at his address were heinous and very much illegal, and we could get him locked up for owning indecent images of children, but I wanted to put him away for murder. Or he might end up a free man after only a brief sentence of five years or so. There were convicted pedophiles on the streets all over Florida.

My hand hovered over the file as I prepared to slide it into my bag, the last item before calling it a night. The station was quiet, the kind of hush that falls when most have gone home and those left are too buried in their work to notice the ticking clock.

That's when the phone rang. I snatched it up, heart already anticipating the worst.

"Detective Wilde," I answered briskly.

"Detective," Sergeant James Ryan, who was manning the calls from dispatch at night, said, "There's another girl. She's gone missing."

"You're freaking kidding me?" I reached for a pen, my other hand steadying the receiver against my ear as I flipped open a new page in my notebook. "Tell me the details."

"I have a number you can call. I am sending a patrol to her house as well, but thought you'd like to know."

"Yes, of course," I said, even if I found it hard to grasp. Was this related to Madison? Or was it another case? I had to calm myself down, telling myself it could be some completely different situation. Yet it didn't help. I had a feeling something was very wrong.

"I'll go with them out there."

I hung up the phone, the weight of another child's life pressing down on me. It was a heaviness I knew all too well, a burden that never quite lifted no matter how many times I faced it.

"Damn it," I muttered, shoving the chair back with more force than necessary.

I snapped on my jacket. I wanted to go to the woman's

home myself alongside the patrol. If this had anything to do with Madison's murder I needed to get on top of this as quickly as possible. I texted Tom and Scott to meet me at the address.

Pulling up to Mrs. Travers' home, the porch light threw a golden halo around the open door where she stood, a thin shawl wrapped around her shoulders, her body trembling like a leaf, despite the warm night.

"Thank God you came." She greeted us, voice quivering with unspoken fears. I signaled for the officers to take a look around the trailer and inside.

"Mrs. Travers, I'm Detective Billie Ann Wilde. Tell me everything you can," I said, stepping into her home, my eyes catching the photos of a smiling girl on the fridge door. "I've been told your granddaughter Kayla is missing. When did you see her last? Or hear from her?"

"I-I know she went to school. Yesterday now. I left early in the morning and she was still sleeping. But her friends said she was in school. She wasn't on the bus home, though; her friend Jessie said she never got on the bus, so she assumed she was getting picked up or maybe had taken her bike. They usually go on the bus together. I don't know if she ever came home here. She hasn't answered any of my calls or texts."

"Tell me about her. Has she ever done anything like this before? Ever stayed away like this?"

"Not Kayla," she began, wringing her hands, "she's thirteen years old. She's a good girl. Doesn't get herself in trouble like many of the other ones..."

"Friends?" I asked, pulling out my notepad. The pen hovered over the paper, ready to capture every detail. There was only one elementary school and one high school in town, but it was still worth noting that both girls disappeared from the same school, and in a very similar manner.

"Neighborhood kids mostly, but I already called them," she replied. "She isn't with any of them."

"Any changes recently? Did she act different? Seem like she was secretive about something? Anything at all?"

Mrs. Travers shook her head. "She's been the same happy child... always."

"Tell me about her parents," I pressed gently, knowing each piece could be the key to finding Kayla in time.

"Her father, my son, died when she was two. Heart attack." She swallowed hard. "And her mother..." Her gaze fell to the floor.

"Never around?" I ventured.

"Never wanted to be," she corrected, lifting her eyes to meet mine. "That's what my son said. Kayla was his world after her mother left."

"So, you've never met her?"

"Never did. No pictures, no calls, nothing."

"All right, we'll need a list of everyone who's come into contact with Kayla lately," I said, clicking the pen shut. "Neighbors, friends, anyone."

"Of course, Detective." She nodded, holding on to the lifeline of my assurance.

"Thank you, Mrs. Travers. We'll do everything we can," I promised.

We moved back outside, the night air clammy against my skin. Time was slipping away, and with it, a little girl's chances. I wouldn't let that happen. Not on my watch. I had to redeem myself for not saving Madison.

Stepping outside, the night seemed to clutch at the edges of my jacket, a strange foreboding whispering through the trees. Madison's case clung to me, the pang of not finding her in time gnawing at my resolve. "Not again," I muttered under my breath, the determination hardening in my gut.

"Billie Ann?" Scott spoke in the darkness. He stood by the cruiser, his curly hair a shadowed halo under the streetlights.

"Got something?" I asked, striding purposefully as I joined him.

"Maybe." He handed over a map, fingers brushing mine. "Wetlands here," he pointed, "kids love it. Could be a hideout or..." His voice trailed off, but we both understood the unsaid.

"Right," I acknowledged, tracing the tangled lines of water and land with my finger. "Tom?"

"Here." Tom emerged, his tall frame unfolding from the darkness. "What's the plan?"

"Search party," I said, handing him a flashlight. "We comb the wetlands. Grid pattern. I know everyone is exhausted from the searches for Madison, but this will be another overnight job."

"Creepy place at night," Tom commented, trying to lighten the mood, but his attempt fell flat in the gravity of our task. He passed on my instructions to the few other officers, leaving one deputy at Kayla's grandmother's door. We fanned out.

"Kayla!" I called into the void between the silhouettes of twisted trees and murky waters. Shadows played tricks on my eyes, every rustle a potential sign. I got into my car and we drove slowly toward the swamps behind the trailer park. Kayla could have gotten lost in there, maybe staying out too late and not being able to find her way back, or she could have met a wild animal; hopefully it wasn't a gator.

"Anything?" I radioed looking out the windows as I drove slowly.

"Negative," came Scott's response, static-laced and terse.

"Keep looking," I urged.

The squad car's tires crunched over gravel as we pulled up to the edge of the wetlands. A heavy blanket of darkness enveloped everything, turning the swaying reeds into ghostly figures that danced at the periphery of the headlights' reach. I killed the engine and stepped out, my boots sinking slightly into the soft earth.

"All right, gear up," I said, popping the trunk to reveal the neatly arranged equipment.

I handed out walkie-talkies with a firm nod, my gaze scanning the looming tree line.

Tom hefted a powerful flashlight, testing its beam against the creeping mist that seemed to rise in challenge. "Feels like walking into a monster's mouth," he said, only half-joking. I clipped my own radio to my belt and checked the batteries in my light.

With a collective breath, we ventured forward, the beams from our flashlights cutting swathes through the night. The air was thick with the smell of damp earth and stagnant water. Every sound was amplified—a frog's croak, the whisper of leaves, the splash of something unseen moving in the water.

"Kayla!" I called out, voice straining against the silence. "Can you hear us?"

"Keep an eye on the ground," I instructed the team. "Look for tracks, dropped items, anything."

"Copy that," Scott acknowledged, crouching occasionally to inspect the underbrush.

"Team," my voice crackled over the radio. "Remember, we need to think like her. Where would a scared kid go?"

"Somewhere safe?" Tom asked.

"Somewhere to hide, somewhere she thinks is safe," I responded, pushing aside a low-hanging branch to peer into a hollow. "Don't just look on the path," I advised.

"Roger that," Tom said, and started checking behind clusters of cattails and fallen logs.

"Anything?" I checked in after several minutes.

"Negative," came the reply.

"Keep looking," I urged, the urgency pushing me on. We had to find her. We just had to.

Mud sucked at my boots with each step. The beam of my flashlight jittered over tangled roots and murky puddles, searching for a sign.

"Kayla!" I shouted again.

"Billie Ann," Tom's voice was steady but thick with concern, "over here."

I sloshed through the muddy ground to where he stood, shining his light on a scrap of pink fabric caught on a bramble. My heart leapt then sank—hope followed by fear.

"Could be hers," Scott suggested, joining us, his eyes scanning the vicinity for any further clue. Rebecca had said that Kayla wore a pink T-shirt and jeans shorts.

"Bag it," I ordered. We couldn't afford to overlook anything.

"Kayla!" Scott's hopeful call echoed mine in the oppressive night. I visualized her small face, imagined her huddled somewhere cold and alone.

"Spread out, but keep within sight," I instructed. The wetlands were a maze, their beauty belying danger.

"Billie, look." Tom pointed to a set of small footprints leading deeper into the swamp.

"Good eyes," I praised, even as my pulse hammered. We followed cautiously, each shadow a potential hiding spot.

"Kayla! It's the police. We're here to help you!" My calls grew more desperate. Minutes stretched into hours, blurring together, relentless. I thought of all the dangers lurking out here at night.

"Damn it," I said, frustration simmering. There was no response, only the unnerving chorus of nocturnal creatures. My thoughts wandered to my own children. I had called them earlier to hear their voices. William was at home playing computer games, Charlene pretended to be doing homework, but was really watching a reality show on TV. I could hear it in the background. And Zack? He was having a friend over from school and they were playing soccer in the backyard.

Find this girl. Bring her home.

"Stay positive," Tom reminded me, likely sensing my growing tension.

"Positive won't find her," I snapped back, immediately regretting the harshness. I tried to soften it up. "Sorry, just... we need to find this kid."

"Understood," he replied, undaunted. "We're not giving up."

"Never," I affirmed, squaring my shoulders against the creeping doubt. "We'll find her."

"Kayla!" Our voices merged, willing the darkness to give up its secret.

SIXTEEN

BILLIE ANN

The swamp swallowed the beams of our flashlights, thick foliage and hanging moss reducing their reach to feeble pools of light in the oppressive darkness. My boots sank into the muck as I led the way. We were all running on fumes, the kind of bone-deep exhaustion that comes from hours of fruitless searching. Many of the officers who had joined me had scoured the area around Madison's house all day. But if Kayla had just gone missing, these hours following her disappearance were crucial.

"Kayla!" My voice tore through the silence, bouncing off the water and trees before falling flat, unanswered. "Kayla, can you hear me?"

No reply came, just the distant croak of a bullfrog and the hum of insects that were too comfortable in this desolate place. Scott swung his flashlight to the left; Tom did the same to the right. Their faces were etched with weariness, eyes reflecting a shared, unspoken fear. This was not just another search; it was a race against time, against all odds.

A mosquito buzzed near my ear, and I swatted it away, the sound unnaturally loud in the stillness. The swamp seemed to hold its breath, waiting for something, anything, to shatter the quiet. But there was nothing—no cry for help, no rustling of someone moving through the underbrush. Just the heaviness of despair settling over us.

"Nothing," Tom grumbled, frustration bleeding into his voice as he scanned the murky water's edge.

"Keep looking." My command came out sharper than I intended, but how could we stop? Somewhere out there was Kayla, a girl whose life hung by a thread, and it was my job to find her—my responsibility. It wasn't just about proving myself capable, about fighting the courts and their snail's pace to see my own kids again. It was about saving someone else's child when they couldn't.

"Kayla!" The echo of her name became a mantra, a desperate plea to the universe to give us a sign, any sign. But the swamp remained indifferent, holding its secrets close, leaving us to chase shadows and hope.

The K-9 unit arrived, slipping into the marshland. The dogs, nostrils flaring, began their meticulous search, weaving through cypress knees and underbrush with a purpose that reignited a spark of hope in my weary heart. I followed close behind.

"Find her, boys," I murmured, my gaze fixed on the dogs as they snuffled along the moist soil, their handlers quiet and focused beside them.

The swamp was a labyrinth, a tangle of life and decay. It seemed to breathe around us, alive with hidden dangers. My flashlight swept over the gnarled roots and hanging moss, but it was the canines we depended on now.

Suddenly, a bark shattered the silence—a sharp, urgent sound that sent ripples through the still water. We all froze.

"Rex has got something!" one of the handlers called out.

"Where?" Scott asked, his voice tense as he adjusted his grip on his flashlight, the beam jittering across the undergrowth.

"Over there, near the bank." The handler pointed toward

an area where the murky water lay still, reflecting the half-moon above.

"Damn it," Tom hissed, taking a step back. "That's gator territory."

"Are you kidding me?" Scott added, his face paling under the brim of his cap.

My stomach clenched, but I pushed the fear aside. "We have to check it out. Kayla could be there." I glanced at the water's edge, thinking of what might lie beneath.

"Billie Ann, it's too risky," Scott protested, his fingers pushing his curly hair out of his eyes.

"Kayla's life is on the line," I shot back, trying to keep my voice steady despite the dread that crawled up my spine.

"Let's go, but stay alert," I ordered, knowing full well the risks but also knowing what was at stake.

Tom sighed, his broad shoulders tensed. "I'm not going in."

As we approached the spot Rex had marked, every shadow seemed to move, every splash a warning. We were intruders here, in a world ruled by tooth and scale. But somewhere in this foreboding wilderness, a girl was waiting to be found, and I wasn't about to let fear stand in our way—not now, not ever.

"Guess I'll do it then," I declared, my voice betraying none of my inward trepidation. I extended an arm toward Scott, then to Tom, relinquishing my flashlight to each in turn. "Keep those beams steady on me," I instructed, steeling myself for what was to come.

The murky water lapped at my boots as I took the first tentative steps into the swamp. My muscles tensed, ready for any sudden movements. I had faced down perps with nothing but a glare, but the primordial gaze of alligators was something else entirely—a dance with prehistoric devils. Yet I was the one who had grown up not far from here, hunting with my brothers in the swamps very much like these. I was the one who could do this, if any of us.

Gator eyes dotted the surface like sinister stars in an obsidian sky, unblinking and calculating. A chill ran down my spine, yet my resolve did not waver.

"I used to wrestle gators just like you as a teenager," I whispered under my breath. The words felt like a talisman, warding off the danger as I moved deeper into their domain.

The water rose to my waist, warm and unforgiving, cloaking whatever lay beneath. Every step had to be deliberate, purposeful. I knew that one misstep could mean disaster—not just for me, but for the case, for Kayla.

"Careful, Billie Ann," Scott's voice carried over the water, a lifeline in the darkness.

"Watch for movement," Tom added with focused concern.

"Keep the lights on me," I reminded them, pushing forward. The gators watched, but they didn't move—yet. I couldn't afford to think about the court's warning to stay out of trouble, out of danger. This was both, but the kind you don't walk away from when someone's life hangs in the balance.

"Almost there," I grunted, feeling the mud suck at my legs, making every inch gained a victory against the swamp. The beam from my team's flashlights opened the night, guiding me, a tether back to the world.

"Stay sharp," I murmured, more to myself than to Scott and Tom. I was in this now, deep enough that turning back was no longer an option. Forward was the only way, through the dark water and past the guardian beasts that called this place home.

The water was still, too still. My boots sank into the silty bottom, sending up clouds that disappeared in the murky depths. The chorus of insects fell silent as if the swamp held its breath. I strained to hear over my own hammering heart.

"Kayla!" My shout bounced off the trees, unanswered.

Rex whined behind me, high and anxious.

"Go, go," I commanded myself, wading through the dark

water, the lights behind me casting long shadows ahead. Every splash I made seemed to scream danger.

"Billie Ann, there's something…" Scott called out, his voice tight with worry. His light shone ahead of me.

"Stay focused," I replied, though my throat clenched around the words.

A shape bobbed on the surface. I reached out, water swirling over my wrists, cold seeping into my bones.

I touched fabric—sodden and heavy.

"God, no," I whispered, fingertips tracing the outline of a shoulder, an arm, and then a face. A young girl's face, eyes closed as if in sleep. Her chestnut hair floated like a halo in the black water, trailed over her forehead.

"Jesus," Tom breathed, the beam of his flashlight trembling slightly as it landed on her.

"Is it—?" Scott didn't finish.

"Kayla," I confirmed, my stomach churning as grief knotted in my chest. I recognized her from the photo in the trailer. "I think it's Kayla."

"Dammit." The curse came out strangled from Scott, pain etched in every syllable.

"Come on, we have to get her out," I urged, steeling myself against the wave of sorrow threatening to pull me under.

"Watch for gators," Tom reminded us, though it sounded like he was reminding himself just as much.

"Help me here," I called out, my hands sliding under the girl's back, lifting. Waterlogged clothes dragged her down, but I wouldn't let go. Not now. Not after coming this far.

"Got you, Kayla," I murmured through gritted teeth. "I've got you."

A ripple was in the water, and I spotted a glint of scales. My heart thumped a frantic warning.

"Gator," I hissed, eyes locked on the reptile's unblinking gaze.

"Billie, be careful!" Tom's voice was a distant echo against the pounding in my ears.

The beast's interest was piqued—by Kayla or by me, I couldn't tell. It didn't matter. Not to the gator. Not to me.

"Keep that light steady," I barked, muscles tensing for a struggle I hoped to avoid.

"Come on, Billie Ann," Scott urged, but fear sharpened his words.

I reached deeper, fingers brushing Kayla's cold skin. "Not today," I said to the gator, to myself. Adrenaline surged as I pulled, dragging the weight of death through the clinging grasp of the swamp.

"Move, move!" Tom's command spurred me on.

Water erupted around us. A thrashing tail, a warning. My breath caught. No time.

"Got her!" I grunted, half-dragging, half-carrying Kayla's body toward the muddy bank.

"Watch it!" Scott's shout was too late.

Teeth snapped shut inches from my leg. Instinctively, I kicked, sending a spray of murky water into the air.

"Go, go, go!" Tom yelled.

With one final heave, I tumbled onto the bank, Kayla beside me. The gator's eyes disappeared beneath the surface, defeated for now.

"Is it...?" Scott's question died in his throat.

"Jesus, Billie." Tom crouched down, his hand on my shoulder.

"I'm safe," I whispered, more to reassure myself than them.

"Good work," Scott offered quietly, but his eyes told a story of wrenching helplessness.

The warm night air did nothing to ease the fire burning through my veins. I lay there, on the ground next to Kayla, the fight gone from my limbs. We had won this small victory against nature, but the loss—the loss was immeasurable.

"Another life... taken," My voice cracked, tears unbidden and unwelcome stung at my eyes.

"Billie Ann..." Tom started, but what comfort could he offer?

"Let's get her out of here," I said after a moment, pushing past the pain, the sorrow. For Kayla, for all the others, I would keep fighting. "Call forensics."

"On it," Tom said.

"Scott, light here," I croaked, my throat raw.

He obliged, his beam trembling slightly as it landed on the girl's face. The swamp was silent save for the distant hum of insects and the sound of our own ragged breaths.

"God..." Scott's voice was a mere whisper.

I followed his gaze and stifled a gasp. Across Kayla's forehead, a mark—crudely carved into her skin, stark against the paleness of death.

"Is that...?" Scott couldn't finish.

"Symbolic, maybe," I murmured, my detective's mind trying to piece together this grotesque puzzle even as my heart revolted at the sight.

"Who would do such a thing?" Tom's question went unanswered.

"Let's not jump to any conclusions," I said, but the unease was unmistakable in my voice. Something ritualistic about it sent a shiver down my spine.

"Billie Ann, we need to call this in." Scott was practical, grounding.

"Already done," I replied, gesturing to the radio clipped to my belt.

"Chief's not gonna like this," Tom said, wiping sweat from his brow with a shaky hand.

"Never does," I said, swallowing hard. "But she'll want to know immediately."

"Should we cover her up?" Scott asked, looking anywhere but at Kayla's marred face.

"Preserve the scene," I reminded him. "Forensics will want everything untouched."

"Right," he replied, though the thought of leaving the girl exposed seemed to go against every humane instinct.

"Let's secure the area," I instructed, pushing myself up from the ground with effort. "We can't risk contaminating any evidence."

"Sure thing, boss," Tom replied gravely.

"Billie," Scott said, his voice low, "you did everything you could."

"Doesn't feel like enough," I admitted, my gaze lingering on the cruel mark etched into young skin. Several stab wounds to her chest looked like it had been the cause of her death.

Just like Madison.

"Let's just... make sure we catch whoever did this," Tom added, his eyes meeting mine, fierce and determined.

"Agreed," I stated, taking one last look at Kayla before turning away to shield my eyes from the horror. "Nobody else should have to endure this."

"Nobody," they echoed.

SEVENTEEN

BILLIE ANN

I sat hunched over the cluttered coffee table in my new apartment in the morning hours, swamped by case files and glossy photographs that glared back at me. I traced the outline of Kayla's face in a close-up her grandmother had given me, the lines of fate that had brought her to such an abrupt stop. She was older than Madison, sure, but there had to be a thread linking them. They went to the same school but that was all I had found so far. None of their friends matched up and they didn't live in the same neighborhood.

A knock jolted me from my thoughts. I opened the door, revealing the worried faces of my parents. My dad's brows knitted together in concern, my mom wringing her hands as if she could squeeze out the tension between us.

"Billie, honey, we came to see how you're holding up," Mom said, her voice trembling with concern. They had all seen the headlines by now, thanks to the relentless coverage from reporter Sophia Rodriguez. The unspoken fears weighed heavily in the air as they waited for my response.

"I'm fine, just busy," I replied, my voice sharper than intended. "I've got to get into the station soon."

"But it's Saturday?" Mom tilted her head, confusion mingling with concern. "Can't you take some time off?"

"Time off?" The words felt foreign on my tongue, bitter even. "Two girls are dead, Mom. How can I rest?"

Their silence filled the space between us, thick and heavy like the August air outside.

"Come in," I said, stepping aside to let my parents pass. The apartment seemed to shrink with their entrance, the walls closing in on me, suffocating. I motioned toward the couch.

"Make yourselves comfortable," I murmured, already moving toward the kitchenette. The coffee pot was a relic from better times, but it worked well enough. The scent of brewing coffee began to mingle with the musty air, a small comfort in an otherwise stark room.

"Thank you, dear," Mom said, settling onto the couch with a careful grace. Dad followed suit, his frame dwarfing the cushions as he sat down beside her.

I returned with two steaming cups, handing them over before taking a seat opposite them, my own mug clasped tightly in my hands. The warmth did little to ease the chill of the photographs that littered the table, a mosaic of sorrow and unanswered questions.

"Billie, what's all this?" Dad's voice broke through the silence, his finger hovering over the nearest photo.

"Case work," I replied, keeping my tone neutral. I watched as they both leaned forward, squinting at the images laid bare before them—snapshots of life ended too soon. I tried to gather it all up in a pile in order to remove them from their sight, but my mom stopped me.

"Is this...?" Mom's voice trailed off, her eyes fixed on a close-up of Kayla's face that she grabbed from my hands.

"It's part of the investigation," I said, trying to shield them from the harsher truths that lay just beneath the surface. "You shouldn't be seeing these. It's work."

"Looks like anything but routine," Dad said, his gaze sharp, missing nothing. He was staring at the photograph in my mother's hand.

I sighed, feeling the weight of my responsibilities pressing down upon me once again. The pictures, the victims—they were all part of a world I wished I could keep my parents separate from, a world that demanded every ounce of my strength and focus.

"Let's not worry about that now," I said, forcing a smile that felt more like a grimace. I pulled the photo from between my mother's hands, and put everything away. Then I looked at them forcing a smile back at me. "How have you been?"

But my attempt to redirect the conversation fell flat; the elephant in the room was too large to ignore, its presence looming over us. The photos, the evidence of human cruelty, remained between us, an undeniable truth that we could not simply sip away with our coffee.

I bit the inside of my cheek, the taste of coffee bitter on my tongue.

"That mark there," my mother said. "On the forehead of that girl..."

"I know. It's horrifying," I said. "I'm sorry. I should have removed it all before you sat down. Sometimes I forget that people don't see murder scenes every day like I do. And I wasn't expecting you both..."

"No," my mother said. "I have seen it before. The mark."

I leaned forward. "What do you mean?"

She looked briefly at my father, then continued, with almost a whisper, "it's The Mark."

Dad's hand went to his mouth, and he looked at Mom. Their eyes met, a silent conversation passing between them that I wasn't privy to.

"We've seen it before," Dad said after a heavy pause. "It's important."

"Important?" My voice cracked. "How?"

"It's meant to be a sign of... evil," Mom replied hesitantly, her hands clasped tightly together. "You know... it's the Devil's mark."

"What do you mean?" The question was dense and foreboding.

My parents shared another glance, heavier this time. "It's the mark of the Devil, the Devil's spawn," Dad murmured, almost to himself. "One that will try and stop us from starting a new world."

"New world?" I echoed, the words alien and cold.

"Pastor Amelia saw this very mark in a vision," Mom explained, her voice barely above a whisper now. "Many years ago. God helped her unlock the Seven Seals in the Revelations. She sees things differently, Billie Ann. Clearer. Because she's so close to God. She—"

"Sees things," I cut her off, a hollow laugh escaping me. "Right."

I put my palms down on the table. Could Kayla's death be related to the church that my parents went to? I couldn't believe it. I still remembered coming home for Thanksgiving while in college, and everything had changed. All my parents would talk about was the new church they were attending, and how their lives had changed for the better. It was my older brother who had introduced them to it, and now they were completely hooked. That break, I barely saw them, as they were constantly going somewhere meeting up with members of the church, having prayer meetings at people's houses, or listening sermons by the female pastor, who they absolutely worshipped. People would come to our house, and they'd stand in a circle in our living room holding hands and speaking in tongues, or chanting. They had tried to get me to join them too that week, but I spent ten minutes with these people, in a so-called healing meeting, where I watched a woman roll around on the carpet screaming and crying for God's healing to happen, and then decided I was never going to do that again. My mom didn't even cook turkey that break, because she was so preoccupied with this new thing in her life, and Pastor Amelia apparently didn't believe in celebrating Thanksgiving.

All they could talk about was the church and the newfound life they had gotten. And how I should try it too. I remembered it all so clearly. The pain, the hurt they'd caused me. The fissure that had opened between us. They'd said everything in their lives had been so empty before. Our family. My childhood. Me. But apparently, I was a lost sheep that needed to be recovered and helped; it just became too much for me. I ended up going back to school early just to get away but it all repeated itself at Christmas. I had hoped it was just a phase for my parents, perhaps because they were now empty-nesters and needed something to do, but they were still members of the church now after all these years. I had been angry at them for going there for years, and told them they were being brainwashed, but this? This took the cake.

"You're calling this enlightenment?" I thrust a photograph in their direction, Kayla's lifeless eyes staring up at us. "She was just a kid!"

"Billie Ann, lower your voice," Dad said, his own tone a mix of caution and reproach.

"Lower my voice?" I echoed incredulously. "How can you sit there and talk about new worlds when someone's daughter is dead? With that—that mark on her forehead! Did your pastor put that mark on her? Did she kill her?"

"Pastor Amelia teaches peace, love," Mom interjected, her hands reaching out as if to calm stormy waters. "She would never condone violence."

"Peace? Love?" I snorted, disbelief etching my features

tight. "This is not peace." My finger jabbed repeatedly at the gruesome image.

"Your anger is clouding your judgment," Dad said firmly. "Amelia has helped us understand things we never knew."

"Understand?" I spat the word out. "Understand what? That it's okay to follow someone blindly? To ignore the signs?"

"Billie Ann," Mom's voice softened, "we believe in Amelia. She has shown us a path to spiritual awakening."

"Awakening," I repeated, shaking my head. "Wake up! Look around you. This isn't spirituality—it's madness. And now she might be a murderer?"

"Your work... it's made you cynical," Dad said, sadness creeping into his voice. "You only see the worst in people now. Pastor Amelia would never hurt anyone."

"I see the worst because they show me their worst!" I shot back. My chest heaved with each breath, my heart pounding against my ribcage.

"Amelia is a preacher, a guide," Mom insisted, her resolve unshaken. "She leads us with light and truth."

"Light and truth don't leave marks on children's foreheads." My words were thick with unshed tears.

"Amelia would never harm a child," Dad declared, standing up, his posture rigid with conviction. "Our faith in her is strong."

"Strong enough to blind you," I murmured, sinking back into my chair, the fight draining out of me. "Strong enough to let evil slip right past you."

I squared my shoulders, locking eyes with them. The decision was etched into every line of my face. "I have to do what's right," I said, voice steady despite the chaos brewing inside. "She is now a suspect."

"That's not right," my dad said. "We only mentioned it because we've seen it before. We're not saying Amelia has anything to do with this... this poor child." He shook his head.

I tried to calm down. "I have to speak to her now, you do realize that, don't you?"

"Even if it means going against your own family?" Mom's question quivered in the air, laced with disbelief.

"Even then." My resolve didn't waver.

Dad sighed, his disappointment a tangible thing. "We raised you to be strong, Billie Ann. But this..."

They stood, their movements slow, reluctant. At the door, Mom turned back for a moment, her eyes searching mine. "We only want what's best for you," she said, the words like a plea.

"I know you trust Amelia completely, Mom, but I'm a detective. I can't do that." I met her gaze, unyielding.

With heavy hearts, they left, the door clicking shut behind them. I watched from the window as they descended the steps, their silhouettes growing smaller, their connection to Amelia—a woman shrouded in darkness—still intact.

As their car disappeared around the corner, the image of Kayla's marked forehead flashed in my mind, urging me forward. I had no idea if Amelia had anything to do with it, but I had always worried about that church. This was more than just a case; it was a crusade against the shadows that preyed on the innocent.

The room felt colder, emptier. I stood for a moment, letting the silence wrap around me. I grabbed my jacket, sliding my arms into the familiar weight of it. My badge and gun followed, essentials of my trade, slipping into their respective places as if they were extensions of me.

I locked the door with a click that echoed too loudly in the quiet hallway. Down the stairs, each step was firm, resolute— the beat of a drum marching me onward. The outside air hit my face with a humid slap, a wake-up call to the urgency of now.

Inhaling deeply, I tasted the determination on my tongue, metallic and sharp. The lives of innocent children, the specter of an elusive killer—all of it rested on my next moves. With each step toward my car, resolve pulsed through my veins. This wasn't just another case.

It was a mission. And I wouldn't—couldn't—fail.

The engine hummed, a steady backdrop to the thoughts swirling in my head. I gripped the steering wheel, knuckles white, eyes locked on the road ahead.

I parked with a jerk, the lines of the station blurring into view. The door clanged shut behind me, the sound echoing off the walls as I strode through the corridor. Scott and Tom waited, coffee in hand.

"Got your fuel," Scott said, pushing a steaming cup toward me.

"Thanks," I grunted, taking a sip. "We've got work to do."

"Any updates from IT?" Tom asked, his brow furrowed.

"Still waiting." My voice was flat, impatient. "Harris's phone might be key. He did a factory reset of it after Madison disappeared, that's why we haven't been able to look through it yet, but IT said they could restore it. I'm hoping it will give something even if it takes time."

Scott chimed in, leaning against a desk. "It could be insignificant," he said, "but it could also be crucial. Are there any other leads we can pursue? Have we spoken to Alissa or Madison's other friends? Has John made any statements while in custody? Has he consulted with a lawyer? How did Joanne react to his arrest?"

"She hasn't said anything," I replied. "And until we have Kayla's time of death, he stays put."

"Stuff on his computer's enough for that," Tom added, shifting his weight. "Do we know whether there are any connections between the two victims? Or between Kayla and John?"

"Not that I can see. I've been through Kayla's phone, her

contacts, and the grandmother's friends and family. I can't see anything."

"Are we definitely treating the cases as connected?" Scott asked.

I nodded.

"It would be extremely unusual if two young girls were murdered on the same day and abandoned in wetlands by two different people. The mark on Kayla's forehead is different, of course, but, my instincts say we should consider them linked." Pictures of my parents' faces when they spotted the mark carved into Kayla's forehead still lingered in me. There was something there. A connection, that I couldn't—and wouldn't—let go. No matter if my parents would hate me for it and probably never talk to me again. They were devoted to this Amelia character and would easily choose her over me any day. I knew that much. It was a risk I had to take. I wasn't ready to share my thoughts yet with the others, as I didn't have a lot to go by. Not yet. After all, the mark could mean many things, even if my parents did recognize it. I would have to look deeper into it first, do some research, before I accused Amelia and her church of having a connection to it.

I didn't believe John killed Kayla and had started to question if he killed Madison as well. If their murders were connected, we were looking at a completely different beast.

"We need to know everything about Kayla's last hours, talk to all her friends and family, neighbors, everything. I spoke to the bus driver, and she was on the bus the morning of her disappearance, but not in the afternoon. I need to know her whereabouts after the school is out at 3:30. Someone must have seen her. Talk to the teachers, students at the school. Anyone you can think of."

Scott ran a hand through his hair, looking exhausted. As they discussed their plan of action, I couldn't help but feel a sense of camaraderie between him and Tom. They were more than just colleagues—they were close friends who had each other's backs no matter what. And right now, that bond was needed more than ever as we all worked tirelessly to find the killer.

EIGHTEEN

BILLIE ANN

I parked the cruiser alongside a row of tired trailers, their paint jobs bleached by the sun and neglect. The number seven dangled lopsided on the door of the one at the end. I stepped out into the heat, gravel crunching under my boots, and knocked.

"Ma'am, it's Detective Billie Ann Wilde," I announced through the thin door.

It swung open, revealing Kayla's grandmother. Her eyes were swollen red, a damp tissue clutched in her trembling hands.

"Oh, Detective," she breathed. She buckled slightly, and I steadied her with an arm. Grief, recognizable and raw, gripped my heart. I thought of my own kids, how I'd feel if...

"Can I come in?" I asked, guiding her back inside.

"Of course, of course," she mumbled, shuffling ahead of me. We settled into a kitchen that smelled of stale coffee and something sweet, maybe vanilla.

I walked over to the table at the side of the room and perused the photos of Kayla; in some she had her back to the camera, but in most she had a large toothy grin on her face.

"She was... she was such a good girl," Rebecca sad, noticing what I was doing. "Always smiling, even when things got tough. She didn't have it easy, you know?" A tear snaked down her cheek. "She didn't deserve this."

"None of them do," I murmured, thinking of all the cases, all the lost lives. "What do you mean, she didn't have it easy?"

"Well, what with losing her parents. But, Kayla, oh, she was something..." She continued on, voice thick with tears, recounting how hopeful and happy Kayla was. Plus, the little details only a grandmother would remember—the way she tied her shoelaces, the doodles on her school notebooks.

"Did she have many friends around here?" I prodded, needing her to focus.

"Just Jenna, really, from number twelve. They were thick as thieves." She squeezed the tissue in her hand until it tore. "Please, just find who did this to my baby," she implored, gripping my hand with surprising strength.

"I will do everything I can," I promised, and meant it. Not just for Kayla or her grandmother, but for myself too, to prove that I could make at least this part of the world right again.

"What did she like to do?"

"Sports weren't really an option," the grandmother said, shaking her head. "I couldn't afford it. But she loved riding her bike. She'd pedal around here for hours, or go to the beach with Jenna."

"Jenna from number twelve?" I clarified, my mind already mapping the connections.

"Yes, dear. Always together, those two."

"Did Kayla ever mention a John Harris? Or maybe just a man hanging around she didn't know?" My voice was even, but my pulse quickened at the thought.

"John Harris? No, no, nothing like that." She seemed certain, her eyes welling up again. "Kayla was cautious, always kept to herself and Jenna. Is he a suspect?"

"I can't say," I replied. "And her parents? Her mom was never in the picture, but could she have been?" I asked.

"No, I don't even think she cares that Kayla exists... or that she did... I mean..."

I placed a hand on her arm. "It's okay. It takes time."

"I know I should have been home and been there for her," she said, tears in her eyes. "I took a double shift. I was gone all night and all day. I didn't know that she didn't make it home. I should have known."

"So you last saw her the day before yesterday?" I asked.

"Yes, in the early morning before she left for school."

I wrote it down. I was trying to get the timelines straight but it was getting hard. I had asked Tom to get on it. Timelines for both girls lives before they met their fate.

I could tell she was getting tired and decided to leave for now, letting her grieve in peace.

"Thank you. You've been a great help." I offered a nod, feeling her gaze as I turned away.

"Anytime, Detective."

* * *

I made my way through rows of trailers. Each step crunched on gravel strewn with litter that spoke volumes about the lives within these thin aluminum walls.

At trailer number twelve, I paused, taking in the peeling paint and a child's broken play pram in the yard. The door swung open before I could knock.

"Can I help—" The woman's words cut off as I flashed my badge. "What now?"

"Is Jenna home? I need to speak with her," I said, keeping my voice steady despite the sinking feeling in my stomach.

"Jenna!" she hollered over her shoulder without taking her

eyes off me. A moment later, a girl appeared, her face a mix of curiosity and fear.

The girl shuffled forward, her eyes brimming with tears that streaked mascara down her cheeks. She wiped at them, smearing the black further, but they kept coming, relentless as rain through a leaky roof.

"Hey," I said softly, angling my body to block the view from prying neighbors. "I know this is hard." She had clearly heard the news, and, by the looks of it, wasn't getting much sympathy from her mother. I couldn't imagine my own daughter finding out her best friend had been killed and hollering at her like she was a dog.

Jenna sniffled, a sound that tugged at something maternal within me. "I can't believe she's gone," she whispered, the words quivering in the air between us.

"Kayla was your friend," I said, keeping my voice level. Empathy was a tool, but it was also a bridge. "It's okay to be upset."

"More than a friend," Jenna managed before another sob racked her body. Her knees seemed to buckle, and I reached out instinctively to steady her.

"Let's sit down, okay?" I guided her to a rickety plastic chair beside the door, the sound of it scraping against the concrete setting my teeth on edge.

"Thank you," she murmured, clutching a crumpled tissue in her hand like a lifeline.

I knelt beside her. "Jenna, I'm here to help figure out what happened to Kayla. Anything you tell me could be important."

"I just..." She looked up at me, eyes seeking assurance. "I wish I could do more for her."

"You are," I said firmly. "By talking to me, you're helping a lot."

"Okay," Jenna breathed out, nodding slowly. "Okay."

Jenna's hands clenched and unclenched around the tissue,

her knuckles whitening. "There's something I haven't said," she started, then hesitated, a frown creasing her forehead.

"Whatever it is, Jenna, it could help us understand," I encouraged, my own hands resting on my knees, ready to take notes.

"Kayla... she paid me," Jenna blurted out, and I stiffened, not expecting this turn.

"Paid you for what?" I leaned in, my voice low and steady.

"To be her friend. To hang out with her, make it look like we were close," she confessed, eyes darting away.

"Was there a reason she needed to do that?" I probed, confused. Why would a thirteen-year-old girl need to do that?

"To have a story to tell her grandmother, I guess?"

"So she paid you to lie for her and say you were with her? What did she do instead of being with you? Did she mention anyone specific? Any strange men or people she might have met?" I pushed gently.

Jenna shook her head slowly. "She never talked about that stuff with me. She was extremely quiet and secretive."

"Think carefully, Jenna. Anything out of the ordinary? Even if it seemed insignificant at the time." I kept my voice calm, despite the urgency bubbling inside me.

"Nothing. I swear." She looked up at me, her eyes brimming with sincerity but also fear—a fear of what might lie beneath the surface of her own words.

I sat back. My eyes never left Jenna as she twisted a tissue between her fingers, a storm of emotions crossing her young face.

"Jenna," I started, keeping my tone even, "you've got to understand, anything you tell me could be vital."

She sniffed, nodding slowly. "It's just... when Kayla said we were hanging out, I don't actually know what she was doing."

"Where was she going?" My voice was soft but insistent.

"I-I don't know." Jenna's voice quivered, and she pulled her knees to her chest.

"Did she have any other friends? Anyone else she might've been with?" The questions poured out of me like water from a breached dam.

"Maybe," she conceded, her gaze falling to the floor. "But she didn't talk about them to me."

"Jenna, think. Anything could help." My frustration simmered beneath the surface, but I kept it in check.

"It's all so messed up," she whispered, her eyes meeting mine for a fleeting second before dropping again. "She was always so secretive."

"Secretive how?" I leaned forward, my heart pounding against my ribs.

"Kayla was... She had these moods, you know? One minute she'd be all smiles, the next she'd be lost in her phone, typing like mad. Then she'd vanish for hours."

"Did you ever ask where she went?" My pen hovered over my notepad, ready.

"Once," Jenna admitted, tugging at a frayed thread on her sleeve. "She shut down, told me to mind my own business if I wanted the money to keep coming."

"Money can be a powerful silencer," I said, more to myself than to Jenna.

"Is that why you're a cop?" she asked suddenly, looking up with a hint of defiance. "For the money?"

"No." The answer was instinctive. "To find the truth."

"Even if it hurts?" Jenna's voice was barely audible.

"Especially then." My jaw set firm. "That's the job."

"Then you should know." Jenna breathed out, pausing as if considering her next words. "Kayla once came back scared, really scared. Said she did something she shouldn't have."

"Did she say what it was?" I leaned in closer, my pulse quickening.

"No." Jenna shook her head. "And I didn't push it. I thought she was being dramatic. Now..."

"Now you wish you had," I finished for her, my frustration a tangible thing in the cramped space between us.

"Yeah," she agreed, her voice trailing off into silence.

"Thank you, Jenna," I said after a moment, standing up. "Anything else comes to mind, you call me. Day or night."

"Okay," she replied, but I sensed the word carried more weight than just an agreement to call.

I raked a hand through my short hair, the strands resisting my attempt to impose order as much as the case before me.

"Jenna," I said, my voice steadier than I felt, "the fact Kayla paid you—it doesn't make sense. Friends don't need to pay each other."

She fidgeted with the hem of her shirt, not meeting my eyes. "I know, but... she was desperate. For what, I don't know. And I never have any money, so it was kind of nice, you know?

"Detective Wilde?" Jenna's voice quivered, pulling me back.

"Call me Billie Ann," I corrected gently. "We're past formalities now."

"Billie Ann," she repeated, tasting the name. "I really didn't know her, did I?"

"None of us ever fully know another person," I mused. "But we can try to understand them. And right now, understanding Kayla might be the key to solving this."

Jenna nodded, though her gaze remained fixed on some unseen point in the distance.

"Thank you for telling me the truth," I began, standing up and signaling the end of our conversation. "It's not easy, coming forward like you did."

"Will you find who did this?" Her eyes finally met mine, searching for reassurance.

"We will," I promised, my resolve steeling within me. "We'll find out what happened to Kayla and why. If there's someone out there responsible, they'll face justice."

"Justice," she echoed softly, as if trying out the word, finding comfort in its solidity.

"Stay safe, Jenna. And remember, any time of day, you have something to say, you call."

I considered going back inside the trailer to question Jenna's mother, but it seemed pointless. From her tone she didn't seem as if she'd have been interested in what Jenna was getting up to with Kayla. I touched Jenna's shoulder, attempting to give her some comfort, and left her.

One thing was certain: whatever Kayla had been involved in, whoever she was afraid of, I would uncover the truth. It was the job, after all, and maybe, just maybe, it was also a path back to a semblance of redemption for me.

NINETEEN

Then

Lucy's eyes flickered open. Sleep had once again eluded her grasp. She lay in bed staring at the ceiling, her mind churning with images of Amelia—that silver hair masking intentions as murky as the bottomless night.

With each passing day, Amelia's warmth seemed to twist, contorting into something more sinister, more unsettling. Lucy could feel it, a palpable shift in the air whenever Amelia spoke, her words laced with a hidden agenda that set Lucy's nerves on edge. She couldn't shake the feeling of dread, couldn't unsee the glint of something predatory in Amelia's brown eyes. It wrapped around her thoughts, constricting, suffocating, until she felt she might drown in the fear of what lay ahead. She wasn't the only one who had noticed. Ben and Cassie had become her close allies lately, and she knew she could trust them.

"Lucy?" Cassie's voice was a whisper, barely audible through the thin wall separating their rooms.

"Here," Lucy breathed in response, pushing herself up to sit against the headboard. Her heart was a drumbeat too loud in the silence of the night.

"Can we talk?" Cassie asked with the same worry that gnawed at Lucy.

A floorboard creaked, and then Ben's voice joined in, a quiet rumble, "Something's not right."

"Meet me outside," Lucy whispered back, already swinging her legs over the bed and reaching for the comforting solidity of her boots.

They gathered beneath the skeletal embrace of a leafless oak, the moon casting them in a pale glow that seemed to strip away all pretense. Cassie's face was drawn, eyes wide and searching, while Ben loomed beside her, a silent sentinel whose very presence spoke of the turmoil within.

"Did you see how she was today?" Cassie's question hung between them, fragile as glass.

"Every word feels like a trap," Ben added, his gaze fixed on some distant point, as if trying to discern the shape of their shared fear.

"Her sermons... they're changing," Lucy said, finding her voice amidst the unease. "It's like she's preparing us for something." Her fingers twisted together, knotting in the hem of her sweater.

"Preparing or indoctrinating?" Ben's dark eyes met hers, and the unspoken understanding passed between them like an electric charge.

"Kyle..." Cassie's voice faltered, a tremble betraying her attempt at steadiness. "He's getting pulled in deeper."

Lucy nodded, the image of Kyle's face, so full of trust, cutting her with a pang of desperation. They were all adrift in this sea of Amelia's making, and Lucy felt the tide tugging at them, threatening to pull them under. He was spending more and more time with Amelia and rarely sleeping in same room as

Lucy. And worst of all they had stopped making music together. Now he only sang for Amelia.

"Tomorrow," Lucy said, her resolve hardening. "We confront her. Together."

"Are we ready for the fallout?" The words left Cassie's lips, but the uncertainty in her eyes mirrored Lucy's own fears.

"Ready or not," Ben murmured, "we can't let this go on."

Silence settled around them, heavy with the promise of a storm on the horizon. Lucy looked from Cassie to Ben, their faces etched with the same resolve that now bolstered her own. Together, they would face the coming dawn, and whatever darkness it might bring.

The next day Lucy was in the shadow of the community hall, her eyes tracking Kyle's every move. Amelia, with her silver hair catching the sunlight, stood too close to him, her laughter mingling with the notes drifting from Kyle's guitar. Lucy felt a tightness in her chest as she watched them, an invisible hand squeezing her heart.

"Stay away from her," Lucy murmured under her breath when Kyle glanced her way, his eyes searching for her.

Kyle offered a small nod, almost imperceptible, but it was enough. He understood the unspoken plea in her eyes, the protective edge to her presence. As Amelia leaned in closer, whispering something that made Kyle's brow furrow, Lucy felt the stirrings of defiance swell within her.

"I can't let this happen," she said.

"Stay strong, Lucy," Cassie's voice reached her. But it was enough. Enough to remind Lucy of the pact they'd made under the cover of night—a pact of loyalty and resistance.

"I'm trying," Lucy responded, her voice steady despite her racing pulse. She needed to get Kyle away from Amelia.

· · ·

Lucy walked in the moonlight toward Amelia's compound. Her hands were clammy with sweat. The door loomed before her and creaked open with a light push.

"Lucy?" Amelia's tone was friendly, but her eyes were sharp. "What brings you here at this hour?"

"Can't... I can't let this go on," Lucy stammered, her resolve hardening with every word. "I can't let you have sex with my boyfriend. It's not right."

"Is that why you've come? To tell me what is right?" Amelia countered, stepping closer, her presence imposing.

"Yes," Lucy affirmed, her voice gaining strength. "This... whatever you're planning with Kyle, it stops now."

"Lucy," Amelia began, but Lucy cut her off.

"No. I won't stand by and watch you manipulate him—us." Lucy's stance was firm, her eyes locked onto Amelia's. "We see through you."

"Seeing through me?" Amelia echoed, a hint of a challenge in her voice. "Who is *we*? I only see you here?"

"Enough games," Lucy pushed on; she knew she had Cassie and Ben's silent support behind her even if they weren't there. "We're done playing your twisted version of faith. I've come here to tell you that we're leaving."

Amelia scoffed. "I knew you were never truly one of us. I knew you wouldn't understand what we're doing here. Kyle does, though. He is truly becoming one of us."

"Because you brainwashed him. But I will show you that you can't take him away from me, I won't let you," Lucy shot back, bracing for the storm she knew was coming.

Amelia's lips curled into a tight smile, but there was no warmth in it.

"Be careful, Lucy," Amelia warned. "You have no idea what you're meddling with."

"Neither do you," Lucy retorted. "You underestimate our strength."

"Strength?" Amelia scoffed, her gaze piercing. "You're children playing at rebellion. And again, I only see you here. No one else."

"Maybe," Lucy conceded, "but I do have backup, and even children know when enough is enough."

"Is that so?" Amelia's voice was deceptively soft, dangerous. "And what will you do, little singer? Sing me a lullaby while your world crumbles?"

"Watch us," Lucy said, her voice steady. "We're leaving this place, Amelia. And you can't stop us."

"Leaving?" Amelia's eyebrow arched in amusement. "And where will you go?"

"Anywhere but here," Lucy replied, unwavering. "Away from your control."

"Control is such a harsh word," Amelia mused.

"Then what would you call it?" Lucy challenged.

"Guidance," Amelia offered, her tone almost convincing.

"Guidance? Pah."

"Lucy, my dear," Amelia began, voice smooth as silk, "you don't understand. This is all part of a greater plan."

Lucy's pulse thrummed in her ears, a relentless drumbeat that matched the fury building inside her.

"Plans?" Lucy's voice cracked like a whip. "Your plans have a cost, and we're the ones who pay it."

"Ah," Amelia sighed, her head tilting with feigned empathy. "The cost of enlightenment can indeed seem steep to those not willing to ascend."

"Enlightenment?" Lucy echoed, disbelief sharpening her tone. "That's what you call this?"

"Of course." Amelia's eyes glinted in the dim light, warm brown now appearing bottomless and dark. "And I want to lift you all with me."

"By tearing us down?" Lucy countered, her fists clenching

at her sides. "No. I won't let you manipulate us anymore. We deserve better than this."

"Lucy, sweet girl." Amelia stepped closer, her presence looming. "You mistake my intentions. I guide you because I care."

"Guidance should not suffocate," Lucy shot back, her breathing shallow but her stance unwavering. "It shouldn't control or coerce."

"Sometimes," Amelia whispered, close enough for Lucy to feel her breath, "we must be led through the shadows to see the light."

"Then consider us blind," Lucy retorted. "Because we refuse to follow you into the dark any longer."

Amelia's composure crumbled like a cliff face under siege; fissures appeared in the serene mask she wore day by day. "Lucy, do not test my patience," she said, her voice no longer the honeyed cadence of sermons.

"Patience?" Lucy's laugh was brittle. "What about *our* patience? *Our* trust?"

"Trust is for those who have faith," Amelia snapped back, and there it was—the simmering anger beneath her words, making them hiss and spit like oil in a fire. Her eyes, once pools of warmth, now narrowed into slits that seemed to strip Lucy bare of her defiance.

"Faith doesn't excuse manipulation." Lucy's voice was a flickering flame, refusing to be snuffed out. She locked eyes with Amelia, unblinking. "It's over."

"Child, you think you can simply walk away?" Amelia's laughter was a thunderclap in the tense silence, reverberating off the walls of the room they stood in.

"Watch me," Lucy shot back. "I won't let you destroy us. We're leaving this place, and there's nothing you can do to stop us."

"Lucy Everhart," Amelia's voice rose, each syllable laced with venom, "you've always been so naive. Do you think you can escape my reach?"

"Escape?" The word felt foreign on Lucy's tongue, tasting of freedom and fear all at once. "No. I'm not escaping. I'm choosing. And my choice is a life without your shadows."

"Your choices are nothing!" Amelia's control slipped further, her facade cracking wider. "Without me, you are nothing!"

"I am everything I need to be," Lucy declared, her heart pounding a ferocious rhythm against her ribs. "With or without you."

"Then go," Amelia said, the volume of her voice crashing down to a deadly whisper. "But remember this: outside these walls, the world is cruel and unforgiving. You'll come crawling back, and I-I may not be here to welcome you."

"Then we'll take our chances," Lucy replied, the finality in her voice leaving no room for argument. "We're done here, Amelia."

The preacher stared, her fury a palpable force in the room, and for a moment, Lucy saw the storm clouds gathering behind those narrowed eyes. But she stood her ground, her resolve guiding her out of this darkness.

Amelia's silhouette loomed in the doorway, her frame rigid with unspoken threats. Shadows played across her face, transforming her features into an ominous mask. "You think you can walk away?" Her voice was a low growl, menace dripping from every word.

"Watch me," Lucy retorted, her own shadow merging with the darkness of the night, giving her an ephemeral courage.

"Lucy, my dear, the bonds we've forged here—"

"Are chains," Lucy interrupted. "And I am breaking them."

"Ungrateful child," Amelia hissed, stepping forward, her

presence overwhelming, suffocating. "I gave you purpose, meaning!"

"Your 'purpose' is a prison," Lucy snapped back, her eyes flaring with defiance. "Your 'meaning' is manipulation."

The air between them crackled, electric with fury and fear. For a heartbeat, they stood locked in a standoff, two forces of nature on the brink of chaos.

"Fine," Amelia spat. "Leave. See how far you get without my protection."

"Farther than you think," Lucy replied.

"You'll falter," Amelia warned, her voice rising to a crescendo that echoed off the bare walls. "You'll fail. And when you do, don't dare seek my grace."

"I won't need it," Lucy shot back, already turning away.

"Lucy!" Amelia's call halted her escape. "You're nothing but a moth, drawn to flames that will consume you!"

But Lucy didn't flinch, didn't turn. She left Amelia's room behind, each step a silent vow of liberation. The door slammed shut with a resounding thud, sealing her departure.

The compound lay silent, its inhabitants lost in slumber, unaware of the storm that had just erupted within its walls. In the distance, a flash of lightning split the sky, its jagged edge mirroring the turmoil inside Lucy's chest.

She paused, the taste of freedom bittersweet on her lips. What lay beyond the gates? Would Kyle follow when he'd heard what happened?

Lucy's breath came in shallow bursts, the echo of her heartbeat loud in her ears as she navigated the labyrinthine hallways of the compound back to her own room. Every shadow seemed to whisper Amelia's warnings; every gust of wind through the corridors felt like a caress from watchful eyes. The taste of defiance still lingered on her tongue, a potent mix of fear and exhilaration.

"Lucy?" Cassie's voice, barely louder than a sigh, drifted from a darkened doorway. Her silhouette was small, her movements hesitant.

"Over here." Lucy's reply was terse, her steps not slowing.

Cassie fell into stride beside her, with Ben's tall frame looming moments later. They moved together, a trio bound by secrets and silent pledges made in the night. Their gazes met, darting quick and sharp, each one an unspoken question:

What now?

"Amelia... I told her we would leave, that we are done," Lucy whispered, her voice brittle.

Ben's jaw clenched.

"Kyle," Cassie murmured, the name a fragile shard of hope amidst uncertainty. "We have to tell him."

"Tomorrow," Lucy asserted. "First light, we act. We pack up and leave. Hopefully Kyle will come with us."

Their pact solidified in the gloom. They separated at the crossroads of the corridor.

Back in her room, Lucy sank onto the edge of her bed, knees weak, her hands trembling. Kyle was still asleep, snoring lightly. She had stood up to Amelia, had tasted the intoxicating power of her own voice raised in dissent. Yet the thought of retaliation loomed large. In her head, Amelia's last words reverberated, a chilling prophecy or a curse.

Nothing but a moth...

Lucy shook her head, casting off the image. She was no moth; she was fire—wild, untamed, and burning for truth. But even fire could be smothered, and in the silence of their room doubts crept in like tendrils of smoke.

"Kyle," she breathed, the name steadying her fraying nerves. The thought of him—strong, steady Kyle—was both an anchor and a reminder of what was at stake.

Morning would come, bringing with it a new set of challenges, and Lucy Everhart would face them with a song in her heart—a melody of freedom and fierce resolve. But tonight, enveloped in the quiet before the storm, she allowed herself to tremble, to feel the full extent of her fears and the magnitude of what she was about to do.

TWENTY

BILLIE ANN

The phone buzzed on the counter. I snatched it up, desperate to be told Tom and Scott had found something on John. I had just come back from work, and sat by my laptop, researching Amelia and the church online. The display told me it was Danni, and I felt a ripple of anxiety run through me. I hadn't talked to my best friend in a long time, and every part of my body missed her desperately.

"Billie Ann, you free for wine? I'm dying to see your new place." Danni's voice was like a balm, smoothing over the jagged edges of my day. I looked at my case files, work, spread out on the table, and thought for a second that I didn't have any time, but then decided against it. It was, after all, Danni. She had been out of town for two weeks visiting her grandmother in Wisconsin who was sick. Hearing her voice made my heart flutter with joy. I missed her so much, it almost hurt. I would do anything for her. Anything.

"Sure. I'll text you the address. Come over."

I ended the call and surveyed the chaos of unpacked boxes. No time for that now. I removed the case files, and rushed into the bedroom. I riffled through my clothes, settling on a clean shirt that didn't scream "off-duty homicide detective." The mirror reflected someone trying to piece herself back together—short blonde hair tousled just right, a stroke of mascara to hide the fatigue.

Excitement bubbled up as I dabbed on lip gloss. Seeing Danni always did that to me.

The purr of an engine cut through the stillness outside. I peered through the window just as her car slid into a space right in front of my building. My heartbeat picked up. I flicked the lock and swung the door open.

"Hey," Danni called out. A breeze toyed with her hair, loose strands dancing around her face.

"Over here," I said, leaning on the doorframe.

Her smile reached me before she did, warm and familiar, melting away the day's tension. She climbed the steps, her boots echoing on the concrete.

"Place looks great from the outside," she said, her eyes scanning the facade.

"It's not much on the inside," I said.

She crossed the threshold and we wrapped each other in a hug that spoke volumes. Her presence was a comfort, something I'd been missing. I was a little embarrassed about how small my place was, and hoped she wouldn't notice.

"Come on, let's get that wine," I said, my voice muffled against her shoulder.

"Lead the way." She stepped back, but our fingers lingered together for a moment longer.

I fetched the Merlot from the fridge, popping the cork. The glug of wine into glasses underscored the quiet hum of anticipation between us. We always had wine; it always quelled the anxiety between us. Back when we hadn't yet admitted our feelings to one another, it helped us overcome our nerves and open up. Wine had become a ritual we both needed.

"Cheers," she said, clinking her glass lightly against mine.

"Cheers."

We settled on my couch. I swirled the wine in my glass, watching the red liquid climb up the sides before settling back down.

"So how are you holding up?" Danni asked.

I shrugged. "I'm okay."

She tilted her head. "You're not okay. Don't give me that. I know you. Don't shut me out, please."

"I'm not. I just... well, you have your own stuff. Getting separated and dealing with being alone with young kids and all that. You have enough on your plate."

"I do, but that doesn't mean I don't have room for you," she said. "You're going through a lot right now, with the divorce, losing the children, moving..."

"Divorce is a beast," I muttered. "I just... I miss the kids so much, you know?"

Danni reached over, her fingers intertwining with mine, a silent strength. "I know you are. You can talk to me. How are you feeling?"

"Feels like I'm treading water." My voice, usually steady, faltered. "And this case isn't helping any."

"Case?" Her brows knit together in concern.

"Yeah. Ever heard of The Last Days? That cult?"

"Those folks secluded in that compound in North Merritt Island?" She knew of them; everyone did, whispers and rumors. It was a huge estate and no one knew exactly what was going on there.

"Exactly. They're private, elusive even, but..." I paused, took a breath. "One of the victims in the case I'm working on had a mark carved right into her forehead. I think it might have to do with them."

Danni's hand tightened around mine, her face drained of color. "That's horrific."

Nodding, I glanced at my laptop, open on the coffee table,

its screen littered with tabs of research on the cult. A thought struck me. I released Danni's hand and grabbed my phone from the armrest.

"Billie Ann?" Danni leaned in, peering at the flurry of windows on my computer.

"Something just clicked." My thumbs flew across the screen, seeking out the information that had been nagging at the back of my mind all evening.

"Whatcha got?" Danni's voice was curious, a note of concern lingering underneath.

"I found their Facebook page." I tapped the app icon, a smugness in my voice. Even cults couldn't resist social media.

"Of course they have one," she quipped, leaning closer.

"Was scrolling through earlier, but..." My thumb hovered over the screen, swiping back to a post I'd glossed over before.

"Thought of what, Billie?" Danni's eyes met mine, searching for the piece of the puzzle I was silently piecing together.

"Look here." My fingers pinched the screen, zooming into an old grainy photo. A group of solemn faces stared back at us from years gone by.

"Early members," I mumbled, more to myself than to her. The faces blurred and then sharpened under my ministrations. "Maybe, just maybe..."

"Maybe what?" Danni leaned in, her breath warm on my neck.

I didn't answer right away. My heart thudded, a drumbeat echoing the breakthrough. "Bingo."

"Billie, you're killing me. What is it?" Her voice was a mix of exasperation and excitement.

"Gotcha," I whispered, almost to myself, staring at the proof that had been hiding in plain sight.

"Who's this?" Danni squinted at the woman I'd zeroed in on, her finger hovering just shy of the screen.

"Joanne," I said, a twinge of triumph lacing my voice. "Madison's mom."

"Who is that?" Her brows knitted together, a frown tugging at the corner of her lips.

"A mom of one of the victims." I set the phone down, the image of Joanne's face burned into my thoughts. "I needed a link between my two victims and The Last Days. And there she is."

Danni's eyes flickered back to the photo, then to me. "I'm, not sure I understand fully, but it sounds big, Billie."

"Could be everything." I leaned back, the wine glass cool in my hand.

Her hand brushed mine, a current of something unspoken passing between us. "You're so good at this," she said softly.

"Have to be." My gaze settled on our interlocked shadows. "For the kids."

"Always for the kids." She squeezed my hand, gentle but firm.

The air between us was charged as our eyes met. The room felt smaller, the world outside fading to a soft blur. We were two souls momentarily untethered from our troubles.

"Billie Ann," Danni whispered, her voice thick with emotion.

"Yeah?" I replied, my voice barely above a breath.

She moved closer, and for a second, all my cases, all my worries about my children and the courts slipped away into the background. Her lips met mine, a kiss that spoke of the years we'd known each other, the battles we'd fought side by side, and the love that lingered despite it all. It was deep, filled with the ache of longing and the warmth of familiarity.

Suddenly, she pulled away, her chest heaving as if she'd just run miles instead of crossed inches. "I-I have to go," Danni stammered, avoiding my gaze.

"What? Why?" I was confused.

"I just... I need to think." She was up now, gathering her things in a hurry, her movements brisk and jittery.

"About us?"

"Everything, Billie Ann." She paused at the door, her silhouette framed by the hallway light. "We're moving very fast. With everything going on in both of our lives. This isn't easy."

"Wait, Danni—"

But the door clicked shut behind her, leaving me alone with the echo of our kiss. I sank back onto the couch, the cushion still warm from where she had been. Love, longing, determination—they swirled within me like a tempest, each vying for dominance.

"Great job, Wilde," I told myself, grabbing the wine glass she'd left behind. Its rim still bore the imprint of her lipstick—a ghost touch.

I stared at the blank computer screen, the earlier discovery of Joanne still fresh in my mind. That thread could unravel everything or lead to a dead end. My gut said it was the former. I needed it to be.

"Justice," I whispered; justice was the light guiding me through the fog. The kids, the case—everything hinged on what came next. I couldn't afford to lose myself in heartache. Not now. Not yet.

The glass slipped from my fingers, shattering against the tile. Crimson drops mingled with clear shards. I barely noticed the sting as a sliver pierced my skin.

"Damn it," I hissed, reaching for paper towels to mop up the mess. My hand trembled, betraying me.

"Get a grip, Billie Ann." The whisper was harsh, a self-reprimand.

I studied the blood welling from my palm, then wiped it away. No room for weakness. Not when Madison's trustful eyes haunted my every thought, not when Joanne's secrets wove through the case like poison ivy—entangling, suffocating.

"Joanne Harris," I said, pressing a bandage over the cut. "What are you hiding?"

A tear betrayed me, trailing down my cheek. I swiped it angrily. These tears weren't for Danni's abrupt departure or the hollow space where her warmth used to be. They were for the children I missed, for the justice that seemed just beyond reach. How would I ever get them back?

The screen beckoned, and I obliged, pulling up the cult's page again. There, amidst the smiling faces, lay the answers. Joanne's image was a key; I just needed to find the lock it fit.

"Madison, your mom is the link," I said, as if the girl could hear me. "And I'll find out how."

Determination settled over me like armor. I had a job to do. Someone else could be targeted and I needed to stop anyone else from losing their life.

TWENTY-ONE

BILLIE ANN

I pushed the front door open, slamming it against the wall, and it echoed like a gunshot in my childhood home. Memories were flooding back of lazy Sunday afternoons spent playing board games with my siblings. The familiar scent of cinnamon and vanilla still lingered in the air, a reminder of our mother's famous apple pie. As I gazed around the room, my eyes landed on the family portraits hanging on the wall, capturing moments of laughter frozen in time. My sneakers hit the hardwood as I hurried into the living room.

"Mom? Dad?" My voice carried through the large house, but I couldn't see or hear my parents in the hallway or through the open doors that led to the adjoining rooms.

They emerged from the kitchen, worry creasing their faces. "Billie Ann, what's wrong?" my mother asked.

"The Last Days... I need to know everything about it."

My father tried to usher me into a chair, noticing how worried and frantic I was, but I wouldn't budge. "I'm telling you, she won't have anything to do with your case," he said, his voice a feeble attempt at calm. "What's going on?"

My body felt rigid with tension. I couldn't stand their attitude toward the church—I never could. All their prayer circles coming to our house, chanting and speaking in tongues sounding like they were possessed. And how they always had a ready answer for everything, treating every feeling I had like it was an attack from the Devil. *Just don't feed into it. Pray it away.*

I know we as a family had been through a lot this past year and I felt awful to have to confront them with this, but it was necessary.

Disappointed, I studied their faces for any sign of guilt, any flicker of recognition. They exchanged a glance that spoke volumes, yet they remained silent.

"You're both well aware that I think there's a connection between The Last Days and the case I'm working on. There might be children at risk." My voice spiked, a plea beneath the command.

"Billie, we just— We knew this would happen one day. Amelia has taught us how to deal with it. Don't believe what you read online. People call our church all kinds of things, we're used to that, Billie Ann. You must understand that our purpose is more"

"No." I cut my dad off. "I don't want to hear the words Amelia has told you to say." I collected myself. I needed to be smart about this. My parents weren't going to land Amelia in trouble on purpose. "I've found evidence that suggests the church has had something to do with the two murders I'm investigating." My mother's eyebrows rose. I'd caught her attention. "Amelia may know what to say, but she won't be able to do anything about the connection I've found between my victims and her organization. But if you tell me a little bit more about how things work on the inside, perhaps I can help her." I felt bad lying, but I had to.

My mother smoothed her apron, a nervous tic of hers I'd come to recognize over the years.

"It's just a church, Billie," she said, her voice fluttering like a trapped bird.

"Churches don't demand life savings," I retorted. "They don't isolate their members."

I wanted to say they don't kill young girls and carve a mark on their foreheads either, but I needed to control my anger. And I couldn't prove Amelia had done anything yet.

"Billie Ann, we're not in any trouble," my father chimed in, his hands outstretched as if he could push away the reality with his palms.

From my jacket pocket, I pulled out printouts. Bank statements, transaction histories, figures highlighted in neon yellow. All evidence I had come across during my investigation into the cult with a little help from Scott who knew his way around stuff like this. I had wanted to look into the church for a long time, but I'd never had a reason to. I always thought my parents were caught up in something odd. That they were being taken advantage of. What I'd found so far didn't further connect Amelia to my cases, but it was bad. And I knew my parents wouldn't just take my word for it. They needed to see it on paper.

"Look!" I rushed into the kitchen and slapped the papers down onto the table. "This is your 'church'."

Their eyes skimmed the documents, widening with each line they read. Silence stretched out, heavy and accusing.

"I know you think Amelia is looking after you," I said tentatively. I needed to try a different tack. "But she's been funneling your money into The Last Days. Into her own accounts."

"No, she's just holding that until our retirement..." My mother's voice cracked.

"Billie, we—" my father started, but I didn't let him finish.

"No, she's not," I said, the room closing in around us. "Look at the papers."

The room felt colder, the air thinner. My parents refused to look at me, or the bundles of documents I'd set down on the table, a barricade of stubborn denial rising between us.

"Billie Ann, we've made our choices," my dad said, his voice steady but his eyes still avoiding mine.

"Choices?" I echoed, incredulous. "You call squandering everything on a cult a choice? You gave them everything."

"Enough!" Mom's hands clenched the edges of her apron, knuckles whitening. "We trust Amelia."

"Trust?" The word came out as half-laugh, half-sob.

"Your brother believed in their message," Dad interjected.

"Peter." His name was acid on my tongue. After losing his son last year, Peter had moved down south to Palm Bay, and we hadn't spoken since. But I knew my parents spoke with him regularly. "He didn't just believe, he led you into this mess!"

"Billie, it's not that simple," Mom pleaded.

"Simple?" My voice escalated, bouncing off the walls. "You're broke because of him. Because of this... leader and her promises."

"Your brother loves us," Dad shot back, his defensiveness a shield guarding a wound.

"Love?" I spat out. "It's all a lie!"

"Billie Ann," Mom's voice trembled, "please."

"Please what? I've watched you destroy yourselves for years. I've stood by and let you do what you wanted. But there are other people at risk now—two girls are gone..." I let my comment hang in the air.

"Billie, you don't know the full story." Mom's voice was a whisper now, but it cut through the tension. "The church does so much good. For people in need, for children. We want to help."

"I want to get the full story of what is going on at that compound. You can help me. Instead of hiding in delusions."

"Delusions?" Dad's face reddened. "Our faith—"

"Is blindness!" Words erupted from me like bullets. "You're

victims, and you can't even see it!" I had lost all control. I couldn't hold my anger in anymore.

"Victims?" The word hung between us.

"Billie Ann, we are not victims," Mom's voice cracked, but her eyes were steel. "We made our choices."

"Wrong ones." My stance was firm, unyielding. "And now you're paying the price."

"Enough!" Dad stood, chair grating back. "This is our belief, our life."

"Your cult," I corrected, standing toe-to-toe with him. "It's devouring you."

"We've heard enough." Mom's hands trembled, but her gaze never wavered.

"Have you?" I shot back. "Because there's more, so much more."

"Billie, you're just..." Dad struggled for words, his face contorted in frustration.

"Trying to save you!" I shouted, feeling the vein in my neck pulse with fury. "From yourselves, from this insanity that Peter got you into!"

"Insanity?" Mom echoed, aghast.

"Exactly." My breaths came fast, hot. "And it ends here. It has to."

"Billie Ann Wilde." Dad's use of my full name was a warning. "You're overstepping."

"Am I?" My challenge was clear, unwavering. "Or am I the only one stepping up?"

"Stop this," Mom's plea was barely audible over the ringing in my ears.

"I can't." I straightened, resolve hardening. "Not until this is right."

"Right?" Dad scoffed. "What do you know about right?"

"More than you," I retorted, the detective in me refusing to back down. "More than any of you."

"Billie Ann…" Mom reached out, a gesture meant to bridge the gap, but I stepped back.

"Look at it!" It placed it all on the kitchen counter in front of them. Bank statements fluttering beneath my palm. Scott had gotten ahold of these statements when I asked him to look into the cult's finances. All the donations they had received over the years. It terrified me. I didn't know it was this bad, that they had given this much over the years. I had to confront them about it, to try and talk some sense into them before it was too late. "The numbers don't lie."

Silence.

"Billie, we—" Mom's voice wavered, a reed in the storm.

"The symbol," I said and showed them a drawing of the symbol carved into Kayla's forehead. "I know you know about it. What does it mean?"

"It's the Devil's mark," my dad said. "A new world is coming."

"A new world? What new world?" I said. "Is that what she is telling you?"

"You wouldn't understand," my mom said.

I sighed deeply, rubbing my forehead in desperation. This was worse than I thought. They were completely brainwashed.

"Peter dragged you into this mess," I repeated. "It's all his fault."

"Peter is our son," Mom whispered.

"And I'm your daughter!" The betrayal stung, a slap across my conscience. "Doesn't that count for something? Why won't you listen to me?"

"Of course we will, but—"

"No buts!" I leaned in, the investigator resurfacing. "You've been conned, and it's hurting people."

"Billie Ann, please," Dad said, his tone softer, almost pleading.

"Please what?" I demanded. "Please ignore the lies? The victims?"

"Victims?" Mom repeated, as if the word was foreign.

I stared at her. There really was no way for me to get through to her, was there? I was wasting my time. "I can't do this anymore."

"Can't do what?" Mom reached out, fingers trembling.

"Watch you fall apart." My voice broke, splintered resolve. "Watch you destroy everything for a cult."

"Billie, we love you." Mom's plea bordered on despair.

"Believe what you want. But until you see what is really going on here, I'm done."

"Done?" Mom echoed, disbelief painting her features.

"Done." I affirmed. "No contact. Not until you're out. Out of the cult, out of the madness."

"Billie, you can't mean that," Mom said, tears cresting.

"Mean it?" I nodded, once, sharply. "With every fiber of my being."

"Please..." Mom's hands were clasped before her. "Don't do this."

"Already done." My final words fell heavy, a gavel's sentence.

Their faces blurred as I turned away, steps echoing with resolve.

I pivoted on my heel, a compass needle spinning from true north. The floorboards creaked beneath me, each step a drumbeat of the war inside. Anger, sadness, determination, they churned in a tempest, threatening to tear me down, but I wouldn't let them. Not then.

I had hoped to find out some more information about Amelia. I had hoped my parents would introduce me, but perhaps I'd gone about it the wrong way. Should I have pretended to be interested in joining The Last Days? But my parents would have seen right through that. I was angry at myself for letting my pain get the better of me. I'd let Madison and Kayla down again.

"Billie Ann." Dad's voice cracked behind me.

I didn't turn back. Couldn't turn back. My hand found the doorknob, cold and unyielding, like the wall between us now. I grasped it, fingers white-knuckled, and pulled.

"Please."

Mom's whisper sliced through the air. I hesitated—a flicker, a fracture. But the dam held.

"Be safe," she added, quieter still.

The door swung open, a gust of warm air rushed to greet me, like the world inhaling sharply at the sight of a child leaving home for the last time.

TWENTY-TWO

JENNA

Jenna's legs pumped rhythmically, propelling her bike down the quiet street. A cool breeze whispered through her hair, and the tang of salt air teased her senses. She was going to school, but every morning she'd take a little detour to the beach and check on the waves. Jenna knew she had no time to go surf, but she loved the endless blue freedom of the ocean.

"Almost there," she murmured, the corners of her mouth lifting in anticipation.

The soft hum of her bike tires on pavement was a soothing soundtrack to the morning calm. But then, a different sound crept into the mix—a low, persistent growl that grew louder with each passing second.

She glanced over her shoulder. A car, nondescript and dark, crawled behind her. Too close. Way too close.

"Hey!" Jenna called out, her voice edged with annoyance. "Back off!"

The car didn't obey. It shadowed her every move as if tethered invisibly to her bike. Jenna's heartbeat quickened—not from exertion now but from a budding fear.

"Give me some space, why don't you?" Her demand sliced through the quiet, but the car refused to yield.

The engine roared—a predatory snarl that split the quiet morning. Jenna's fingers clenched around her handlebars. The car was an unwanted shadow, looming just inches from her back tire.

"Too close!" she spat out, breathless.

It was as if the driver fed off her panic, the car inching forward even more. The revving grew frenetic. A surge of power taunted her from behind, pushing her to pedal harder. Her legs burned with the effort, each stroke a desperate plea for distance.

"Stop!" Jenna threw the word over her shoulder like a stone.

But the car clung to her, insistent. It was no coincidence—this was intentional, a deliberate chase. Fear twisted in her gut, sharp and cold. She could almost feel the driver's eyes on her, a silent threat pressing down on the gas pedal.

"Leave me alone!"

Jenna's legs pumped furiously, every muscle screaming. The car lurched. She risked a glance back, her heart hammering against her ribs. It was still there.

Then she felt a deafening crash.

Jenna catapulted through the air, the sky and earth trading places in a dizzying dance. Her bike, once a trusted companion, now twisted metal discarded in the wake of violence.

She struck the pavement, the impact stealing the breath from her lungs. Her head smacked the ground, reality jarring with a sickening thud. Silence rushed in, punctuated by the distant echo of screeching tires. Consciousness flickered.

Grit crunched under Jenna's cheek. Hot asphalt pressed against her skin. She blinked rapidly, trying to clear the haze from her eyes. Colors swam into each other, a nauseating kaleidoscope. Her ears rang, the aftermath of the crash still vibrating through her body.

"Stay down," a voice hissed, almost gentle.

Pain lanced through her as she attempted to move, a symphony of hurt signaling parts of her body she hadn't known could ache so acutely. Her thoughts churned, sluggish and fragmented. The smell of burnt rubber filled her nostrils.

"Help," she croaked, but her voice was a mere thread of sound, lost in the void that seemed to have enveloped her.

Hands—cold and unyielding—clamped around her arms. They dragged her. The world tilted, and her sense of direction was lost. She tried to resist, to dig her heels into the ground, but her limbs betrayed her, heavy and uncooperative.

"Please, don't," she whimpered, but her plea was swallowed by the growl of an engine, close and menacing.

"Shut it," the voice snapped, hard and commanding.

The trunk loomed before her, a dark maw ready to swallow her whole. Panic clawed its way up her throat, bile burning behind her teeth. She twisted, trying to see her captor, to etch their faces into her memory, but her vision betrayed her, offering only shadows and the glint of metal.

"Stop!"

Her heart thundered. The hands were relentless, rough. She was lifted up.

Jenna's body convulsed, a feral creature caught in a snare. Her legs flailed wildly, the rubber soles of her sneakers seeking purchase on anything tangible—they found only air. She bucked, her spine arching in defiance, muscles corded with the raw energy of survival.

"Let go of me!" she barked, her voice ragged with exertion.

"Easy, easy," the assailant grunted, their breath hot against her ear. They were more shadow than substance, their features obscured by Jenna's blurred sight. But they were undeniably real, as were their intentions.

"Let go!" Her fist connected with something soft—a cheek, perhaps—and a curse splintered the charged silence. But it was like striking water; it yielded, absorbed the blow, and then returned to its original form.

"Damn it!" the commanding voice yelled, a thread of annoyance now woven through the coldness. The grip tightened and she felt bands around her wrists.

Panic surged, lending her new strength. Jenna thrashed, her head lolling from side to side, hair whipping across her face. Her knee jerked upward, connecting with a solid mass—maybe a gut. A satisfying *oof* followed, but the triumph was short-lived.

"Enough!" Suddenly there were hands everywhere—on her shoulders, her waist, her thighs—pinning her down with brutal efficiency.

"Stop, please—" Her plea cut off as her body was folded, compressed into the dark cavity of the trunk. Fabric rasped against her skin; the world shrank to fit the confines of the small space.

The lid descended, a guillotine blade of finality. Light was out. Sound muffled. Air turned stale and thick. Jenna's chest heaved, her breaths shallow gasps in the suffocating darkness.

The thud of the trunk locking reverberated through Jenna's bones. Silence, then the distant rumble of the engine coming to life.

The car's engine hummed, a predator's purr. Jenna lay motionless, her breaths shallow echoes against the trunk's tight walls.

Wheels crunched over gravel, slow at first then steadier. The car turned a corner, and Jenna's world tilted. She slid, skin scraping metal, her mind clawing for purchase in the blackness.

"Quiet back there," a voice hissed through the partition.

Jenna's heart pounded, each beat a timer counting down. She shifted, the darkness an oppressive weight. Her thoughts spiraled—where were they taking her?

The car started moving again, slower this time, cautious. Jenna's mind raced, terror a cold hand squeezing her chest.

Jenna felt every turn, every acceleration, her body rolling with the movement. She tried to scream, but her voice was a whisper.

The car slowed, tires crunching on a different surface—dirt, maybe gravel. It stopped; a door opened and closed. Silence returned, thick and all-consuming.

"End of the line," the voice said, almost inaudible.

The trunk opened; light invaded. Jenna squinted, disoriented. Hands reached in, dragged her out. Her knees hit the ground, gravel biting flesh. The world spun, sounds and sights blurring. Something was pulled over her head and all she could see now was darkness.

TWENTY-THREE
BILLIE ANN

My cruiser rolled to a dusty stop at the edge of the compound, gravel crunching beneath the tires. The place rose up like a fortress, surrounded by high fences topped with barbed wire that cut it off from the outside world. I killed the engine and stepped out.

As I approached the gate, a group had gathered on the other side. Their faces were ashen under the harsh sun, their eyes narrow with suspicion. They were a motley crew—men, women, and children—all dressed in drab clothing and bearing signs of hard labor and sacrifice. Some wore grime-streaked overalls, others ragged dresses or tattered suits. Their hair was unkempt and their skin was weathered from years spent living off the land. Yet despite their worn appearances, there was an air of strength and resilience about them.

"Can I help you?"

I looked into the sea of wary glances and saw the determination etched on each face. These were not just lost souls looking for direction; they were true believers devoted to their leader and their way of life. And as I stood there face to face with them, I couldn't help but feel a sense of unease settle over me.

This was no ordinary cult, I felt—this was a well-armed community ready to defend their beliefs at any cost.

"Detective Billie Ann Wilde," I said, holding up my badge for them to see. It glinted briefly in the light, a beacon of authority. "I need to talk to your pastor."

Murmurs hummed. None moved to open the gate. Their eyes flicked over my short blonde hair, my squared shoulders.

A tall man stepped forward, his arms crossed.

"Amelia's a busy woman," he drawled, skepticism in his tone.

"Then she'll want to clear this up quickly." I met his gaze evenly, planting myself firmly on the ground like an unmovable force.

He hesitated, then jerked his head in a nod. A signal passed between them, and the gate creaked open just enough to let me through.

"Follow me." It wasn't a request. I stepped into their world, leaving the gate—and an easy escape—behind.

As I approached the main hall, the grand double doors creaked open ominously. The low hum of chanting grew louder as I stepped inside. The room was lit by a single row of flickering candles, casting long shadows against the stone walls. And there she stood at the center, Pastor Amelia Hawthorne, her sharp features almost regal as she surveyed her followers with an unwavering gaze. She was dressed in all black, her silver hair pulled back tightly into a bun. Despite her small frame, she exuded an aura of authority and power. My stomach twisted nervously as her piercing eyes found mine, and I couldn't help but feel a sense of unease at being granted an audience.

The autopsy results for Kayla had arrived before I'd left the station, revealing her time of death to be midnight. I hadn't yet shared my theories with the team; I needed more evidence before presenting them. What I had gathered so far was still not enough to draw any solid conclusions. Meanwhile, Scott and Tom were busy investigating Kayla's family and friends, checking alibis for the time that she died. Scott may have helped me with the financial records but so far I told him it was for something else, and not related to this case.

"Detective Wilde," she intoned, her voice smooth like silk over glass. "This is an unexpected surprise."

"Pastor Hawthorne," I acknowledged, each second stretching between us. We stood there, measuring each other up. It wasn't the first time I had met this woman. My parents had brought her to their house many years ago, when I was just married and pregnant with my first child. They had arranged for me and Joe to be there for dinner, not telling us about their true intentions. They wanted to convince me and Joe to join them, for the sake of our future children. So they wouldn't be lost the way we were. Obviously, they hadn't succeeded.

"To what do I owe the pleasure?" she asked. "You're here due to your work, I understand? How can I help?"

"I'm working on a murder case."

"Murder. A heinous word to speak in such a peaceful place," she began, her tone woven with a sweetness that didn't reach her eyes. "I'm sure we won't know anything that would be helpful."

I studied her, the practiced ease of her denial. "People are dead, Amelia. And some trails lead here." My voice was level, but inside, doubt gnawed at me. Her serenity was too well crafted, a facade I was determined to shatter.

"Trails can be deceiving, Detective. We spread love, not death." She clasped her hands together, a depiction of pious innocence.

I showed her the picture of the symbol that had been carved into Kayla's forehead. I was hoping for some sort of reaction, and her face froze.

"What do you know about this symbol?" I asked.

She shook her head.

"It was carved into a little girl's forehead," I said. She didn't react. "Where were you on Friday night?" I asked, leaning forward. Kayla's time of death had been set to just after midnight but according to autopsy she didn't die right away. Bruises on her body told a story of being tormented and beaten for hours before her death. Madison's body had told the same story. Water found in her lungs showed she was still alive when thrown in the creek.

"Where I always am, Detective," she replied, her voice steady as a heartbeat. "Spreading the light among my flock."

"Apparently you have talked about this symbol before, as the symbol of the Devil? Something about a new world coming? Help me out here?" My tone was ice, my gaze drilling into hers.

"Symbols can easily be misinterpreted by those unenlightened." Amelia's lips curled into a patronizing smile. "You see shadows where there is only sun."

"Sun doesn't bleed, Amelia. I need facts, not philosophy."

The air grew thick with tension. From the corners of the room, her followers crept closer. It was clear that they didn't approve of my presence. I could hear them whispering.

"Detective, your presence disrupts our harmony," Amelia said, her voice a melody of feigned concern.

"Harmony? Is that what you call manipulation?" I didn't flinch as the circle tightened around us. "They deserve to know the truth."

"Truth is a matter of perspective," she countered, her brow arching in challenge.

"Then let's adjust the view." My words a gauntlet thrown. "Start talking, or I'll have this place turned inside out."

Her followers bristled, a forest of bodies swaying with unease. But their movement didn't mask my purpose—it sharpened it.

"Enough," Amelia declared, her command cutting off the murmurs. But her eyes, oh, they flickered with something wild, something cornered.

"Tell them to back off," I demanded, refusing to be cowed by numbers or by her.

"Back off," she echoed softly, yet it boomed like thunder. The crowd hesitated, then parted reluctantly.

"Good choice." I locked eyes with her. "Now, let's talk about those murders."

"Leave this place," Amelia demanded, her voice suddenly sharp.

I planted my feet more firmly on the ground, feeling the grit beneath my boots. "I'm not done here," I said.

"Detective Wilde," Amelia's voice took on a sweet poison, "you test my patience."

"Then we have something in common." I met her gaze squarely, unblinking.

"Billie Ann, please, we both know you have nothing on me, no right to detain me." She used my first name as if it were a weapon. "We wouldn't want an incident."

"Neither would I." My words were calm, but inside, adrenaline was a river bursting its banks.

I stared at her and noticed her hands were trembling. Was it fear? Or anger?

"You're scared," I said to her.

"Silence!" Amelia snapped.

"Of course," I replied, "the truth can be unsettling."

"Out!" Amelia pointed toward the gate. I could feel her authority slipping like sand through fingers.

"I'll be watching you." My stance was steady though my heart thundered against my ribs.

The cultists shuffled, unease rippling through them. They glanced at each other, at Amelia, uncertain.

"Don't push me, Detective." Her threat was a noose waiting to tighten.

"Pushing is my job." I stood tall, despite the tightening circle. "Especially when lives are at stake."

"Go now," she ordered.

Her followers began to part, creating a path to the exit.

I took a step back, eyes still locked with Amelia's. "This isn't over," I said quietly, the threat implicit in my tone.

"Leave, Detective Wilde," she responded, her voice steady but her eyes betraying a flicker of concern.

"Fine." My voice was ice, a contrast to the heat coursing through me. It would be foolish to push harder now, I realized; I needed to regroup, reassess. The investigation was at stake. I couldn't let my personal emotions take control here or I'd lose it all. And I hoped I'd scared her enough to stop whatever she was planning next. If she was hurting people, perhaps I'd bought her next victim some more time. I turned on my heel, dismissing the silent audience with a sweep of my gaze.

"Until next time," I said, stepping through the divide, my vigilance unwavering as I walked out of the lion's den.

As I walked away, an unnatural hush fell over the compound. The murmurs and shuffles that had filled the air moments ago were swallowed by a quiet so deep it buzzed in my ears. I could feel their eyes boring into my back, each step I took amplified against the gravel path.

"Detective," Amelia called out from behind me. Her voice sharp and commanding.

I paused but didn't turn around. "Yes?"

"Remember, we're watching."

"Likewise." The words left my lips without looking back. The gate loomed ahead.

I stepped through the threshold, the change immediate. The compound's oppressive atmosphere couldn't follow me past those gates. Yet, the silence clung to me, whispering secrets

I had yet to decipher. Something dark lurked in the shadows of that place, something that went beyond the surface piety and communal living.

I reached my car, the metallic click of the door handle piercing the quiet. As I sat behind the wheel, the compound in my rearview mirror, I felt relief. Amelia's hold on her followers was strong, but there was something else, something more sinister at play.

The engine roared to life, disrupting the eerie calm. As I drove away, the silence of the compound was replaced by the familiar sounds of the outside world. But the disquiet remained, a haunting melody that promised this was only the beginning. The road unwound before me, each mile taking me further from the compound's suffocating grip. Amelia's cryptic parting shot echoed in my mind—a veiled threat or merely an acknowledgment of the chess game we were both playing?

I gripped the steering wheel tighter, focusing on the hum of the engine and the thrum of tires against asphalt. It gave me something to hold on to, something normal compared to what had just unfolded.

"Watching, huh?" I said. Maybe. But so was I—every move, every word, every glance. My eyes caught sight of a hawk soaring above, its predatory gaze scanning the ground below. We weren't so different, that bird and I. Both hunting, both waiting for the right moment to strike.

I'd need a new plan, a way to peel back the layers of secrecy that Amelia wrapped herself in. The truth was there—I could feel it in my bones. And I would find it, for my own peace of mind and for the victims who deserved justice.

And hopefully for my parents.

Stay out of trouble, my lawyer's words repeated like a mantra. But trouble was my element; it's where I thrived.

. . .

I pulled into the station's lot and gathered my thoughts in the silence that followed the engine cut-off. I strode through the precinct doors, the familiar buzz of activity a stark contrast to the eerie calm of the cult's lair.

"Listen up," I announced, my team turning to face me.

They huddled around, their faces etched with concern and determination. I laid out the facts, sparse yet significant, the pieces of the puzzle begging to be put together. I told them my suspicions, that something was going on at that compound and how I feared it had to do with the murdered girls. I told them of my meeting with Amelia and how her responses were worrying to me. But I also told them I had no evidence to back it up. We needed to find that. Tom and Scott both told me they had been following up on all our leads so far and found nothing interesting. They both agreed the mark on Kayla's forehead was significant enough for us to go after my angle. Scott had found pictures online of the mark of the beast, and showed them to us. It sent a chill through us all.

"Amelia won't go quietly," I warned them, meeting each gaze squarely. "She's got her hooks deep, and she'll fight dirty to keep her secrets."

"Then we'll fight smarter," Tom declared, his jaw set.

"Exactly." I slammed my palm onto the table. "We'll use every resource, every ounce of wit. We'll protect the potential victims and pry the truth from her cold hands if that's what it takes."

"Billie Ann, this could get messy," Scott cautioned, his voice low.

"Let it," I replied without hesitation. "We can't let fear dictate our moves. Not now. We need to find out what is really going on. Starting by having the compound under observation around the clock. One little mistake and we get them. Tom, you make sure of that."

"Yes, ma'am."

"All right," I said. "Scott, you keep looking into the financials. Anything out of the ordinary, enough for us to take her in, you tell me. Be it a tax evasion or anything else illegal, and we got her."

"I'm on it."

"Good. I will investigate the girls' connections to the cult. Let's get to work."

The room was a hive of activity, each of us taking on specific tasks as we prepared for the inevitable confrontation. Our tension-fueled determination made us a well-oiled machine, ready to face any challenge that came our way. Losing was not an option, and we were willing to do whatever it took to emerge victorious.

TWENTY-FOUR

Then

Lucy's heart thudded. She was being dragged down a narrow hallway that seemed to stretch into forever, her feet stumbling and scraping against the cold, unfeeling floor. She fought, her voice rising in a crescendo of desperate cries, her body twisting and turning in a futile attempt to break free from the iron grip of her captors.

"Let me go!" Her words echoed off the walls. She thrashed with more force but the people holding her were stronger.

The isolation box loomed before her. It was a small, windowless room that she'd heard whispers about. As she was thrust inside, the starkness of the space assaulted her senses. The walls closed in around her, oppressive and unyielding, the ceiling just out of reach for her to stand tall. A single bulb hung precariously from above, casting a dim, jaundiced light that barely penetrated the gloom. The air was still, heavy with a heat that settled on her skin like a suffocating blanket.

For a moment, Lucy sat there motionless, her breaths coming in short, sharp gasps as she tried to process the reality of her imprisonment. Disbelief clouded her vision, painting the dreary confines of the box in surreal shades. She reached out, her fingers tracing the rough texture of the walls, each bump and groove a testament to the countless others who had known this same despair.

"Help! Someone, please!" Her voice cracked as she pounded on the metal door, the sound reverberating through the tiny space, mocking her with its futility. There were no comforting objects here, no personal belongings to anchor her to the world outside. Only the relentless claustrophobia of the box and the creeping dread that slithered into her thoughts.

Would she ever be able to leave here again?

"Can anyone hear me?" Lucy's screams were raw and ragged as she beat against the door with the strength of her desperation. But there was no reply, only the echo of her own voice coming back to haunt her, a ghostly reminder of her isolation.

"Please!" Her pleas rose in a crescendo of terror and disbelief, dissolving in the stifling air of the isolation box. Alone, she faced the harrowing silence that followed, a silence that threatened to consume her resilient spirit with every passing second.

Lucy threw her body against the walls, the dull thud of flesh and bone meeting metal ringing in her ears. "Is anybody there?" she shouted, her voice becoming hoarse. But the compound remained silent.

"Please! I just want to talk!" she yelled, hoping for even a whisper through the walls, some sign that she wasn't utterly alone. Yet no comforting words came, no footsteps, not even the creak of a door—only suffocating silence.

With every passing moment, the heat intensified. Sweat beaded on her forehead, trickling down her temples. The air was saturated with her breaths, each inhale a struggle against the oppressive atmosphere, her thrumming pulse a stark contrast to the stillness outside the box.

She shifted her position, trying to find relief from the cramped space, but as she moved, something skittered across her foot. A gasp escaped her lips as she jerked back, her eyes darting down to catch sight of rats scurrying in the shadows and ants marching in a relentless line. They nipped at her skin, their tiny bites a reminder that she wasn't completely abandoned—just not in a way she longed for.

"Get away from me!" Lucy cried out, stomping her feet.

"Damn it!" she spat, swiping at the insects that seemed to multiply by the second. Her movements grew frantic, her skin crawling with the sensation of dozens of tiny legs. Bites turned into welts, itching and burning.

"Help me," she whispered this time, her resolve wavering, strength sapped by the unrelenting heat. Lucy's eyes closed briefly, seeking solace in the darkness behind her lids, but even there, she couldn't escape the reality of the isolation box—the unending nightmare that held her captive.

They'll let me out soon. They'll come soon. Any minute now.

But they didn't.

As the days passed the walls closed in, and each breath became a struggle. Lucy's fingertips grazed the rough surface, her nails chipped and bloodied from days of clawing for escape. Her heart thrummed a wild rhythm, a soundtrack to her unraveling mind. Sleep eluded her, a distant memory now replaced with fitful dozing and jolts of panic.

"Please," she said, her voice hoarse, almost foreign to her own ears. The darkness laughed back, a mocking echo. Time warped. She lost count. The isolation box, a relentless captor, offered no answers, only more questions—each one etching deeper into her psyche.

"Kyle," she whispered, the name a lifeline in the suffocating silence. She imagined his face, the blue of his eyes that always seemed to hold a melody. In her mind's eye, he strummed his guitar, notes floating through bars and walls, reaching for her. But reality bit hard, cruel fangs reminding her that melodies didn't penetrate steel.

"Help me," she croaked, pressing her forehead against the cool metal door. "Anyone." The word cracked, a brittle plea. Silence was her cruel companion, never faltering, never comforting. The ache for human touch, for Kyle's hand in hers, gnawed at her insides.

"Talk to me," she said to the emptiness. "Just talk." Memories of laughter, of shared dreams under open skies, swirled in her head like taunting specters. She clung to them.

"Kyle, I need you," she breathed out, imagining his arms around her, a shield against despair. But arms didn't materialize, and her own embrace felt hollow. The absence of his warmth was a void no amount of self-soothing could fill.

"I have to get out of here," she resolved anew, each day a fresh battle against an invisible foe. "For him. For me." Words became mantras, a fragile bulwark against the tide of madness lapping at her mind. Lucy Everhart, the singer, the dreamer, now the prisoner—she wouldn't let this be her final stage.

Finally, the sound of footsteps approached. Sitting cross-legged, she perked up. She pressed her ear against the cool metal door, hoping for a voice, a sign of life. As the food slot opened with a metallic scrape and a slice of light appeared in the darkness, her pulse quickened.

"Hello?" Her voice wavered. The tray clattered onto the floor, a plastic cup teetering on its edge before settling. No words came in reply, only the retreating cadence of boots against concrete.

"Wait! Please!" Lucy's fists pounded the door, the hollow sound mocking her efforts.

"Look at me when you give me my food. Say something!"

she demanded, but the silence that followed was as stifling as the thick air around her.

Every day, the same. The silent server departed, leaving behind a taste of solitude more bitter than the tepid water she sipped. Alone again, her head drooped to her chest, despair coiling tightly within her.

In the crushing silence, Lucy turned inward, searching for an ember of herself not yet snuffed out by the darkness. She hummed, softly at first, then with more conviction—a melody from a time when her voice soared freely beneath spotlights, not swallowed by steel walls. The tune was shaky, notes frayed at the edges, but it was hers.

She sang a familiar song about a place over the rainbow, the lyrics caressing her parched throat. Her voice grew stronger, weaving through the stale air, crafting a bridge to the world beyond confinement. Each verse was an act of defiance, a declaration of her spirit's refusal to be caged.

Eyes closed, she envisioned vast expanses of freedom beyond her reach. The song was a lifeline back to the woman with auburn waves and dreams larger than this box, larger than fear. Lucy's song danced alone in the dark.

"Please," she whispered between verses, not to the ghosts of her captors, but to herself, to the memory of who she once was. "Hold on, Lucy." Her own voice, tender and resolute, cradled her through the night, a lullaby for the weary and lost.

Lucy's fingers traced the coarse seam of her makeshift pillow, a tangle of torn clothing that barely cushioned the unforgiving concrete. The vibration of footsteps neared, then faded, the promise of human contact dissolving with each receding echo. Her stomach ached, an empty cavern.

"Water," she croaked, a ghostly rasp as the slot opened and a plastic bottle skidded across the floor. She lunged with an urgency born of desperation, her movements sluggish, her body an assemblage of brittle bones wrapped in paper-thin skin. The cool liquid kissed her cracked lips.

"Thank you," she whispered to no one, the words unanswered.

A muffled cough racked her frame, each convulsion a reminder of her frailty. But in the quake of her body, the spark that her song had ignited deep within burned more brightly, refusing to be extinguished.

"Kyle," she breathed, the name fueling her resolve. "I must survive. For him. For us."

She closed her eyes, summoning visions of her boyfriend, her lover, her best friend—his laughter, his courage. They were the antidote to her despair, a reason to endure, to fight.

"Amelia won't win," she promised the darkness, her voice gaining strength. "I'll expose her lies."

With each repetition, her spirit stitched itself back together, weaving resilience into the fabric of her being. Lucy Everhart, the singer with dreams as vast as the sky, would not fade into oblivion.

"I'll escape," she vowed, her determination crystallizing into clarity. "And make them see."

Lucy's fingers grazed the door's cold surface, her nails catching on the metal's imperfections. She pressed her ear against it, straining to hear beyond its confines—a whisper, a footstep, any sign of life. The silence mocked her efforts. She stepped back, eyes scanning the room's dimly lit corners for something, anything she might have missed.

"Think, Lucy, think," she mumbled under her breath.

A loose bolt in the corner caught her attention. She knelt down and wrapped her fingers around it. The bolt resisted at first, but desperation lent her strength, and soon it gave way with a groan. Her heart surged with hope. If there was one loose piece, there could be more—a hidden passage or a weak spot in the walls.

"Come on," she urged herself, fingering along the rough edges of the wall, searching for anomalies. But the walls held firm, indifferent to her plight.

"Help!" she shouted suddenly in a wave of panic and madness, pounding her fists against the metal door. "Can anyone hear me? Please!"

Her pleas evaporated into the stifling air.

"It's useless," she hissed in frustration.

Lucy slumped to the floor, her back against the wall, her breathing rapid. A drop of sweat trickled down her temple. Every shadow seemed to shift, every creak a deliberate torment. They're watching me, she thought. Monitoring my every move.

"Kyle," she whispered, the name a talisman against her rising panic. "I'm doing this for you."

She closed her eyes, focusing on the rhythm of her own breath, trying to still the tremor in her hands. When she opened them again, her gaze fell upon the tiny ventilation grill near the ceiling. Too small to crawl through, but perhaps...

"Hello?" Her voice was hoarse as she called out, directing her words toward the vent. "If you can hear me, I'm not giving up. You won't break me."

But the silence that greeted her felt heavier than before. Lucy shivered despite the heat, her skin prickling with unease. She had the unsettling feeling of being observed, studied like a specimen in a jar.

"Stop it," she scolded herself, shaking off the paranoia. "Focus on getting out, not imaginary watchers."

Determined, Lucy rose to her feet once more, even if she couldn't stand upright. Her eyes were vigilant, darting from shadow to shadow. She refused to succumb to fear. Her resolve was a blade, cutting through the darkness, carving a path toward escape. And she wielded it with all the strength she had left.

Lucy's fingers traced the gritty texture of the floor, her nails scraping against the compacted sand. Each line etched was a silent testament to the days spent in this suffocating cell. She carved another mark, adding it to the tally that represented both the passage of time and her enduring spirit. The lines were crude, uneven, but they were hers—a small rebellion.

She leaned back against the cool wall, drawing her knees up to her chest. Her body ached from the cramped space, muscles yearning to stretch, to run, to break free. But it was her mind that waged the fiercest battle, teetering between hope and desolation.

"Freedom," she murmured, the word dancing on her lips like a prayer. It was that singular thought which fortified her resolve, an anthem pulsing through her veins.

Each day melded into the next, an indistinct blur of heat and darkness, punctuated only by the scratch of her nails against the earth. Rats scurried in the periphery, their whiskers twitching as they sought out crumbs. Lucy shooed them away with a lethargic wave, her movements slow, conserved.

"Get lost," she hissed, her voice carrying no real threat. Even the rats seemed to know it.

The isolation could have devoured her whole, but Lucy clung to fragments of song, melodies that haunted her waking moments. They reminded her of who she was, who she would be again. Humming, she filled the void with strains of music, each note a lifeline that tethered her to sanity. She repeated scripture, verses from the Bible that would give her hope. Amelia might be a phony, but God wasn't. Lucy knew that much.

Then, without warning one day, came a sound that didn't belong—the metallic groan of the door hinge. Lucy froze, breath caught in her throat, disbelieving.

Could it be?

Light spilled into the box. She squinted, shielding her eyes with a hand that trembled uncontrollably.

"Out," rasped a voice.

Lucy crawled forward, her limbs weak but spurred by a surge of adrenaline.

"Come on," urged the voice again. It held no warmth, no comfort. It wasn't Kyle.

Pushing herself onto shaky legs, she stepped forward.

"Move," barked the guard, a silhouette against the burgeoning light of the hallway.

He pushed her onwards, past the line of cabins, where she could see a sliver of the world beyond.

"Keep moving." The command snapped her back to the present, back to the gravel path outside of the compound. But instead of heading to freedom, they neared the main building.

"Inside," grunted the guard, nudging her toward the door.

Lucy's frame passed through the entryway. She hoped this was the path to her freedom. Not the end.

TWENTY-FIVE

BILLIE ANN

I knocked three times on the peeling wooden door of Joanne's dilapidated home. My heart raced in anticipation, hoping she would be home. The lock finally clicked and the door creaked open, revealing Joanne's tired face framed by the dark hallway. Her eyes held a hint of worry and I couldn't help but notice the new lines etched around them. It was clear that things had changed in her life.

"Detective Wilde," she breathed, stepping aside to let me in.

"Joanne." My greeting was curt as I crossed the threshold.

I swept a glance around the living room. Each detail could be a piece to the puzzle: the worn couch, the stack of magazines, the faint scent of lemon cleaner. My eyes flickered to a photo on the wall—a family portrait, smiles frozen in time. I filed it away for later.

"Is everything okay?" Her voice cracked with nervous energy.

"Let's talk."

"Please, have a seat," she said, her arm sweeping toward an

armchair that faced the couch where she would sit. The fabric on both pieces of furniture was faded, betraying their age and history.

"Thanks." I lowered myself into the chair, my muscles taut as coiled springs. The room seemed to shrink with our shared unease.

"Can I get you anything? Water? Coffee?" Her voice wavered slightly.

"No, I'm fine." I clasped my hands together, grounding myself for what needed to be said. "Joanne, first off, I want to say—again—I'm sorry about Madison."

Her eyes glistened, a well of sorrow threatening to overflow. "Thank you. That means a lot."

I wondered if I should tell her I was sorry about John and us finding those pictures and videos on his computer. It had to be difficult to find out about someone you loved and lived with. I had told her earlier that I didn't believe John murdered Madison, as I believed Kayla was murdered by the same killer, and John was in our custody at the time of Kayla's death. But we were still keeping him for what we had found. It was a Federal crime. We had found other material on his computer and in the material he deleted off his phone that we were able to regenerate, and it was bad. I knew he would at least have to serve five to seven years in jail for that. Everything had been turned over to the prosecutor and he would go to trial for it soon. The judge hadn't granted him bail. He wasn't seeing daylight anytime soon. But then I realized I wasn't sorry. I was glad he was behind bars for this. I just felt bad for Joanne. She was the one who finally brought it up.

"I can't... I can't believe I didn't see it. I mean, we lived here, together, for eight years. We raised a child together. I need you to know that I never saw what was on his computer. I swear to God, I didn't know..."

I raised my hand. "It's not uncommon for the partner to be

unaware in these sorts of cases. We don't suspect you of being involved in it at all, Joanne. That's not why I'm here."

She cleared her throat nervously. "That's good. 'Cause I didn't know... about him."

"I know."

"So why are you here?"

I took in a deep breath. "It might be unpleasant, but I need to ask some questions—about your past."

"Okay," she replied, a guarded note creeping into her tone.

"Your involvement with the cult... with The Last Days," I leaned forward, locking eyes with her. "Can you tell me about that time?"

A line formed between her brows, a tiny crease of resistance. I could tell she was surprised at hearing the name again, and at the fact I knew she had been a part of it. "It's been years since I left all that behind," she murmured, her fingers tracing the armrest. "I really don't remember much."

"Joanne," I pressed gently, "anything you can share could be crucial."

"I don't have anything to do with those people anymore," Joanne's voice quivered, her face a tight mask of denial.

I watched her closely, my detective's instincts on high alert. The shifting of her gaze, the slight tremble of her hands—was she scared, or was it guilt?

"Are they connected... Madison and the other girl?" Her question seeped into the thick air with hidden meaning. "The news mentioned something about it."

"We are investigating it as the same case, yes," I confirmed, my tone steady despite the churn in my gut.

I kept my voice even, though inside I was getting frustrated with the lack of information I had on Amelia. I had to get this conversation back on track. It was obvious she didn't want to talk about her time in the cult, but that just made me more curious.

"Why did you leave The Last Days? And when?"

"I left more than ten years ago, and I wasn't there very long." she murmured, her hands clasping and unclasping in her lap. "It was all before Madison, before I knew I was going to be a mother."

I leaned back, the pieces of the puzzle shifting, searching for a fit in my mind. What did she mean by that? Was The Last Days an unsafe place to become a mother?

"Go on," I urged quietly, watching as regret painted Joanne's features in somber hues.

"I left them." Her voice cracked. She shook her head, wavy brown hair catching the light. "I wanted a fresh start. It was just a bunch of hippies thinking they could change the world."

I didn't believe her. She clearly wanted to be done with the conversation, but I knew they weren't "just a bunch of hippies" and I felt like she knew it too.

"Joanne." My voice broke through the hush, firm as the resolve hardening within me. "Anything you know could be crucial. You understand that, right?"

Her eyes lifted to mine. She looked scared. She nodded, a slight movement almost lost in the gravity of the moment.

"Was there anyone... any talk of rituals, involving branding?" I pressed. I showed her the picture of the symbol branded on Kayla's forehead. "Do you recognize this?"

"Detective, I swear..." She trailed off, her gaze drifting toward the window.

"Swear later. Right now, just talk." I edged my chair closer. "Help me protect other Madisons out there."

Her lips parted, closed, then parted again. A battle waged behind her eyes, one I understood all too well. Truth versus safety. Silence could cost lives; speaking up could cost hers.

"Please, Joanne." I reached across the space between us, professionalism giving way to empathy. "For Madison."

Tears streamed down her face as she spoke. Her fingers twisted in her hair, a nervous habit that I had noticed before.

"I had to leave them," Joanne choked out. "It was a cult, Billie. A dangerous one. They promised us a new way of life, but it was all a lie."

I could tell when memories flooded back to her of the tight-knit group my family used to be a part of; the free-spirited community that seemed so appealing to them at the time. Joanne's words shattered that illusion once and for all.

"They were brainwashing us, controlling every aspect of our lives," she continued, her voice trembling. "We could do nothing without Amelia's consent. And if we did we would face punishment. Everyone was watching everyone. If you didn't follow the rules, someone would snitch. I couldn't take it anymore. So I ran away."

Joanne's eyes darted away, her fingers twisting a loose thread on the hem of her shirt. She opened her mouth, words hovering on the brink of revelation, then snapped it shut. Her breath quivered.

"There's more, isn't there, Joanne?" My voice was softer now, coaxing secrets like a confidante rather than demanding them as an officer. I wasn't surprised by anything she said. I knew Amelia was controlling. "What aren't you telling me?"

She glanced up, her eyes awash with a fear that wrenched at my gut. "I-I can't," she whispered, the struggle in her voice resonating with a mother's protective instinct—a chord that struck deep within me.

"Joanne." I leaned in, close enough to share the weight of her dread. "Madison deserves this. We can help protect her memory. Protect you."

A tear escaped, tracing a path down her cheek. She looked at me then, really looked at me, and in that gaze, I saw the dam break.

"It's... the symbol..." Her voice cracked, a dam of emotions bursting forth. "I know it. From before. From them. The symbol on that other girl's..."

"Them?" I prodded gently, handing her a tissue from the box on the coffee table.

"The cult." She took the tissue, dabbing at the corners of her eyes. "It was their mark. The one they'd... they said it was the Devil's mark, meaning someone who has it is the spawn of the Devil."

"And what does that mean?" I asked, my pulse quickening with each word that fell from her lips.

"They would have rituals," she said, a shudder passing through her. "Dark rituals. I never... I never thought..."

"Thought what?" I urged, aware that each piece she gave could be vital, could be the key to saving another life.

"Thought they'd... hurt someone outside. Someone innocent like Madison." Her body shook, grief and terror mingling in a bitter cocktail.

"So you believe they might have hurt Madison?" I asked.

She cleared her throat and nodded. "As soon as I saw the mark that they said was on Kayla's body. I knew. They took her. I just know they did. And maybe they took Madison as well. As a revenge for me leaving. That's what I believe. But I can't prove it, you know? I can only tell you what I think. To be honest, then I didn't think you'd believe me if I told you."

"Joanne," I reached out, squeezing her hand lightly, a bridge of trust in the dim room. "You've done the right thing by telling me."

Her tears continued, but there was a faint glimmer of relief in her eyes—a burden shared, if not yet lifted.

"Joanne," I said. "Look at me."

She lifted her gaze, eyes rimmed red.

"I can't imagine what you've been through," I continued, "but Madison deserves justice. And you—you deserve peace."

My hand found hers, the gesture surprising us both. "I will do everything I can to keep you safe. To find whoever did this."

Her fingers trembled against mine.

"Can you trust me with that?" I asked.

She nodded, lips pressed into a thin line.

"Good," I said, squeezing her hand before letting go. It was a promise—a lifeline for both of us. "I will need you to talk to me about the compound. Do you remember the floorplan?"

"Yes."

"Okay, tell me about it. And then tell me where these rituals took place?"

"I-it was in the swamps. By the creek by the compound."

"I'm gonna need you to show me on a map. And can you help me find those children? The ones who were branded."

"They're probably still at the compound," she said.

"Okay. And then the big question is—would you be able to testify to all this should it be necessary?"

It took her a few seconds, but she nodded. "Y-yes. If you promise to protect me."

"Of course."

* * *

Once we were done, I stood, every muscle tight. The quiet that filled the room seemed to press against my ears. We were two women, bound by tragedy and a quest for truth, yet separated by an ocean of unspoken fears.

"Thank you, Joanne," I said, my voice barely above a whisper. "For telling me the truth."

Her eyes tracked my every move, but she didn't speak.

The silence hovered with the things we couldn't say as I reached the door. With a final nod, I stepped out into the fading light, leaving behind the warmth of the house and the cold shadow of the secret we now shared.

The door clicked shut behind me. A chill brushed against my skin, a stark contrast to the stifling tension that had cocooned Joanne's living room. I stepped off the porch, gravel crunching beneath my boots.

The silence of the neighborhood wrapped around me, deceptively peaceful. Somewhere in this quiet suburban maze, answers lurked, shrouded in secrets and fear.

TWENTY-SIX

Then

Lucy edged toward the door.

She had been out of the box for three days now and was finally allowed to move around with no one guarding her. She hadn't seen Kyle and had gone looking for him. As she passed a door, she thought she heard his voice and approached it, then peeked inside.

A soft glow illuminated the room within, casting a halo around the figures entwined at its center. Kyle and Amelia, locked in an embrace so tender it cut like glass. His hands, those familiar hands that had strummed melodies into the night, now traced gentle circles over Amelia's clothed midsection.

Lucy's heart seized, a vice of shock and disbelief. Breath hitched in her throat. Time slowed, each second a note held too long, a chord unresolved. The world narrowed to this single frozen moment: the intimate whisper of fabric against fabric, the warm amber light, the shadow of betrayal. Lucy stood motionless, unseen, bearing witness to the unraveling of her reality.

Amelia was pregnant. And it had to be Kyle's.

Betrayal. The sting felt sharp, visceral. Lucy's mind raced, a tempest of disbelief and hurt. How? Why?

"Kyle..." she breathed, the name a blade in her chest.

Images flashed—laughs shared, songs co-written, nights entwined. All tainted now. Her trust crumbled like dry leaves underfoot. The room spun, walls closing in, suffocating.

"Why would you do that to me?" she murmured, each word a shard of her shattered illusions.

Her eyes fixed on them, betrayal searing into her very soul. Kyle's touch, once hers, now Amelia's. A caress of the protruding stomach that spoke volumes, unwritten lyrics of a song she was never meant to hear.

"Amelia," she whispered, the pastor's name was now a curse, a question, an enigma.

The tendrils of fear that had clutched her heart now twisted into something fiercer. She couldn't stand idly by, a spectator in her own demise.

Lucy's fists clenched, nails biting into palms—a physical anchor amidst the chaos of her emotions. Jaw set, a line drawn in the sand.

Lucy pivoted on her heel, a silent phantom as she slipped from the threshold. The door clicked shut, a soft accusation in the stillness. She sped down the corridor, her strides long and purposeful, each footfall a drumbeat of urgency reverberating against the cold, unyielding walls. The hallway stretched before her, an endless tunnel. She blinked rapidly, willing the tears that threatened to blur her vision into submission.

"Focus," she commanded herself, the word barely a breath on her lips. "You can't let this take you down."

Her hands shook as she delved into Amelia's quarters, a place once sanctified, now tainted with duplicity. Drawers slid open with hushed protests, their contents scattered—a chaotic testament to her frantic search. Papers rustled and whispered secrets as she sifted through them, her pulse whooshing in her ears. Every fiber of her being strained for signs of deceit, for proof that might take Amelia down.

TWENTY-SEVEN

BILLIE ANN

The screen of my phone lit up in the darkness of my cramped apartment. It was early evening and I had just gotten home.

"Wilde," I answered, the name fitting more than ever.

"Detective, it's Tom."

His voice was a low rasp, like the drag of a boat through marshy waters. "I talked to some neighbors down by the creek earlier today, and there was a guy named Hank who said he saw something that day Madison was murdered. I thought maybe you'd want to talk to him."

He gave me the address, and I was already grabbing my keys, slipping into boots worn thin from too many miles. The drive to the swamps was a blur of streetlights and shadows.

His porch light flickered as I knocked on the door. It swung open to reveal his weathered face, eyes darting behind thick lenses. Tom had been re-interviewing everyone in the vicinity of both Madison's and Kayla's crime scenes, and this was the first lead we had, the first time anyone had claimed anything unordinary had happened in the lead-up to either girl's disappearance. We had no understanding of how either girl was snatched, just the fact that they both failed to get on the same school bus. No one had reported seeing them alone in the local area or being taken. So, it must have been done quickly and by someone who had experience in doing so quietly.

"Evening." I showed him my badge before I stepped inside, the smell of mildew greeting me.

"Detective." He nodded, then glanced outside before closing the door.

"So my colleague says you saw something the other day?"

"Yeah, I saw something odd, is all."

"Odd how?" I pressed, my gaze fixed on him.

"Late-night wanderer, down by the creek. Carrying a bag, heavy-like." Hank's fingers twitched.

"Did you recognize this person?" I leaned in, searching his eyes for clues.

"Stranger to me," he admitted. "But the way they moved, quiet and deliberate, made my skin crawl." This could have been the dumping of Kayla's body. She was taken after school, branded sometime during the afternoon, and killed around midnight then dumped that same night. I wondered if there were any surveillance cameras between the creek and The Last Day compound. There weren't a lot of houses or business out here. A few small neighborhoods was all. Perhaps a Ring camera had picked up something in the nearby area. I made a note to follow up.

"Anything else?" I pushed, knowing the importance of every scrap of information.

"Seemed like they knew the swamps. Knew where to step. That's about it. Couldn't see a face or anything."

"Thanks, Hank." I jotted notes in my pad, the ink barely keeping up with my thoughts. Tom would have got Hank's own alibi. "If you remember anything else—"

"I'll call," he finished.

I stepped back into the night. Amelia's shadow loomed

large, but I was closer now. Closer to answers, closer to justice for Madison and Kayla.

The swamp embraced me like an old friend, one you can't trust. My boots squelched in the mud, and I clutched the flashlight, its beam a thin line, opening the oppressive dark.

Mangroves loomed over me. The air was thick with the smell of decay and life all at once, a reminder of nature's indifference. The swamps were big, and this was an area we hadn't searched.

I swept the light side to side methodically. The tip from Hank was sparse, but it was all I had—a wisp of smoke suggesting a fire.

A noise. Soft, but out of place in the still night. I froze, every muscle tensing.

"Police! Identify yourself!" No response, just the echo of my own voice against the dense foliage.

Heart hammering, I edged closer, my flashlight's halo revealing a scene that seemed to belong to another world. It was a campsite, haphazard and crude. A circle of blackened stones marked a recent fire, its warmth long dissipated into the cool night air.

My eyes caught on the food wrappers strewn about, a breadcrumb trail left by someone who didn't care or didn't think they'd be followed. I crouched, examining a faded label, trying to glean some sense of who I was chasing.

My fingers brushed over the ground, the damp earth embedding under my nails as I searched for clues. And there it was. A child's shirt among the belongings.

Adrenaline surged. Instinct took over. In one swift motion, I pivoted on my heel, drawing my gun with an ease that belied my pounding heart.

"Freeze!"

The flashlight's beam swept the darkness, landing on the figure before me. Tall, broad-shouldered, their features were obscured by the shadows. They stood still, watching me with an intensity that set every nerve on edge.

"Who are you?" I demanded, my voice steady despite the tumult inside. "What are you doing here?"

The figure didn't move, didn't speak. We were statues in a twisted tableau, locked in a moment fraught with danger and unanswered questions. The swampland held its breath, waiting for the next move.

"Talk," I ordered, my weapon unwavering. "Now."

The figure's lips twisted into a half-smirk, half-snarl. "I don't have anything to say to you, cop."

"Wrong answer." The edge in my voice was as sharp as a knife. This wasn't just some random swamp dweller. The shirt told me something else.

"Think carefully," I pressed on. "Why are you here? What do you know about the girls who were murdered out here?"

Silence was his stubborn reply. Eyes narrowed, he seemed to assess his odds, calculating whether he could outrun a bullet or outfight a trained detective.

"Last chance," I warned, my finger tense against the cold metal of the trigger guard.

He lunged.

I sidestepped, reflexes honed by years on the force snapping into play. My gun hand remained steady, but I didn't shoot. Not yet. We grappled, his bulk surprising me with its force. But I was quicker, more desperate. I had kids to think about, a life to rebuild. If I shot him there, I risked getting in trouble. I couldn't afford to. No shadowy figure in a swamp was going to hold me back from getting my kids.

"Get off!" I spat out as I drove my knee into his midsection.

He grunted, the sound mingling with the nocturnal chorus of the swamplands. We were a whirlwind of motion, two predators fighting for survival. But only one of us fought for justice.

With a swift move, I hooked his arm, twisting it behind his back. He yelped—a small victory in the silence of the swamp.

"Down!" I commanded, pushing him to the muddy ground.

I cuffed him quickly, metal clinking in the quiet night. His evasion had told me everything I needed to know; he was involved somehow. And I would find out exactly how.

"Start talking," I ordered, breathless but resolute. "Or we can chat down at the station. Your choice."

He glowered up at me, defiance etched onto his face even through the pain. It was clear this wasn't over.

He lay on the ground, chest heaving, eyes darting. I towered over him, my flashlight beam trained on his face like an interrogator's spotlight.

"I didn't kill no one," he protested weakly.

"That's what they all say."

"Look," he whispered, "I don't wanna go to jail. I didn't do anything wrong. Amelia... she—"

"What do you know about her?" I asked, shocked. Had I stumbled on my strongest lead yet?

"Nothing. I didn't mean to..."

"Help me bring her in, and we can talk about keeping you out." I offered the bait, watching him squirm mentally.

"Okay... okay," he relented, a bead of sweat rolling down his temple. "But you gotta protect me from her."

"Deal," I snapped; and I knew any deal with me was better than what Amelia would offer him.

Time was slipping through my fingers slowly, like the murky waters of the swamp. I needed to move now.

TWENTY-EIGHT

Then

Lucy's pulse quickened as she slipped through the narrow, unguarded doorway at the far end of the compound. She had intended to run, but this door, a forgotten relic with peeling paint and rusted hinges, had always been there—unnoticed, blending into the monotony of the endless concrete walls. And today, driven by an unnerving intuition, Lucy felt its silent call. She knew she needed to find out Amelia's secrets if she was going to save him, and his child. She had to do this for them.

Darting a look back over her shoulder, she feared the consequence of being discovered. She could almost feel the cold isolation box still, its stark walls pressing in on her, punishing her for her curiosity. She would end up in there again, if she was caught. She had located the keys in Amelia's drawer and finally found what it belonged to. She knew it was dangerous. But she couldn't shake the feeling that behind this door lay answers she needed, dark secrets at the edges of her consciousness.

She stepped inside, and the door groaned a protest, closing with an ominous click behind her. A single bulb, swaying gently from a cobwebbed ceiling, cast a sickly yellow glow over the room. Shadows pooled in the corners, deep and thick, hiding what lay beyond the weak circle of light.

The air musty with the scent of disuse, the room thick with dust and decay, the kind that wraps around you. It was a smell that spoke of things long forgotten, of time slipping away unnoticed. Her nostrils flared as she inhaled the dank atmosphere, the pungent odor mingling with the taste of fear on her tongue.

"Keep it together, Lucy," she whispered to herself, her voice barely audible.

She moved forward, her hands reaching out to graze against cold metal shelving, feeling the slight tremor in her fingertips. Every step seemed louder than the last, her boots echoing off the concrete floor, betraying her presence in this secret space.

"What secrets are you hiding down here, Amelia?" she murmured. And with each hesitant step, Lucy delved deeper into the heart of the unknown, driven by a mix of dread and an unquenchable thirst for the truth that might lie buried within these walls.

A low creak from the floorboards beneath her teased out the silence. Shadows hovered at the edges of her vision, but it was the outline of an anomaly against the far wall that seized her attention—another door, concealed by the very darkness that shrouded the room.

The dim light from her handheld flashlight flickered as she approached, its beam revealing the subtle contours of a hidden doorway. Her breath caught in her throat, fingers skimming over the cold surface of the door, feeling for a latch or a knob. There was nothing but the smooth expanse of aged wood and a faint outline where the door met the wall.

Lucy pressed her ear against the cool wood, straining to hear any signs of life beyond. Silence answered back. She withdrew, chewing on her lower lip, the weight of decision anchoring her to the spot.

"Secrets don't stay buried," she whispered, as though the words could lend her strength. "Not today."

Gathering a quiet courage, Lucy found the seam with her fingertips and pushed. The door groaned in protest, a sound that seemed far too loud in the stillness of the storage room. She went on, even as her instincts screamed for caution.

As the hidden door swung open, a new world revealed itself —a room bathed in the sickly glow of overhead bulbs, their dim light struggling against the encroaching shadows. Walls lined with steel shelving loomed like silent sentinels, each one laden with a meticulously organized arsenal.

Her eyes darted across rows of firearms—a chilling array of handguns, rifles, and shotguns. Boxes of ammunition were stacked with precision, a pyramid of potential violence. On hooks above, tactical vests and helmets bore the bleak promise of protection. It was a collection vast enough to arm a legion, each piece a testament to a plan far more sinister than anything Lucy had imagined.

"Jesus," she breathed.

She stepped inside, the temperature seeming to drop with each inch she ventured further, the chill seeping through her clothes to her skin. Her hand hovered over a rifle, not daring to touch, yet feeling the latent power that emanated from the sleek metal and oiled wood.

"Who are you preparing to fight?" The query was for herself, for the walls, for the ghosts that might linger in this place of preparation and dread.

In that moment, the reality of her discovery anchored itself to her bones—a heavy, sinking truth that threatened to drag her down into the abyss of fear and revelation. But Lucy was no stranger to adversity; her music had carried her through darker times, her voice finding strength even when her spirit faltered. Now, standing among the implements of war, she knew that silent songs would not suffice.

"Find your voice, Lucy," she urged. "Before it's too late."

She assessed the arsenal. Rows upon rows of guns, from sleek handguns to matte-black assault rifles, each meticulously arranged like a macabre museum display. Shelves brimmed with boxes of ammunition, the rounds glinting dully under the faint light. Grenades huddled together, their pins ominously still.

"Unbelievable," she whispered.

She moved deeper into the space that smelled of metal and oil. Fingers trembling, she reached out, her touch grazing the cold barrel of a rifle. The realization that these weapons were meant to be held, to be used by human hands, sent a shudder through her.

"Amelia, what have you done?" It was more than zealotry now; it was mobilization.

Lucy's thoughts churned. The sermons, the passionate speeches about deliverance—they weren't just words. They were a call to arms, a battle cry she hadn't understood until now.

"Preparing for war..." Her own voice sounded foreign in her ears, the pieces clicking together in a terrifying clarity. She thought of the faces in the compound, the eyes filled with reverence for Amelia, not knowing the depth of darkness they were being led into. And she knew she couldn't leave yet either. She couldn't leave Kyle and his child in danger.

TWENTY-NINE

JENNA

Jenna's breath hitched, stifled by the coarse fabric against her lips. She writhed, the ropes biting into her wrists, ankles raw from the relentless friction. Darkness engulfed her, the blackness beneath the hood absolute, suffocating. The room was a tomb, air heavy with the scent of mildew and despair.

"Please," she whispered. "I want to go home."

The walls seemed to press closer at her plea, the room no larger than a closet, a casket crafted for the living. A chill crept up from the concrete floor, seeping through her clothes, a cold embrace from the shadows that held her captive.

"Mom..." Jenna's voice broke.

Tears soaked the blindfold, her sobs a muted soundtrack to the oppressive silence. The small space robbed her of any sense of direction, of time. It could have been hours, days since she last heard a human sound other than her own fractured breathing.

"Help," she managed, the plea strangled, lost to the void that encased her. "Somebody, please..."

The silence jeered back, cruel, unyielding. Jenna shivered, the terror a living thing within her chest. Each breath became a battle, each heartbeat counting down the moments of her captivity.

The door creaked, a harbinger of dread. Footsteps, deliberate and heavy, approached. Jenna's heart thundered against her ribs.

"Who's there?" Her voice quivered, strangled by the thick air. "Why-why are you doing this?"

Each step seemed louder, closer. Shadows danced across the thin fabric over her eyes, playing tricks with her mind.

"Please," she begged, her words tumbling out in a rush. "I just want to go home."

The footsteps halted, a few paces away. Jenna held her breath, waiting, fearing.

"Who are you?" she choked out, her voice trembling. "What do you want?"

No answer came, only the sound of shallow breathing.

"Please," she whimpered, the blindfold clinging to her wet lashes. "I need to go home. My mom... she's waiting for me."

The silence stretched, taut as a wire. Then, a low chuckle, devoid of humor, filled the void.

"Let me go," she pleaded, her voice breaking.

"Shhh," the voice soothed, mockingly.

Jenna sobbed harder. For a second she thought the mysterious presence had left, but then she sensed movement behind her back.

"Who's there?"

"Someone you should be afraid of," the voice replied, tone dipped in darkness, malevolent as the space around her.

"I don't understand," she said, twisting against her restraints. "What do you want from me?"

"Want?" A pause followed, thick with implication. "I'm fulfilling a purpose."

"Please." She was begging again, her voice loaded with desperation. "You have to let me go."

"Let you go?" The voice seemed closer now, a whisper against her ear. "The Devil doesn't release what belongs to Him."

"Devil?" Jenna's pulse hammered. "I've done nothing wrong."

"Wrong is a matter of perspective. You're the Devil's spawn, they say." The words were almost playful, baiting her terror.

"Spawn? What do you mean?" Her confusion bled through, a stark contrast to the cryptic calm of her captor.

"Caught between worlds, Jenna. A life indebted, a soul ensnared. I can set you free."

"Whose soul?" She fought the rising hysteria, the urge to scream and never stop.

"Questions, questions," the voice tutted. "All in due time."

"Please, just tell me—" Her plea cut off as something brushed her cheek, soft yet chilling.

"Shhh." A finger pressed to her lips through the fabric. "Patience is a virtue."

Jenna recoiled, but the touch lingered, insistent. Her breath came in shallow gasps as the dark room seemed to shrink around her, the musty air clinging to her. Sweat beaded on her forehead, trickling down the sides of her face, mingling with tears that had long since dried.

"Who are you?" she cried out again, her voice barely above a whisper, constricted by fear and the oppressive darkness.

The footsteps halted mere inches away from her, the silence that followed stretching into eternity. She could feel the presence of her captor as a tangible force; she could hardly breathe.

"Please," she whimpered, her body trembling uncontrollably now. "I need to go home."

Panic surged, lending her strength she didn't know she had. Jenna writhed against her bonds, the ropes biting into her flesh, the scrape of coarse fabric against her skin adding to the sensations overwhelming her.

"Struggle all you want," the voice whispered, closer now, breathing life into her darkest fears. "It won't change a thing."

The scent of damp earth and decay that filled her nostrils was overpowering now, a sickly sweet aroma that made her stomach churn. And there was something else—a metallic tang that hinted at unseen horrors lurking in the shadows.

"Let me go!"

Her pleas dissolved into incoherent cries in the rustling movement that surrounded her, the brush of something cold and unyielding against her arm. Darkness closed in, a living entity that devoured hope and left nothing but the chilling embrace of despair.

The cold touch lingered, then retreated. She listened for any sign of life beyond her own frightened whimpers.

"Please," she whispered into the void. "I want to go home."

No answer came, only the quiet mocking her plea. The bag over her head seemed to tighten, darkness pressing against her closed eyelids.

A sudden creak in the quiet. Footsteps receded, the faint echo of a door closing, leaving her alone with the creeping dread that something terrible loomed on the horizon. Jenna's heart raced, her mind reeling with the cryptic exchange.

"Wait!" she cried out, but only silence answered.

The room felt colder now, emptier. Her thoughts scrambled, every dark possibility racing through her mind. She knew what had happened to Kayla. Was it her turn now?

"Help me. Please, someone, help me," she whispered, but the plea held no power against the encroaching terror.

THIRTY

BILLIE ANN

The station's lights flickered overhead as I marched the suspect down the stark hallway. The scent of stale coffee and worn-out leather filled the air, a comfort in its familiarity. He began to slow and I nudged him forward with a firm hand at his back. He had sweat beading on his brow, and his eyes were darting around as if everyone in the station knew why he was there. Was he ashamed? Embarrassed? Or perhaps looking for an escape. I grasped his shoulder and pushed him on.

We reached the door marked "Interrogation." Just as I was about to usher him inside, a noise from behind made me pause —the sound of a door swinging open with urgency.

"Billie Ann!"

Chief Harold's voice cracked across the quiet of the precinct. I turned sharply.

She was emerging from her office, her usually stoic face washed out, the lines around her mouth deeper than I remembered. Her hands trembled visibly, a sight so disconcerting it rooted me to the spot. Chief Harold never showed weakness, yet here she was, looking as if she'd seen a ghost.

"Chief?" I asked, a deep frown creasing my forehead.

"Inside. Now." Her voice was a low growl, commanding immediate action.

I took the suspect into the interrogation room, told him to wait and closed the door, then followed Chief Harold into her office. Something big was up, something that had rattled her—and that scared me more than any criminal ever could.

"Chief," I said, keeping my tone even, "what's wrong?" The pounding in my chest felt like it was trying to break free from my ribcage.

"Billie Ann," she began, her voice strained, "I'm afraid we have another one."

"Another what?" I asked, my brain already ticking through possibilities.

"Missing girl. Jenna Hart." Not another kid. *Dammit, not again.*

"When?" I demanded, the urgency in my voice now mirrored the Chief's.

"Her mom just called it in. She didn't make it to school today and never came home. Her mom went to look for her and found her bike and backpack in the side of the road down by the beach. The bike was all crumpled up, looking like she had been hit by a car."

Chief Harold's words hit me like a physical blow, knocking the wind out of me.

"She must have been missing for hours. Why the hell are they only reporting it now?" My frustration boiled over, the raw edge of fear creeping into my voice.

"Dammit, Billie Ann, you think I'm not asking myself the same questions?" Chief Harold snapped, then visibly collected herself. "We need to move fast."

"Understood."

A chill ran down my spine, icy fingers of fear squeezing my heart. I'd met with Jenna at her home, and talked to her just a few days ago.

"Teams are rolling out as we speak," Chief Harold barked, her orders shaking me out of my fog of disbelief. "I want eyes on every street, every alley. She could be anywhere, Billie Ann."

"Understood." The words were automatic, but behind them lay a quiet promise. This wasn't just about following orders. It was personal. I hadn't been able to save Madison or Kayla, but I was going to save Jenna. Whatever it might cost me.

"Good," she said with a nod, her voice firm with an undercurrent of concern.

"I think I have a lead, something I need to pursue first," I said. My words were clipped, fingers flexing at my sides. "I need to talk to my suspect. He might know something. He lives out there, camps by the creek. I found evidence that connects Kayla to a religious organization, and he has ties to it too."

"All right. Then interrogate him, while we initiate the search. Tom will talk to the family and friends. We're doing everything we can. I will get search teams out there, combing every inch. And this one will give us something. I trust your instincts."

"Harold, I—"

"Listen," she interrupted, placing a hand on my shoulder. It felt like an anchor, steadying my frantic energy. "You've got the best team working with you. You have instincts sharper than anyone I've seen. Trust them. Trust yourself."

"Jenna doesn't have time for trust."

"Keep your cool, Billie Ann. For Jenna. For yourself." She squeezed my shoulder before letting go. "Go get him to talk. We're all behind you."

"Thanks, Chief." I took a deep breath, pulling strength from her words. "Let's bring Jenna home."

"Go," she urged.

I stepped toward the door, resolve pulsing through my veins. *Jenna Hart, I'm not letting you down.*

THIRTY-ONE

Then

Lucy's fingers trembled, the pregnancy test falling into the sink with a clatter that echoed off the sterile tiles. The plus sign was unmistakable, glaring at her from amidst the white plastic like an omen. They had a small store at the compound. That's where she was able to find a test.

She closed her eyes, battling the surge of emotions. She hadn't had her period for months, but she thought it was because of being in the isolation box for so long that it had stressed her body out. She never thought this could be the cause.

She needed Kyle back.

She made her way through the maze of corridors, the soft hum of prayers and hymns seeping from the chapel. She arrived at Amelia's office, pausing for a moment to steady her breath before knocking.

"Come in," called a voice, mellifluous and calm.

The door creaked open to reveal the dimly lit sanctuary of Amelia's world. Shadowy corners, flickering candles casting dancing lights upon the walls adorned with crosses and ancient symbols of protection.

"Lucy, child, what brings you here so flustered?" Amelia stood, concern furrowing her elegant brow.

"I-I'm..." Her confession stuck in her throat like a fishbone.

"Speak, Lucy. Fear has no home among these walls."

The weight of her secret tipped the balance of her composure, and Lucy found herself blurting out the truth. "I'm pregnant."

Amelia's warm eyes widened, her lips parting slightly as if the words had physically jolted her. Silence was dense and suffocating.

"And it's Kyle's and I want him back," she added.

"Lucy," Amelia finally spoke, her tone measured, "this is unexpected." Her fingers absentmindedly traced the silver cross hanging at her neck.

Lucy's gaze fixed on that gesture, the symbol of faith that now seemed to judge her very being.

Amelia's fingers lingered on the cross, her eyes locked onto Lucy's with an intensity that sent shivers down her spine.

"Lucy," Amelia said slowly, "this-this is no ordinary conception. Can you not feel it? The air has shifted, the light dimmed. This child"—she shook her head—"it harbors darkness."

"Darkness?" Lucy's palms were slick against the cool wood of the chair she gripped for support.

"Evil," Amelia whispered, her voice a serpent slithering through the room. "This child is the Devil's spawn, come to kill my child—God's chosen. We must act, swiftly and decisively."

"No!" Lucy's eyes blazed with a fire Amelia had never seen. "This child is mine. And I will protect it with every breath in my body."

"Lucy, think of what you're saying," Amelia urged, stepping closer, her brown eyes searching Lucy's face. "The prophecy..."

"Your prophecy does not dictate my life, or my child's."

Lucy stood, her body a pillar of resolve amidst the wavering candlelight.

"Child, please—" Amelia reached out, but Lucy stepped back, out of reach.

"Amelia," Lucy's voice now held a steely edge, "I will not let fear rule me. Nor will I allow your beliefs to steal my future. My child will live."

Amelia's hands slammed onto the oak desk, a thunderclap in the dim room. "Lucy Everhart, you defy not only me but the very word of God!"

Lucy recoiled as if struck. The office felt smaller, the shadows cast by the flickering candles now menacing.

"God's wrath is mighty," Amelia continued, her voice rising with fervor. "To harbor such sin within you invites His divine punishment."

A cold sweat broke out on Lucy's brow, the silver cross on the wall catching her eye, glinting ominously. She swallowed hard; she felt her resolve fading, a fragile shield against Amelia's onslaught.

"Sin?" Lucy whispered. "My love for Kyle, our child... how can love breed sin?"

"Love?" Amelia scoffed, her eyes narrowing. "It is deception. A veil over your eyes, blinding you to the path of righteousness."

"Kyle and I—we believe in love, in music, not..." Lucy trailed off, torn. Her dreams with Kyle, their shared melodies, now discordant. He had been so distant ever since she was released from the box. She had tried to talk to him, but he had barely said a word to her. He belonged to Amelia now, the others said. But she knew that he was still in there somewhere. Amelia was just controlling him. Lucy could get him back, and this was how. If she too was carrying his child, he had to change his mind, right? She was, after all, his first love.

"Belief without obedience is rebellion," Amelia intoned. "And rebels must be cleansed."

Lucy clenched her fists, battling the image of Kyle's gentle smile with the dread Amelia sowed. "Our baby is innocent," she said, more to herself than to Amelia.

"Your baby," Amelia spat, "will be your downfall."

"Then let me fall," Lucy breathed. "With Kyle, with our child, away from here."

Lucy's palm pressed against the wooden door to hers and Kyle's room, easing it open with a whisper of a creak. Her fingers trembled as they left the door and found sanctuary in the folds of her skirt. Kyle was hunched over a book Amelia had written, containing the words that had ensnared them both.

"Kyle," she began.

He didn't look up. He was lost in the scripture of Amelia's world, a world that promised everything and suffocated them in fine print. Sunlight filtered through the lone window, casting a halo on the dusty floorboards and touching the edge of his shaggy brown hair.

"Kyle," Lucy tried again, louder this time. Her heart thrashed frantically against her ribs.

"Hello," he murmured without lifting his gaze, his thumb flipping another page.

"Can we talk?" Her throat constricted, as if the very air in the compound conspired to silence her.

Finally, his eyes met hers, a flicker of concern crossing his features.

"Something... I need to tell you something important."

She closed the distance between them, her steps hesitant yet resolute. The book in his hands seemed to weigh more than just paper and ink—it was the gravity that held them in orbit around

Amelia. She had approached him after being released from the box, but he had held no compassion for her, only said he believed it was what was best for her. If Amelia believed it was, then so did he.

"Sure, Luce." He marked his place with a finger, setting the book aside, and patted the bed beside him. "What is it?"

Lucy perched on the edge of the mattress, the springs creaking beneath her. Inhaling deeply, she fought for control over the quake in her lungs, the quake in her soul.

"Kyle, I'm—" She broke off, the enormity of her confession catching in her chest.

"Lucy?" His hand reached out, briefly brushing hers. "Whatever it is, we'll face it together. We're all together here."

She met his earnest gaze, saw the trust he placed in her, in them. Her resolve solidified. It was now or never.

"I'm pregnant, Kyle." Her voice was barely more than a whisper. Her fingers entwined nervously as she waited for his reaction.

His eyes widened, the brown depths clouding over with something dark and tumultuous. He swallowed hard, the Adam's apple in his throat bobbing with the effort.

"Baby?" His voice cracked in disbelief.

She nodded, her own eyes pleading. "Our future, our love—made real."

For a moment, there was only the sound of their breaths, uneven and strained, filling the small room with an invisible tension. Then he shot up, his movement so sudden that the book of Amelia's teachings tumbled to the floor with a soft thud.

"It's a sin," Kyle spat out the word like it burned his tongue. "This can't... It mustn't..." His face twisted, a visage of confusion warring with anger. "Amelia says that only she can"

"Kyle, please—" Lucy reached out, her hand trembling as she sought him, but he recoiled as if her touch seared him.

"No!" The force behind the word seemed to shake the very walls. "It's wrong. We have to end it, Lucy. It's what Amelia teaches, what we believe. This child will destroy everything." His chest heaved, and his gaze bore into her, fervent and unyielding.

"Beliefs?" Her voice broke, the single word a plea for the man she knew, the man who dreamed with her under the stars and spoke of love and music as their salvation.

"Amelia's way is life. This"—he gestured wildly, his finger pointing at her abdomen—"is not our path."

Tears welled in her eyes as she faced the stranger before her, his features sharpened by ideologies that were never their own.

"Kyle, listen to me!" Lucy's voice clawed its way out, raw and urgent now. She stepped closer, her shadow merging with his in the dim light. "Amelia's teachings—there's something wrong with them. Deeply wrong."

"Wrong?" Kyle's brow furrowed as he backed away, pressing against the wall. His hands clenched into fists at his sides.

"Think about it, please." Her words rushed out, a torrent of fear and conviction. "She twists everything, makes us fear. She's dangerous, and we're in danger if we don't leave this place."

"Leave?" He scoffed, his laugh short and hollow. "And go where? This is our sanctuary!"

"Sanctuary?" Lucy's hands were shaking, but she forced them still. "Or prison? Look what she did to me!"

"Stop it!" His voice rose, louder than she'd ever heard it. "You're confused. Amelia saved us. You're talking like the Devil now, Lucy."

"Like the Devil?" A sob caught in her throat, strangled by disbelief. "Kyle, can't you see? It's manipulation, all of it!"

"Enough!" He shook his head. "We follow Amelia. We obey. That's final."

"Kyle." Her plea was a whisper, one last flicker of hope against the tide of his conviction.

Lucy's vision blurred, tears carving clear paths down her cheeks. Kyle's accusations echoed in the hollows of the room, reverberating against the stark white walls that had once promised purity and peace. She gasped for breath, each one a shuddering sob that refused to quiet.

"Kyle," Lucy choked out. She blinked rapidly, trying to steady herself, to see the man she loved beyond the veil of her sorrow.

But as she looked at him, really looked, she saw it—the iron-clad grip of conviction in his posture, the unyielding glint in his eye. There was no reaching him; he was lost in Amelia's labyrinth of lies. She stepped back, her heel catching on the threadbare rug they'd once danced upon. The room felt smaller, suffocating.

"Kyle," she tried again, this time with newfound clarity cutting through the fog of her emotions. "I can't—I can't stay here." Her hands instinctively moved to her belly, cradling the life inside her—a secret flicker of existence that deserved a chance.

"Can't stay?" Kyle's voice cracked. "What do you mean?"

She nodded, swallowing hard against the lump in her throat. "This place, what she's doing—it's wrong. And our baby —" She paused, bracing for his reaction.

"Baby?" His face paled, words lost. "It's the Devil, Lucy, can't you see?"

"It's our child," she continued, her resolve hardening to ice. "Our child needs to be safe—from Amelia, from all of this."

"Lucy." Kyle's hands reached out then fell limp.

"I have to protect our baby, Kyle. Even if it means leaving... without you." Lucy's eyes never left his, willing him to understand.

"Leave?" he finally murmured in disbelief.

"Leave," she affirmed, steeling herself against the tremor

threatening to unmake her. "Because I love our child. And I love you too much to let this... madness claim us."

Her footsteps were soft but final as she turned away, each one an echo of the dreams they'd shared, now crumbling beneath the weight of a truth too heavy to bear.

"Lucy, please," Kyle's plea sliced the thick tension. His eyes were panicked. "Amelia, she-she'll guide us. We're safe here."

His words strangled her heart, a desperate tether trying to bind her to a fate she refused to accept. The room felt smaller, the air heavier, as if the very walls were urging her to yield.

"Safe?" Lucy's voice was a whisper, but it carried the weight of their reality. "Kyle, look at me." She waited until his eyes met her gaze, a silent battle raging between hope and fear.

"Amelia's protection is a cage," she said, each word deliberate and clear. "I can't—we can't—let our child grow up in that. The weapons, the war she is getting ready for. It's too much. It's dangerous."

"Lucy, don't do this." His voice cracked, the edges rough with an emotion he couldn't name. "We belong here. With Amelia. With the family."

Her head shook, a small, decisive motion. "No family would ask us to make this choice. I love you, Kyle. With everything I have, I love you. But this?" She gestured around them, to the compound that had become their world and now their prison. "It's not love. It's control."

"Lucy..."

"Please understand." Her eyes never left his, a silent plea for him to see the truth. "I can't stay. Not anymore."

The muscles in Kyle's jaw clenched, his face twisting into a mask of raw emotion. "You're just going to leave?" he spat, the words laced with betrayal. "After everything we've shared, Lucy? What Amelia and the people here have done for you? You turn your back on us—on me!"

Lucy flinched as if struck, her resolve wavering for the

briefest moment under his accusation. She drew in a shaky breath, steeling herself against the pain that lanced through her chest. "It's not that simple, Kyle."

"Simple?" He laughed, a harsh sound devoid of any humor. "What's complicated about it? You're choosing to walk away from our life, our future!"

"Kyle..." Her voice was a fractured whisper, begging him to understand.

"Leaving will have consequences, Lucy. Grave ones." His eyes bore into her, hard as stone. "Amelia won't just let you go. And you think I'll stand by and watch?"

Tears threatened, but she blinked them back fiercely, turning away to shield her face from his tortured gaze. With trembling hands, she pulled a duffel bag from beneath the bed, the zipper's rasp loud in the charged silence.

Her fingers moved of their own accord, gathering the sparse collection of belongings she could call her own—a few articles of clothing, the photograph of her parents, the worn journal filled with song lyrics and dreams.

"Lucy."

She couldn't afford the luxury of looking back, not when every second counted.

"Please," she whispered to the room, to Kyle, to whatever god might be listening. "Please understand." She stuffed the last of her things into the bag, her movements brisk and mechanical.

"Lucy!" Kyle's plea was a dagger, sharp and cold, but she forced herself to stride toward the door, her grip on the bag's strap ironclad.

"Goodbye, Kyle," she said, and with a last glance at the room—their room—that had been a sanctuary turned jail, she stepped across the threshold and into the unknown.

. . .

With the pack ready, Lucy peered through the crack in the door. The hallway was empty, the dim light casting long shadows that seemed to watch her. She stepped out, her movements fluid and silent, a ghost slipping between realms.

The compound was a labyrinth of corridors and doors, each one a potential trap. She moved swiftly, avoiding the main paths where followers gathered for evening prayer. The sound of their collective chanting reached her ears, a haunting melody that underscored the gravity of her escape.

As she passed Amelia's office, her steps faltered. Through the frosted glass, a shadow moved, erratic and large. Lucy's heart skipped. She pressed herself against the wall, willing her body to become invisible, insignificant. The shadow paused, then continued its pacing dance.

"Stay calm," she whispered to the life growing inside her. There was no room for error, no second chances. She imagined Kyle's voice, once soothing and strong, guiding her through the darkness.

In her mind's eye she mapped the compound's layout, seeking an alternative route. There was a service corridor, seldom used at this hour, that led to the back exit. It was a longer way around, but it promised concealment.

She found the metal handle cold under her fingers. She glanced back one last time before pushing it open and stepping into the narrow passage beyond. Here, the air was musty, the light dim, but Lucy welcomed the obscurity it offered.

Ahead lay the final obstacle: the delivery area where vans came and went, ferrying goods and messages to the outside world. It was her gateway to freedom.

As Lucy approached, her pace measured, she could see the silhouettes of guards near the gate. They were the last barrier between her and the night that cloaked her future in uncertainty. She adjusted the pack on her shoulder, her resolve steeling her for the moments ahead.

Lucy crouched behind a stack of crates, inhaling the sharp tang of oil and metal that permeated the delivery area. Her fingers twitched, gripping the fabric of her bag as she eyed the van idling just meters away, its back doors invitingly ajar.

"Come on, come on," she whispered to herself, a mantra to steady her frayed nerves. The weight of her secret pressed upon her chest, every beat of her pulse a reminder of the life growing within, and the life she was about to leave behind.

She could almost feel the compound's walls closing in around her, the air thick with silent judgments and veiled threats. Outside, freedom beckoned—a vast, open landscape fraught with perils and promises. The unknown; fear twisted inside her like a cold knife.

With a sudden burst of movement, Lucy sprang from her hiding spot, her legs carrying her swiftly to the van. Her breaths came in short gasps. She hoisted herself up, diving into the dark cavity behind stacks of supplies. Heart pounding in her ears, she tucked her body out of sight, among boxes and bags.

The driver's door closed with a thud, and Lucy flinched, drawing her knees tighter to her chest. Footsteps approached, a shadow falling across the opening where she hid. A guard leaned in, his flashlight beam brightening the darkness.

Lucy held her breath, willing herself to become part of the shadows, invisible and insignificant. The guard's presence lingered, a physical embodiment of the threat that chased her even now.

"Everything secure?" a voice asked.

"Affirmative. Ready to move out," another answered.

The engine roared to life, a growl that vibrated through her bones, and Lucy fought to keep her breathing even. The van lurched forward, the motion jostling her precarious sanctuary. She bit down on her lip to stifle a cry as the vehicle rolled toward the gate, each second stretching taut with suspense.

"Stop!" The command rang out, and icy fear stabbed through Lucy.

Her pulse spiked, her skin prickled with the chill of exposure. The van halted, and she could hear the murmur of voices, the shuffling of feet outside. This was it—the moment of truth.

"Routine check. Open up the back!"

The order was followed by the sound of metal clanking, the padlock disengaged with a loud click. Lucy's thoughts raced, a jumble of prayers and plans. She braced herself, ready to fight or flee, whichever the fates decreed.

"Let's make it quick. We've got a schedule to keep," the driver grumbled.

"Sure thing. Just a formality."

The back doors opened, a rush of fresh air invading her cramped hideaway. Lucy squinted against the sudden light, her muscles coiled tight.

"Looks good here." The guard's boots appeared in her line of vision before retreating. "All clear."

"All right. Move along."

The doors closed once more, the lock snapping into place. Lucy exhaled, a silent sob of relief escaping her lips. The van resumed its journey, trundling past the gate, past the guards, past the compound walls that had been her cage.

As the distance grew, Lucy allowed herself a single thought: *I'm doing this—for me, for my child, for our future.* Whatever lay ahead, she would face it with the strength that had carried her this far. And with each mile that passed, she moved closer to the promise of a new dawn.

The van finally rolled to a stop. The vehicle's silence louder than any symphony she'd ever sung. She waited, seconds stretching into eternity, muscles knotted with anticipation. A sliver of light crept through a crack in the van's wall—freedom beckoned.

She pushed against the rear doors, her breath quick and

shallow. They gave way with a reluctant groan, protesting their part in her escape. Lucy tumbled out, landing on unsteady legs, gravel biting into her palms. The air tasted different here, free of the compound's stifling control. She gasped it in, savoring the rush of the night against her skin.

Lucy stumbled forward, her first steps erratic but determined. Every sense screamed for her to run, to put distance between herself and the place that had threatened to swallow her whole.

"Keep moving," she whispered to herself, an incantation against the fear gnawing at her resolve.

Her shadow stretched long and thin across the ground as she moved, ghostlike, toward the line of trees bordering the road. Behind it lurked the swamps. With each step, the weight of her decision pressed down, yet she felt lighter than she had in months. The life within her was a silent ally, a secret strength.

Lucy paused at the swamp's edge, the world beyond bathed in moonlight. She closed her eyes for a fleeting moment, letting the reality of her escape wash over her. When she opened them again, the night seemed less ominous, the darkness less absolute.

"Lucy Everhart," she murmured, "you're going to be okay."

Turning her back on the compound, Lucy plunged into the woods. Branches snagged at her hair and clothes, the forest floor uneven underfoot. But she was a melody now, weaving through the night, notes of fear and hope blending into a song of survival.

THIRTY-TWO

BILLIE ANN

I walked into the interrogation room, where the suspect, Kyle Donovan, sat cuffed to the table, a haunted look on his face.

I took my seat across from him. So far, everyone connected to The Last Days had been vague and unhelpful to me, but I was hopeful Kyle was going to give me some useful information, that he was a cog in the machine at that church, and he was willing to give Amelia up.

"Please state your name for the tape."

"Kyle Donovan," he said.

"Kyle, as you know, I'd like to talk about Pastor Amelia Hawthorne."

"I barely managed to escape a few months ago," he stammered, eyes shifty. "I snuck out in the middle of the night. Climbed the fence. They shot at me and grazed my shoulder. But I managed to get out. I stay close. Because she has my child in there." He exhaled.

"Your child?"

"Yes, my son. I had to leave him in there with her. I-I saw things I couldn't agree with. I tried to stand up to her, but ended up having to escape in the middle of the night instead. I have been living out by the marshes since, hiding."

"What kind of things couldn't you agree with?"

He sighed, looking at his fingers. "It's just, if she finds out I betrayed her, she's a dangerous woman."

"Why do you say that?"

He drew in a deep sigh. It felt like a warning. "She's preparing them for war."

I wrinkled my forehead. "War? Has she used those words?"

He nodded, his eyes meeting mine. "Yes. That she wants to create a new world order."

"Do you have proof of that?"

He nodded. "They use Discord, the app. They have virtual communities there where they talk to others outside of the compound. I have it on my phone."

He pulled out his phone and showed me a chat. My jaw almost dropped at the rhetoric used.

"And how is she planning on doing this?" I asked.

"She has weapons, lots and lots of them. My ex tried to warn me about it, saying that it was dangerous, but I didn't believe her. Yes, we were shooting guns, but it was to defend ourselves, Amelia said. And I believed her. Till one day I went into the room myself and saw it. Enough weapons for an entire army. I knew she had a couple of guns because she'd train us in shooting them, but this? This is sick. This is not for self-defense."

I stared at him, and couldn't believe what I was hearing. And then it hit me. Pastor Amelia Hawthorne had been buying weapons with my parents' money that they donated thinking it went to a good purpose. This was insane. It angered me to a whole new level.

I found a picture of Madison and showed it to him. "Do you know this girl?"

He studied her face then shook his head. "She looks familiar but no, I don't think so. Who is she?"

"She's a girl who was murdered recently. We found her body in the creek, out close to where you live."

"Oh. I saw the police there, but stayed away. Couldn't risk being seen."

"Did you have anything to do with it?"

"No. Don't even know what it was about."

I studied him for a few seconds to determine if I believed him or not. Then I showed him a picture of Joanne. "This is her mother. She was part of the cult once too, she told me. You know her?"

Kyle stared at the picture, and I noticed he was barely able to breathe all of a sudden. Tears streamed down his cheeks.

"That's-that's Lucy. My ex."

"Lucy?"

"Yes, that's her."

"She must have changed her name, probably to hide. What happened to her?" I asked.

"She ran away one day. She got pregnant and Amelia, well, she said she needed to get rid of the child, that it was the Devil's spawn. I didn't believe Lucy when she told me about the weapons, and I believed everything Amelia said until one day when I finally opened my eyes… Wait you said she's the girl's mother?"

I saw the terror in his eyes, and felt my heart drop. "Yes."

"And how old is she?"

"She was ten."

He stared at me, unable to speak and barely breathe.

"What's going on?" I asked. "Kyle, are you okay?"

He stared at Madison's photo, then touched it gently like he was caressing her cheek. That's when it hit me.

"You're-you're her dad, aren't you? You were with her while

you two were in the compound, and she was pregnant when she left?"

He nodded, tears streaming across his cheeks. Soon he was sobbing heavily, and I handed him a box of tissues, then gave him a bottle of water. This was horrible. Absolutely awful. Kyle had never seen his daughter and now she was gone. It was almost too much to bear.

"Do you know any of the other girls?" I asked and showed him pictures of Kayla and Jenna.

Kyle stared at them, then shook his head. "N-no."

"Do you know any reason why Amelia would want to kill them?"

"I-I don't know. I have never seen her hurt any children while I was at the compound. Do I think she's capable of it? Heck, yes. That's why I worry about my son. This woman is insane. There's no telling what she might do. All I have of him is the shirt you found at my campsite."

I nodded. "Okay."

I swept the last of the photographs across the table, my eyes burning into each image as if I could force the secrets to rise like ghosts from the glossy surfaces. The faces of the victims stared back at me. I leaned back in my chair, the clock ticking against the wall—time was slipping away, and with it, the chance to stop Amelia before another life was lost. "Okay, thank you. You can leave but don't go far."

I got up and left Kyle in the room. I walked to my office.

"Team, in here," I called out, my voice cutting into the quiet hum of the precinct.

Tom and Scott filed in, each carrying the same resolve that had become etched into my very being. We circled around the evidence, a constellation of determination in the dim light.

"Amelia's playing a dangerous game," I started, tapping a photo where her piercing gaze seemed to challenge us. "And she's not doing it alone."

"Do we have anything we can nail her for?"

I handed Scott my phone. I had asked Kyle to download the app and log in so I could keep the evidence. "Scott, I need you to get on this and pull out everything that is a threat to our society."

He looked at it, then up at me. "This is crazy."

"It sure is. Threatening the security of our government."

"That's terrorism under Florida law," he said.

"Yup. Enough to give us a reason for a warrant," I said, feeling the worry gnaw at my resolve. This could end badly if we weren't careful. "The cult has been gathering weapons. Stocking an army. And the rituals Joanne mentioned to me worry me greatly. There could be something even worse going on here. They could have Jenna."

"We'll need SWAT then, and maybe FBI?" Tom said.

"Exactly." I stood up, pacing now with an energy that seemed to feed off the urgency of our task. "We've got one shot at this. We need to move fast, hit them before they can react, and get Amelia in custody."

"Stakeouts could spook them," Scott said, always the voice of caution. "We could start there."

"Not a choice," I replied sharply. "We sit back, we lose more lives. If they have Jenna Hart, we need to move. Now."

"Billie Ann's right," Tom chimed in.

"All right, I'll set it all in motion. I'll call Judge Cramer, he will be able to move fast on this and then we gear up," I said, clapping my hands together, the sound a call to action. "Communications check at eight o'clock, then we move out. Tom, you're with me; we'll take point on the approach. Everyone else, support and containment."

"Got it, boss," they echoed.

"Remember, Amelia is not just some two-bit criminal," I reminded them, my gaze fierce. "She's smart, manipulative, and deadly. And she has an army. Stay sharp."

"Understood," they responded, their nods solemn.

"Let's bring her down," I said, the finality in my voice reflecting the gravity of our mission. "And hopefully get Jenna back to her mother."

"Let's do it," Tom agreed, determination coloring his tone.

"Stay safe," Scott added. He was always the cautious one.

"Always," I replied, the thought of my children flickering through my mind, the court's warning echoing like a distant thunder. This was exactly why I couldn't have my children. Because of the danger I was around. But this was bigger than personal stakes; this was saving a life, pure and simple. I had to put someone else's child before my own, and that was my job.

I made the call while my team got ready for whatever lay ahead. I spoke to the Chief who gave us the go ahead, then notified the SWAT team and briefed their leader on the situation and how it could potentially get very dangerous. They were ready, they said. The FBI team came out of the sheriff's department in Rockledge, and they would be ready to go in a matter of minutes.

"Let's end this," I said, stepping toward the door, the team falling into step behind me. The precinct faded away as we moved into the growing darkness outside, each of us carrying the weight of the coming confrontation, ready to face whatever horrors awaited us in the heart of The Last Days cult.

"Gear up," I snapped, the words crisp in the charged silence.

Boots scuffed on concrete as my team mobilized, the clink of metal and the rustle of Kevlar filling the air. I checked my own gun, the weight familiar in my palm.

"Rifles loaded?" I asked.

"Check," Tom confirmed, his eyes sharp.

"Comms?"

"Clear and running," Scott replied, tapping his earpiece.

"Good." I holstered my weapon and surveyed the team. We

looked like a storm about to break—dark, determined, ready to unleash.

"Remember, we're not just going up against Amelia," I said, meeting each of their gazes. "We're going up against a belief. These people think she's salvation."

"Delusion can be stronger than truth," Scott said.

"Which is why we stick to the plan." My voice was steel. "No heroes today. We operate as one."

"Copy that," they chorused.

"Visuals?" I eyed the body cams clipped to their vests.

"Live feed to HQ," Scott confirmed.

"Let's make this count." I led the way to the vehicles, the night air clammy against my skin. The faint hum of the swamp in the distance was like a siren call, beckoning us forward.

"Watch each other's backs," I instructed as we piled into the SUVs. "And keep an eye out for anything out of place."

"Always do," Tom said, loading his rifle.

The engines roared to life, headlights cutting swathes through the darkness. We left the safety of the precinct behind, each mile bringing us closer to the heart of darkness.

"Approaching target location," I announced over the radio as the swampland enveloped us.

"Copy, Wilde," came the response from HQ. "Eyes in the sky confirm minimal activity on the ground. You're clear to engage."

"Roger that." I glanced back at my team, our reflections flickering in the rearview mirror. Resolve etched into every line of their faces.

"Time to end The Last Days," I said, and the car fell silent but for the growl of the engine.

We were ready—for justice, for confrontation, for anything Amelia and her followers could throw at us. The road ahead was dangerous, but so were we.

THIRTY-THREE

BILLIE ANN

The parking lot of our building was filled with a variety of law enforcement vehicles. Black-and-white cruisers, unmarked sedans, and heavy-duty SWAT vans all crowded together in a controlled symphony of flashing lights and revving engines. My boots crunched on the gravel as I made my way through the maze of vehicles, my eyes scanning for any signs of trouble. This type of operation didn't happen often, but when it did, things could go wrong quickly. Needless to say, I was on edge, my stomach twisting with worry and anticipation for what was to come.

"Listen up," I called out in the humid air. Heads turned, attention snapping to me like iron filings to a magnet. "We got one shot at this. Our priority is Amelia's safe extraction and the apprehension of any hostile subjects."

"Rules of engagement?" An FBI agent peered at me over a clipboard.

"We need to be on the defensive. Starting a war is not an option." My words were sharp and left no room for argument. I surveyed the faces in front of me: some were fresh out of training, while others showed signs of exhaustion from sleepless nights. They all nodded, knowing the seriousness of the situation.

"SWAT, you're on breach and entry," I continued. "Snipers, I want eyes on every window. No surprises."

"Got it, Wilde," came the gruff acknowledgment from the SWAT commander, his gear rattling with every movement.

"Communications?" I asked, locking eyes with the officer manning the radio.

"Check, Detective Wilde. All channels are live."

"Good. Keep 'em clear unless it's mission-critical."

The convoy formed into a steel serpent, cars and trucks slotting into place. I slid behind the wheel of the lead vehicle, my hands steady despite the nervous energy coursing through my veins.

"Convoy, roll out," I said into the radio, my voice a calm command.

Tires bit pavement, engines growled, and we moved as one toward the cult's compound. I kept the line open, giving orders, receiving updates.

"Approaching target location," I announced. The compound loomed ahead, a fortress of secrets. It was now or never.

"Positions, people."

The compound emerged from the dusk, a cluster of buildings crouched behind a tangle of barbed wire. My pulse quickened as I keyed the mic. "Perimeter teams, take your marks."

"Roger that," crackled the response.

I steered my cruiser to the north side, headlights lighting up the twilight. The rest fell in line, a choreographed maneuver that hemmed in the compound. No one was slipping away on my watch.

"Kill the lights," I ordered, and darkness swallowed us whole. A moment passed, doors opened and closed in soft thuds as my team disembarked. I followed suit, my boots hitting the ground with purpose.

"Ready the megaphone," I ordered, my voice barely above a whisper. An officer nodded, handing it over with a solemn expression.

"Amelia!" My voice boomed as I raised the megaphone, pressing the button. "This is Detective Billie Ann Wilde. We have the place surrounded. Surrender and release any hostages. Do it now.

"Your followers," I continued, a tremor of urgency beneath the words, "lay down your weapons. Walk out unarmed. This is your only warning."

Silence hung heavy for a heartbeat, or two. The compound stood mute, defiant. Then, a light flickered on inside, and shadows moved against the windowpanes. They were listening. Now they had to choose.

"Your threats mean nothing!" A voice echoed from within the compound, raw and scornful. The silhouette of a man appeared in the lit window, arms raised as if to challenge the night itself.

"Stand down," I shouted back, gripping the megaphone tighter. "Don't make this hard."

Laughter, high and unhinged, spiraled from behind the barricaded doors. More figures joined the first, their chants rising into a cacophony of defiance.

My jaw clenched. I fought the urge to hurl the megaphone like a grenade, to shatter their misplaced loyalty with my own hands.

"Last chance," I warned, each syllable a hammer strike. "We're coming in."

As if on cue, the night shattered. Gunfire erupted, an angry buzz saw ripping through the stillness. It was coming from the compound. Bullets zipped past us, close enough to kiss death.

"Down!" I hit the dirt, the world narrowing to my racing heart and the scent of earth. "Cover!"

"Shots fired!" I heard my voice crackle over the radio, instinctively reaching for my sidearm.

"Return fire! Aim for suppression!" Commands peeled off my tongue, automatic, drilled into muscle memory.

The team responded, a volley of controlled bursts answering the compound's wild rage. Dirt kicked up around me, a staccato dance as I crawled to the cruiser for cover.

"Keep your heads down," I barked into the radio. "Stay sharp!"

The night had turned predator, and we were locked in its jaws, every sense strained for survival. This was no longer just about Amelia or proving my worth. It was about making it out alive—for me, for my team, for the slim chance of seeing my kids again.

My breath came in short bursts, eyes darting between shadow and light. The compound loomed, a fortress of fervor and madness, its walls spitting fire at us.

"Bravo Team, hold the line!" I shouted above the din of gunfire. "Charlie, get that SAW singing!"

"Copy, Wilde," came the terse reply, punctuated by the heavy thud of the machine gun laying down a rhythm of authority.

"Delta, move up! Covering fire on my mark!" I was the conductor orchestrating our survival, every note a bullet, every rest a chance to breathe.

"Mark!" Bullets soared overhead, creating a deadly canopy.

"SWAT, this is Wilde." I toggled the radio, crouching behind an armored vehicle. "We need multiple entry points. Front and back, simultaneous breach."

"Roger that," the SWAT leader's voice was calm, collected. "Teams Alpha and Echo are prepped. We go on your signal."

"Three minutes. Sync watches." My thumb pressed down

hard, like I was trying to leave an imprint on the device. "Expect heavy resistance."

"Confirmed. Three minutes."

"Get those flashbangs ready," I added, wiping sweat from my brow with a forearm. "And tell HRT to stand by. We may need them."

"Understood."

The plan was set—a calculated risk with lives in the balance. We had three minutes to turn chaos into precision, pandemonium into order.

"Stay sharp, everyone." I cast a glance over my shoulder, meeting the eyes of men and women who put their trust in me. "We're bringing everyone home tonight. Alive."

"Home," someone echoed softly, almost lost beneath the gunfire.

"Move out!" Above the staccato of gunfire, my voice was a sharp command that had my small unit advancing toward the north end of the compound. Gravel crunched underfoot, while chaos erupted around us.

"Steady," I murmured, eyes locked on the metal door ahead. We snaked between overturned vehicles and debris, a serpentine line of grim determination. A bullet ricocheted off metal nearby, a harrowing ping that sent a shiver down my spine.

"Close ranks," I ordered, hand signals conveying urgency in the dimming light. The team responded in kind, a tight-knit cluster with weapons braced.

"Breaching charges," I said tersely, nodding at the door. Officer Martinez, compact and lithe, stepped forward, his movements precise as he set the charge. Seconds felt like lifetimes as we waited, the digital countdown blinking red.

"Cover your ears!" I shouted over my shoulder, fingers keyed into my earpiece. "Bravo team, we're going in."

"Copy that, Wilde." The response was clear, crackling with static.

"Three... two... one..." Martinez pressed the detonator. A deafening boom shattered the night, the door blown inward in a maelstrom of smoke and splintered metal.

"Go, go, go!" I propelled myself forward, leading the charge into the haze. The world narrowed to the beam of my flashlight revealing dust and debris, the smell of explosives heavy in the air.

"Clear left!" an officer called out, his silhouette sharp against the flash of muzzle fire.

"Right side secure!" another voice barked back, controlled amidst disarray.

"Keep the line open," I instructed, navigating deeper into the belly of the beast. My heart thrummed against my ribs, each beat a reminder of what was at stake—the safety of my team, the lives within these walls, the quiet hope of seeing my children again.

"Status?" I demanded.

"Entry team in position," came the swift reply. "All points covered."

"Good. Eyes peeled, everyone. Let's find Amelia Hawthorne, their leader." My voice was steel; it had to be. For them, for me. For the result we were all desperate to grasp.

"Roger that," they echoed, a chorus of resolve fueling our advance.

"Stack up," I hissed, motioning with a gloved hand. The corridor ahead was narrow. My team fell in line behind me, a silent promise in the set of their jaws.

The next door loomed, a barrier between us and them. I nodded at Martinez, who readied another charge, his movements precise and practiced. But before he could set it, the door burst open from the inside.

"Contact!" I yelled as figures emerged, their silhouettes distorted by the stark backlighting.

Gunfire erupted. I dropped to one knee, sighting down my

weapon. One-two-three, controlled bursts. Cultists fell, but more surged forward, their fanaticism rendering them impervious to fear.

"Push forward!" I called, reloading on the move. My team advanced, covering each other in a deadly dance. The cult members fought with a zeal that chilled the blood, but our training held firm against their fervor.

"Billie Ann, watch your six!" The warning came just in time. I pivoted, blocking a wild swing from a makeshift club, and countered with the butt of my rifle. The cult member crumpled, and I spared no second glance.

"Corridor clear!" Tom's voice cut through the din of battle.

"Keep moving!" My command was redundant; they were already in motion, instincts honed to razor sharpness. We swept room after room, methodical despite the adrenaline that threatened to overrule thought.

"Staircase up ahead," Scott reported, pointing. "Amelia has to be above."

"Breaching stairs!" I took point again, every muscle coiled for the assault. We ascended in a rush, boots pounding on the metal steps.

"Top floor," I whispered into the comm, "get ready to breach."

"Ready," they echoed, a ragged breath shared among warriors.

"Three... two... go!"

The door gave way to our charge, and we spilled into a larger chamber. Resistance met us head-on, a wall of bodies determined to protect their prophet.

"Fall back!" a cultist screamed, but his words were lost in the roar of gunfire.

"Stay tight!" My voice was a lifeline in the maelstrom. We moved as one organism, each officer an extension of my will to end this without further bloodshed.

"Billie Ann, left flank!" The call from Tom snapped my attention to a hidden alcove. I swung around, firing. A few men and women stumbled, taken by surprise.

"Clear!" The shout rang out, almost drowned by the ringing in my ears. I scanned the debris-littered space, chest heaving.

"Amelia?" I croaked, my throat raw from smoke and shouting.

No answer came, just the echo of our victory, hollow against the cost. We'd won the fight, but the war for Amelia's soul was far from over.

The chamber was silent, a stark contrast to the chaos behind us. Amelia sat on a makeshift throne, flanked by her disciples. They were statuesque, eyes fixed forward, betraying no intention of surrender.

"Amelia." My voice was loud in the stillness, steady but forceful. "This ends now. Let's talk."

Her eyes met mine, sharp and calculating. "Detective Wilde, how kind of you to join us."

"Enough blood has been spilled." I stepped closer, my team fanning out, guns trained on every potential threat. "It's over."

"Over?" A wry smile curled Amelia's lips. "You see an end. I see devotion."

"Your followers are scared, Amelia. They're just kids." I glanced at the faces around her, so young and yet so lost. "They need guidance, not manipulation."

"Guidance," she echoed, mockingly. "Is that what you call your laws? Your handcuffs?"

"Better than chains of false belief." I inched forward, trying to reach her humanity. "Come with me. Spare them this."

"Detective..." She paused, her gaze shifting past me. My instinct screamed, turning my head. My heart stopped.

There in the middle of it all, my parents sat among the followers, their expressions serene in the madness.

"Mom? Dad?" My heart lurched.

"Billie Ann," my mother's voice was soft, "we've found peace here."

"Peace?" It was a punch to the gut. "With her?"

"Sometimes we must leave behind what we love for a greater good," my father said, his voice hollow.

"Greater good?" I echoed, the words like ash in my mouth. My eyes darted between the cultists—the unwavering stares, the eerie calm. Then it hit me, an icy dread coiling in my stomach.

"Amelia, what have you done to them?"

THIRTY-FOUR

BILLIE ANN

They were all there, sitting too still, too quiet. A shiver ran through me—something was wrong.

"Hello?" My voice echoed off the walls, a feeble attempt to stir life into the scene. No one moved. It was as if I'd stepped into a photograph, a moment frozen in time. Their eyes were open, but they saw nothing.

My gaze darted around, heart racing. Pill bottles. Dozens of them, empty, littering the ground like casualties of war. I knelt, picked one up. The label was stark, the word "cyanide" hitting me like a punch to the gut.

"God, no..." The bottle slipped from my fingers, bouncing softly on the floor. This couldn't be happening. This was a nightmare.

I stepped over the discarded bottles, my eyes scanning the sea of stillness. I approached my parents.

"Mom! Dad!" The words tore from my lips before I could catch them. My dad turned slightly, and my heart lurched. Clutched in his hand was the unmistakable shape of a capsule.

"Billie Ann," he said softly, his voice a ghost of its former strength.

I lunged forward, stumbling over my own feet in desperation. "Dad, please." My voice broke. "Don't do this."

He looked at me, his eyes brimming with a cocktail of emotions. Fear, love, doubt. The capsule hovered at his lips.

"Put it down," I begged, my tears spilling over, tracing hot tracks down my cheeks. "Please, Dad. For me."

His hand shook. A moment stretched between us, filled with the weight of unspoken words and lifetimes of memories.

"Look at me, all of you!" My voice rose above the silence. The cult members stirred like a field of wheat touched by an uneasy wind. Their eyes found mine, glazed with devotion to a woman who promised them salvation.

"Amelia doesn't care about you!" I shouted, my throat raw with urgency. "She's using you!"

A woman rose, her movements dreamy, detached. "Amelia is our light," she murmured, and others nodded, their faces masks of eerie calm.

"Your light has led you into darkness." My plea bounced off the walls, hollow and ineffectual. "She's not a god. She's—"

"Silence!" a man barked. His gaze bore into me, fierce and unyielding. "We have chosen."

"No, you've been brainwashed!" Desperation laced every syllable.

But it was too late. One by one, they turned away from me, hands trembling as they brought the fatal capsules to their lips.

"Mom! Dad!" I screamed, reaching for them, my hands flailing in the void between us.

"Billie Ann, we love you," my mother said, her voice a whisper lost in the madness. Their eyes met mine, a silent goodbye, before they tilted their heads back and swallowed death.

"Stop!" I cried out, but my words fell on dying ears.

The room filled with a symphony of agony, bodies writhing, lives slipping away in a grotesque dance. I could only watch, helpless, as the people I once knew and loved convulsed, claimed by Amelia's final, cruel command.

Their chests rose and fell, slower, shallower. "No," I whispered, fists clenched at my sides. I pressed my radio and called for help from the ambulance on standby.

"Billie Ann..." My father's voice was barely audible, a breeze that could've been mistaken for the sigh of the room itself.

"Stay with me!" I pleaded, voice cracking, hands reaching out to cradle their faces, to anchor them to life. But their skin was growing cold, the light in their eyes dimming like dusk falling on what used to be home.

"Please, don't leave me," I begged, pressing my forehead against my mother's still hand. Tears spilled over, tracing the battle lines of a war I'd fought too late, too alone.

"Dad?"

"Love... you..." The words tumbled from his lips, disjointed and fading.

"Fight it! You have to fight it!" But even as I screamed, I knew the battle was lost. Their bodies stilled, and something inside me, something vital, fractured. I shook him, trying to get him back to life, but he faded in my hands, his pulse growing weaker by the second.

"Mom? Dad?" My voice was a ghost, haunting the shadows of what remained. Silence answered, a heavy cloak wrapping around my shoulders.

The compound spun, reality a blur of faces and whispers. I fell to my knees, the cold floor a jarring contrast to the heat of my tears. Grief burned my throat, guilt a relentless drumbeat in my chest.

"I'm sorry," I sobbed into the still air. "I should've saved you."

Rage and sorrow clashed, a storm that threatened to sweep me away.

And there I stayed, kneeling among the ruins of faith and flesh, the compound's silence a testament to the cost of blind belief.

Gasping for breath, I raised my head. A lifeless form caught my eye, a few paces away. It was Amelia. Her body sprawled across the ground, eyes staring blankly at the ceiling. She lay motionless.

"Amelia?" My voice was hoarse, disbelieving. No answer came. "You did this," I whispered.

Boots thudded on the floor as paramedics swarmed in, their sure hands and calm voices clearing a path through the fog of despair.

The compound, once filled with murmurs of blind devotion, now echoed with urgent commands and the rasping breaths of those clinging to life. As they worked, the paramedics' efficiency cut a stark contrast to the panic that had ruled mere minutes before.

Tears blurred my vision—tears of grief for lives lost, of relief for those spared, and of guilt for not arriving sooner. My hands shook uncontrollably, each tremor a quiet accusation. I should have known. Should have stopped this.

"Detective Wilde, you okay?" A paramedic, a young man with concern etched on his face, offered me a hand.

"Don't worry about me," I said, accepting his help to stand. "Just-just do what you can for them."

"Of course. We'll take care of them." He turned back to his task, leaving me to face the aftermath alone.

The air was thick with loss. Around me, the reality of Amelia's manipulation lay bare—the price of unquestioned faith written in the still forms of her followers. I had seen it before, the way a single idea could twist and break the human spirit. But never like this.

"Blind faith," I whispered to the empty husk of the compound. "You never see the cliff until you're over the edge."

Tom came toward me, his face twisted in distress. "Please at least tell me we found Jenna Hart," I said.

He shook his head. "We searched the entire compound. We found the weapons, enough for an army, just like we were told."

"But no Jenna?"

"No Jenna."

I stepped outside, into the flashing lights. It was over for the cult, for Amelia, but it would never truly be over. Not for those who'd been lost. Not for those who survived. And certainly not for me. As I looked back at the crumbling facade of the compound, I felt more lost than ever.

If you're not here, Jenna, then where are you?

THIRTY-FIVE

BILLIE ANN

I barged through the sliding doors of the emergency room, my boots clacking against the sterile floor. Each step echoed my frantic heartbeat. I scanned the sea of white coats and scrubs, searching for a face to tell me, *Your parents are going to be okay.* But nobody looked up.

"Chief, any word?" My voice came out sharper than I intended.

Chief Harold was standing there, her eyes a softened steel. "They're still in there, Billie. Docs are doing their best."

"I need to be doing something." I paced, the motion somehow a release valve for the anxiety churning inside me. "Jenna's still out there. I have to—"

"Billie, listen." Chief Harold's voice was firm, her hand reaching out to still my frenetic movement. "My teams are on it. Right now, you need to be here for your folks."

"Being here doesn't help them." I stopped pacing, but my leg bounced with pent-up energy. "Or Jenna."

"Your job is to wait right now," she said, the creases around her eyes deepening. "That's an order."

I slumped into the sterile hospital chair, a cold anchor in the sea of uncertainty. The walls of the waiting room closed in, posters about heart health and flu shots mocking me with their normalcy. My hands, those of a detective who had pieced together uncountable puzzles, now shook, fumbling with the frayed edges of my jacket.

"Billie, you've done everything possible," Chief Harold said, her voice a lifeline.

"Everything but the right thing," I muttered, staring at the linoleum floor, tracking the scuff marks with my eyes as if they were clues that could lead me to some semblance of control.

"Hey." Her tone was softer now, closer. "This isn't on you."

"Isn't it?" I shot back, my voice sharp enough to draw a quick glance from a passing nurse. "If I hadn't—"

"Stop," Chief Harold interrupted, her command leaving no room for argument. "You're only human, Billie Ann."

"Too human," I whispered, the words barely escaping before I clamped my mouth shut, trapping the rest inside. They simmered there, a bitter stew of guilt and fear. The loss of my nephew last year still tasted like bile. All the victims I never managed to save that I should have.

Minutes stretched into eternities, each second ticking by with excruciating deliberateness. I heard the shuffle of footsteps, the distant beeping of machines, the undercurrent of hushed conversations. Sounds that should have been comforting, but instead felt like an auditory assault on my already frayed nerves.

"Detective Wilde?"

My head snapped up. It was the doctor, his scrubs a color that didn't seem to exist outside hospital corridors. His expression was unreadable, a poker face I'd encountered too often in interrogation rooms.

"Please." The word escaped before I could think, a plea wrapped in a veneer of professional composure. "Tell me."

He took a breath, and I braced myself, every muscle tensed for the blow.

His steps halted a mere foot from where I stood, the sterile scent of antiseptic wafting from his green garb. "Detective Wilde," he began, his voice clinical yet not unkind, "I wish I had more definitive news for you."

"Tell me," I urged, my hands balling into fists at my sides.

"Both of your parents are stable for the moment," he said, his eyes holding mine with an unwavering steadiness that both reassured and unnerved me.

"Stable," I echoed, a thread of hope weaving through the tightness in my chest. "But the cyanide…"

He sighed with professional burden. "Cyanide is a fast-acting toxin. It's miraculous they survived long enough to receive treatment."

"Miraculous doesn't sound like a medical term, Doctor." My voice was flat, the detective in me demanding facts over platitudes.

"Fair point," he conceded with a slight nod. "The antidote was administered promptly, which undoubtedly saved their lives. However…"

"However?"

"However, we're not sure about the extent of the damage," he continued, his gaze unwavering. "Cyanide disrupts cellular respiration, and even with the antidote, there can be… complications."

"Complications such as?" I pressed, needing to grasp the cold, hard edges of reality.

"Potential impacts on cardiac function, neurological issues, even peripheral nerve damage," he listed methodically. "We've seen cases where recovery is full, and others where there are lasting effects. Right now, it's a waiting game."

"Waiting," I repeated, the word tasting like ash on my tongue. "For how long?"

"Days, possibly weeks. We'll keep them under close observation," he assured, though the comfort it should have brought was diluted by the gnawing uncertainty.

"Thank you, Doctor," I managed, the gratitude genuine despite the turmoil churning within. "I'll be here, waiting."

"Of course." He gave a curt nod, then turned, leaving me with the echo of his words and a vigil to keep.

My gaze clung to his retreating back as he left the room, the echo of his steps a reminder that we weren't through the worst yet.

Tears broke through, hot and unchecked. They spilled down my cheeks. I felt like I was going to pass out, and the Chief saw it. She rushed to me and grabbed me in her arms. Chief Harold's grip tightened, her arms a bulwark against the waves of despair that threatened to pull me under.

"Harold..." The name came out as a whisper, a plea.

"Let it out, Billie Ann," she urged gently.

"Saved them... but Jenna..." I gasped between sobs, the words tangling with breaths.

"We're still looking. We still have boots on the ground at the compound and we've searched the area and the rooms twice more. There's nothing else incriminating there, but we won't stop until we find her." Her voice was a low rumble, steady in the storm.

"Promise?" My voice cracked.

"Cross my heart." The oath felt sacred, coming from her.

"Thank you," I breathed, my tears soaking into the fabric of her uniform.

"Don't thank me. We're family here."

Family. The word resonated within me, filling spaces hollowed by loss and fear. In the chaos left by the cult, Harold's presence was a constant. Unyielding. A lighthouse in the dark.

"I can't lose anyone else," I said, the words almost lost in her embrace.

"You won't. Not on my watch."

I nodded, clinging to her like a lifeline thrown into tumultuous seas. As minutes stretched, our hold didn't wane. Two protectors amidst wreckage, finding solace in shared strength.

"Stay strong, Detective Wilde," she murmured, her breath warm against my ear.

"Will do, Chief," I managed, pulling back just enough to meet her gaze. "Together."

"Always."

And there, in the sterile halls of the hospital, we held onto each other.

THIRTY-SIX

BILLIE ANN

I stepped out of the hospital, the sliding doors shuddering shut behind me. My legs dragged with every step. The night was almost over, and I was left alone. I needed sleep—the kind that erases and heals—but it dodged me, a slippery shadow just out of reach.

The sterile scent of antiseptic clung to my clothes as I made my way to the car. The quiet hum of fluorescent lights and distant moans filled the air, a constant reminder of the hospital's eerie atmosphere. I tossed my keys from one hand to the other, their jingle a hollow sound in the empty parking lot.

"I'll check on Mom and Dad tomorrow," I murmured, making a mental note as the car unlocked, and I slipped back to work mode. I couldn't help but wonder if I should dig deeper into the interviews with Jenna's parents, friends, and school. Maybe there was something I missed. There had to be.

The streets were lined with the skeletons of trees swaying slightly in the breeze. My mind replayed the hospital—the monitors, the beeping, the hushed tones of doctors. Worry for my parents gnawed at me, a relentless pest.

I reached for my phone. It slipped against the sweat of my

palm. Peter. His name was a splinter lodged deep. I pressed call, my thumb unsteady, betraying the anger churning inside me.

"Pick up," I said, tapping the steering wheel, each tap a tick of the clock, each second stretching longer than the last. The ringing taunted me before it stopped abruptly.

"Billie Ann?" Peter's voice crackled through the speaker, cautious, maybe even guilty.

"Peter, this is on you," I said, my voice raw in the quiet car. "Our parents are lying in hospital beds because of Amelia."

"Billie, I can't—" he started, but I cut him off. I knew he wouldn't want to talk to me about the cult, as he never would, especially not after our fight. But he had to. This time he simply had to.

"No, you don't get to dodge this. You brought them into that-that madness. If not for you—"

"Billie, listen to me!" Peter's voice rose, a sharp edge in his usual calm. "I walked away from all that years ago. You know I did. Mom and Dad, they chose to stay. They believed in it."

"Believed?" My laugh was bitter, hollow. "Is that what we're calling it now? Belief? They're nearly dead because of belief?"

"It's not that simple," he said, and I could picture him, running a hand through his hair in frustration. "I tried to get them out, but they wouldn't listen to me either."

"Convenient, Peter." The words were like venom, and I hated the way they sounded, even as I spat them out. "You introduce them to a poison and then wash your hands clean when it starts to kill."

"Damn it, Billie! It's not fair to put this on me. They're adults. They made their choices!"

"Fair?" I echoed, laughter devoid of humor coloring my tone. "Tell me about fair when I'm standing over their hospital beds, wondering if they'll even wake up! And you're talking about choices?" My voice cracked in the cramped space of my car. "They're in comas, Peter. Choices don't land you there; manipulation does."

"Billie—"

"Save it!" I shouted, the phone pressed so close to my ear I could feel the heat of my own rage emanating from the speaker. "You can't undo this. You can't."

The line crackled with our heavy breathing, his attempts at reconciliation, my refusal to hear them.

"Goodbye, Peter." A guillotine blade severing the call.

I tossed the phone onto the passenger seat, its bounce echoing in the silence that now filled the car. Alone. With each breath, I tried to draw in calm and exhale the storm inside me.

The road led me on autopilot, and before I knew it, the beach was beside me, the early morning's sunrise lurking below the horizon. I rolled down the window, letting the salt air rush in, mingling with my erratic breaths. The rhythmic crash of waves against shore reached out like a lullaby for frayed nerves. For a fleeting moment, the chaos within was quieted by the ocean's timeless song.

Jenna, Kayla and Madison, their faces flickered like broken film reels behind my eyelids. How many nights had they spent fearing the dark? How many secrets did they keep that could unravel this whole twisted case? I clenched the steering wheel as if I could squeeze the answers out of it.

I opened my laptop and began sifting through all the leads, searching for any errors or missed questions that could lead me closer to finding her. I reread every statement the team had gathered from neighbors, friends of each girl, and witnesses. There were new testimonies from those closest to Jenna, from the bus driver who was supposed to have taken Kayla to school, but nothing stuck out to me as a fresh lead. I needed to figure out what to do next, who to talk to. I couldn't let my emotions get in the way; I needed to be focused and methodical in my search for Jenna.

Every instinct as a detective screamed that time was slipping through our fingers like sand. Jenna's safety hung by a
thread, woven into the cult's sinister fabric. If I could just pull
the right one, the whole thing would come undone.

"Kayla didn't make it," I whispered, the words a bitter taste
in my mouth. "But Jenna... Jenna might still have a chance. But
where is she?"

The silence answered back, indifferent.

Then, like a lightning strike, it hit me. My heart pounded.
The clue, the one detail I had overlooked—it danced at the edge
of my memory, elusive yet insistent.

"Think, damn it, think!" I growled, racking my brain. There
was something Jenna had said, a fragment of a conversation so
mundane I had nearly missed its significance. But what?

I couldn't let it slip away, not when Jenna's life might hinge
on this slender recollection. My hands shook, adrenaline
replacing exhaustion, as I forced my mind to replay every inter-
action, every word exchanged.

"Come on, Billie," I urged myself. "You're so close."

The secret clawed at the edges of my consciousness,
demanding to be acknowledged. A shadowy puzzle piece
waiting for its rightful place in the light. I exhaled slowly,
allowing the waves' rhythmic crashing to anchor me back to the
present.

"Remember," I breathed. And there, in the space between
the sea's whispers and the sunrise's embrace, it surfaced.

My fingers curled around the steering wheel, knuckles
whitening. The pieces clicked, connections forming in my
weary mind. I threw the gear into reverse, tires biting into the
gravel as I spun the car around. No time for second-guessing.
No time for what-ifs.

The engine roared to life, its growl mirroring the fierce
resolve settling in my chest. Streetlights blurred into streaks of
amber and white as I accelerated, each one propelling me faster

toward an answer that had been hiding in plain sight. The road stretched before me, a taut ribbon in the darkness, leading me to where instinct told me I needed to go. An urgency pulsed within me, each beat a reminder of the stakes at play.

As the cityscape gave way to open roads, my thoughts sharpened, homing in on the task ahead. The investigation's weight mingled with personal battles—a custody fight, a reputation to mend—each demanding its due. But now, they forged a steel resolve in my core.

I could feel the change coming, the precipice of truth just within reach. The night air whisked through the cracked window, carrying the salty tang of the ocean, a fleeting comfort amidst the chaos. My grip on the wheel was steady now, each turn bringing me closer to a revelation that could shatter lives or salvage them.

"Everything changes with this," I whispered to the empty passenger seat. The road stretched onward, and with it, my will to unearth the truth. For Jenna. For Madison. For Kayla. For every innocent caught in this twisted web.

I realized it wasn't over as I jolted my car forward, speeding into the darkness, a lone comet under the morning sky, racing against time itself.

THIRTY-SEVEN

BILLIE ANN

I sat there, shoulders hunched, eyes burning from the glow of the computer screen, following up on my lead. My fingers rested on the keyboard, static but ready to spring into action as soon as my brain unearthed the next clue. The station was quiet, the kind of stillness that seems to amplify every little sound—the hum of the vending machine, the distant echo of footsteps. I rubbed my temples, willing away the fatigue at the edges of my mind. The lead I'd found could only be investigated from the office. My own laptop housed a limited amount of data from our central server.

"Billie Ann?" Scott's voice broke the silence. "Why the early call?" His long curly hair looked like it hadn't seen a comb since yesterday, and dark circles shadowed his eyes.

"Got something," I said without turning. The words came out flat, heavy with the weight of unspoken details.

Tom loomed in the doorway behind Scott, his wide frame making Scott look even more disheveled by comparison. He stifled a yawn with one hand, the other rubbing his neck. "You better have a pot of coffee brewing if you want us to function at this hour."

"Check the break room." My gaze didn't waver from the screen. Every second counted, and I was not about to let exhaustion be the thief of time.

"All right, lead the way, Scott," Tom said, already heading toward the promise of caffeine. They had been working tirelessly for way longer than they should and deserved a longer rest, but there was no time to waste. Tom had been going from door to door in the neighborhood, while Scott had gone through Jenna's computer looking for connections to any of our other suspects, or suspicious activity. So far, he'd found nothing of consequence.

Scott lingered, studying me for a moment before shrugging off his concern and following Tom. I listened to their retreating steps, allowing myself a brief moment of stillness before delving back into the abyss of data.

Scott and Tom shuffled back into the room moments later, cradling steaming cups of coffee, bringing me one as well. They settled in with creaking chairs and sighs.

"Spill it," Scott said, brushing a lock of hair from his eyes. The steam from his coffee fogged up his glasses momentarily.

"Here's what we've got," I started, flicking a glance at both of them. Their attention, undivided and expectant, anchored me to the moment.

"Okay, Billie Ann, we're all ears," Tom added, his voice still rough with sleep. He took a slow sip, the muscles in his jaw working as he braced for my next words.

I pointed at my computer screen, where tabs lined up like suspects in a line-up. "I went online. Thought outside the box."

"Surfline?" Scott raised an eyebrow.

"Exactly." I clicked on a folder labeled "Beach Cams." "They have webcams all over the beach. Footage for weeks."

"Smart." Tom leaned forward, his interest piqued as he set his coffee down.

"Footage from when?" Scott asked, scooting his chair closer.

"Focused on the weekends." I scrolled through files. "When Kayla's grandmother swore she was with Jenna. On the beach."

"Any luck?" Tom's voice cut through the hum of my tired machine.

"More than luck," I replied. "We've got eyes on the past."

I double-clicked the file, and the beach scene bloomed to life on the screen. The sun cast a golden hue over the sand, shadows of palm trees stretching like long fingers across the beach. There she was, Kayla, her figure small against the vastness of the ocean.

"Wait for it," I murmured, my finger hovering over the pause button.

"Who's that?" Scott leaned in closer, his face reflecting the blue light from the monitor.

"Shh," Tom elbowed him softly, his eyes never leaving the screen.

The video played on. Kayla trudged through the sand, her body language uneasy. She stopped, scanning the beach—then he stepped into frame. John Harris.

"Jesus," Scott whispered. He looked at me, then back at the screen. "That's—"

"Madison's stepfather," I finished for him. "This is who she was meeting when she asked Jenna to lie for her."

Tom's hand froze mid-air, coffee cup halfway to his lips. His eyes were wide as saucers. "Is he...?"

"Yup." No denying it. Onscreen, John's arms enveloped Kayla in an embrace. Not fatherly. Not innocent.

"Did Joanne know about this?" Scott's voice was tight, almost accusatory.

"Can't say." I shrugged, keeping my tone even. "But this changes the game. I was wrong. I might have lost us time by focusing on Amelia."

"You don't know that." Tom set his cup down with a thud, coffee sloshing over the rim. Amelia had been declared dead on arrival, so there was no way we were getting any more answers from her.

"This is twisted. But what we found at that compound was extremely alarming. And I for one am glad we were able to confiscate all those weapons. It could all be connected."

"Do you think John could have murdered both girls?" I posed the question to both of them, knowing it hung in the air, heavy and dangerous.

I clicked off the video, the image of John Harris and Kayla frozen in my mind. "He was paying her," I said flatly, staring at the blank screen. "You will see it at the end of the video. He hands her a couple of bills."

Scott's jaw clenched. "For what?"

"Guess." I met his gaze, letting the implication hang heavy between us. "Kayla needed money. She came from poor conditions and didn't have what her peers had. We know that much. And John... we know he had particular interests. He could have been paying her for photos? Videos?"

"Christ." Scott ran a hand through his curly hair, pushing it back from his forehead. "And Madison?"

"Maybe she saw something. Maybe he..." I didn't finish the sentence. Didn't need to.

"Disgusting," Scott spat out the word like it tasted foul.

Tom leaned back in his chair, the wheels squeaking under his weight. Then he tapped on his computer and let out a small gasp. "John isn't in custody anymore. He was granted bail yesterday."

I rose to my feet. "What?"

"You heard me," he said and turned the screen so I could see the records.

"You've got to be kidding me! Why? Why hasn't anyone told us? I was so sure that no judge would ever grant him bail."

"This one did," Tom said. "It was a hundred and fifty thousand that the judge probably didn't think he would be able to pay, but he did."

"Holy..." My brain started ticking through the timeline.

Scott and Tom exchanged a look, the same question in both their eyes.

"So where is he now?" Scott asked.

My fingers drummed on the desk as I pieced it together aloud. "Let's go."

"Where, Billie?" Tom pressed, urgency in his tone.

I started for the door. "Just come with me."

"Billie," Scott started, caution in his voice, "you sure about this? We should probably talk to the Chief before we do anything rash. Especially you. You're tired. You've been pushing hard. You just said you made a mistake with—"

I cut him off with a raised hand. "Don't patronize me, Scott. I'm onto something. This isn't about proving myself to some damn court. I can't think about myself here and whether or not it might destroy my chances of ever getting my children back. I know I'm supposed to stay out of trouble, but I have to do this. It's about justice and saving a life."

"All right," he conceded, but I could see the concern etched in the lines around his eyes.

"Time to unravel this mess," I affirmed, stepping toward the door, my mind already racing ahead to the confrontation that awaited us.

THIRTY-EIGHT

JENNA

Jenna's breath hitched. Shadows cloaked the room, every corner an inky abyss. A cold sweat broke across her forehead.

"Hello?" she whispered, her voice a mere wisp in the void.

No answer. Only the creak of the old house settling—or something more sinister lurking beyond her field of vision? She strained her ears, seeking the comfort of a familiar sound, but found none. Then, a faint groan of hinges. The door edged open, a sliver of light from the outside world lighting up the darkness. It widened, an ominous creak accompanying its slow movement.

"Who's there?" Jenna's voice quivered, betraying her fear. Her eyes darted frantically, trying to penetrate the gloom that now seemed to advance toward her.

"Please," she begged, "say something."

But there was no answer.

"Who are you?" Jenna's pulse whooshed in her ears.

The silence was a tangible force, smothering her cries. Then, without warning, rough hands fastened around her arms. They were vice-like, unyielding. Jenna gasped, the sound sharp in the quiet room.

"Let go of me!" Her voice rasped with terror, but the hands clamped down harder, their grip relentless.

She twisted, trying to throw off her unseen assailant. A grunt, the only acknowledgment of her struggle. Jenna's fingertips clawed at the wood floor as she was yanked forward, her nails catching on the uneven planks. Splinters bit into her flesh, and she winced, the sting a cruel reminder of her reality.

"Please—stop!" Her plea echoed back at her, mocking, unanswered. The dragging persisted, every motion an agony of fear and confusion. Each jolt sent shots of pain racing up her arms, muscles straining against the force that propelled her deeper into darkness.

"Help! Somebody, please!" Jenna's voice cracked as she yelled. The words bounced off the walls, a hollow sound. The hope of rescue was dwindling with each passing second. Her breaths came out in short, sharp gasps, each one panic-infused.

"Anyone... please..." The tremble in her voice was palpable.

The hands released their grip abruptly. Jenna's body hit the ground with a thud, her limbs splayed across the cold, hard floor. She lay there, a shivering heap, the chill seeping into her bones.

"Is anyone there?" Her teeth chattered as she spoke, her body convulsing with uncontrollable tremors. Silence, heavy and oppressive, was her only answer.

"Devil's child," the voice slithered through the darkness, a hiss that seemed to come from everywhere and nowhere. Jenna's heart clenched. "You cannot hide what you are."

"Who are you?" she gasped, her voice thready.

"Your judge." The reply was cold, detached.

Jenna felt a presence looming over her, a weight of malice that pressed down on her chest. She tried to scramble backward, but her limbs were heavy, unresponsive.

"Let me go," she pleaded, barely whispering.

There was a pause, a moment suspended in time where

only her ragged breathing filled the space. Then pain erupted in her abdomen, sharp and all-consuming. Jenna screamed, a raw sound torn from her throat. Her body arched off the ground, hands clutching at the invisible blade of agony.

"Please, stop!" Her cries shattered the silence, but there was no mercy in the shadows that held her captive.

Jenna felt the blood as it was soaking her clothes. She winced, her breath hitching. "What have you done?" she whispered through the pain, her voice shaky. "Help," Jenna choked.

"Nobody can hear you." The voice was taunting, close yet disembodied.

"Please..." Jenna sobbed, her plea trailing off into silence. She knew the truth; she was in peril, alone and wounded in the dark.

Jenna's consciousness wavered, each heartbeat a drum of agony in her ears. The metallic tang of blood filled her mouth, mingling with the tears that streamed down her temples into the cold embrace of the floor. Gritting her teeth, she tried to muster the strength to move, to escape, but her body refused, leaden and betraying.

"Am I going to die like this?" she whispered.

The silence was her only answer, mocking her, confirming what she already knew. There would be no heroic rescue, no last-minute reprieve. The pain was a relentless tide, pulling her under, and Jenna felt herself sinking, the edges of her world blurring and receding.

"Mommy..." She whispered it like a prayer, an apology. She would never know what happened, why she didn't come home. It pierced her heart sharper than her physical wounds, this thought of leaving her behind, lost and wondering.

"Fight," she urged herself, the word a hiss between clenched teeth. But her body ignored the command, too damaged to obey.

Her eyelids fluttered, heavy as stone. Jenna let out a shuddering breath, the act itself a monumental effort. The darkness crept closer, a comforting blanket ready to smother the flames of her life.

"Keep fighting," she murmured, the mantra weak but determined.

In the abyss that cradled her now, amidst the throes of a pain so profound, Jenna held onto that sliver of hope, fragile and flickering. It was the stubborn spark within her, unwilling to be extinguished, that carried her through the night, waiting for dawn or deliverance, whichever came first.

THIRTY-NINE

BILLIE ANN

We burst through the door to John's house, our guns leading the way. My pulse hammered in my ears, a rhythm set to the pace of danger. Tom's broad frame shouldered past me, his movements surprisingly graceful for a man his size. Scott followed, his curly hair a dark shadow across his intense eyes. I had no idea if the evidence we had found even gave us the right to confront John again, but I'd had enough. Perhaps I'd lost all sense of logic. I was using my experience, following a hunch. And if Jenna was in here, I needed to find her. I was glad to have my two friends by myself supporting me in this.

"Clear," I whispered, peering into the murky stillness of the living room. Tom nodded, his gun sweeping the corners with precision.

Scott's calm voice came from behind, "Kitchen's all clear."

I could sense his low hum of concentration as he surveyed the room. The kitchen was spotless, with gleaming countertops and a sparkling sink. Pots and pans hung neatly above the stove, and the smell of freshly brewed coffee lingered in the air. It was a stark contrast to the chaos that we'd been anticipating.

I could feel Tom's presence beside me, a solid reassurance.

Scott's steps were nearly soundless as he checked behind doors, under tables.

"Anything?" Tom asked, his voice barely above a breath.

"Nothing yet." The words felt heavy on my tongue. We knew this house like the backs of our hands by now after countless searches. Every room told the same story: absence, emptiness.

"Stay sharp," I urged. We advanced, our weapons ready, our senses straining for the hint of a threat that had brought us charging into this place.

A scream sliced through the tension like a knife. My heart skipped, then doubled its speed, beating against my ribs.

"Back of the house!" Scott's voice was urgent, his words a trigger.

We ran, our boots pounding on the hardwood floors. Tom's gun was first, aimed and ready. The hallway stretched before us, and I was certain the girl's voice had come from just beyond the door in front of us. The scream echoed again as we reached the old wooden door to the kitchen. We burst through it. A tableau of horror greeted us—Jenna, sprawled like a discarded puppet, her clothes soaked in crimson. Over her hovered a shadow, a black pillowcase shrouding her head.

"Stop it!"

The woman's hands stilled, hovering above Jenna's still form.

Her head swiveled, slow, deliberate. Her eyes locked with mine, wide and wild. Madness gleamed there, a fervor that chilled my blood.

"Joanne?" I said, surprised.

"I'm saving us," she hissed in icy certainty. She placed the knife on the girl's throat.

And that was when the last piece of the puzzle fell into place for me. I had expected to find John here, but it wasn't him we had been chasing all along.

It was Joanne.

"You're-you're Lucy, aren't you?" I said. "You're Lucy Everhart, Kyle Donovan's girlfriend, and together you were the parents of Madison? You were in the cult together."

"One step closer and I will slit her throat," she hissed. "And don't think I won't. It needs to be done. Jenna is... she's the Devil's spawn. I'm saving her."

My grip on the gun didn't falter, but my voice trembled with emotion. "Saving? What are you talking about, Lucy?" I demanded, trying to make sense. "And what does Madison have to do with this? Tell me everything!" I glanced over at Scott and Tom, who were in readiness nearby. They remained silent, allowing me to take control of the situation for now. I exchanged a meaningful look with Joanne, hoping she would give me some answers before it was too late.

"Madison?" A twisted smile curled her lips. "Oh, she was just the beginning."

I closed in, my determination solidifying. "Speak up!" My eyes scanned Jenna's body, assessing the severity of her wounds. Was it necessary to act quickly? Had she lost too much blood? I couldn't ignore the sight before me: Jenna's pale skin, her trembling hands, and the pool of blood slowly spreading beneath her. I assessed the situation, quickly determining that Jenna needed help urgently before it was too late. I moved closer, ready to take action and save her at all costs, keeping the conversation going to distract Joanne from hurting her more.

"Did you hurt your own daughter?"

"Everything I did, I did for a reason." Her answer was a serpent's whisper, coiling around the room. Her gaze never left mine, as if she was trying to make me understand some unfathomable truth.

"Reason? There's no reason for this!" I spat out, disgust and disbelief tangling together.

"Madison... she seduced him!" Joanne's words slithered out,

poison laced with a perverse sense of justification. "She wanted him, embraced the sin—"

My stomach churned, a vile wave in my throat. "Seduced? She was just a child, Joanne. Your child!"

"Age is but a number for a soul corrupt." Her voice was eerily calm, as if discussing the weather instead of a monstrous act.

"Your husband, Joanne," I pressed. "Where does he fit into this madness?"

"Where he always has." A shrug, cold and dismissive. "At her side, where she wanted him."

"Dammit, Joanne!" The space between us crackled with unspeakable tension. "You're talking about murder."

"Justice," she corrected, a manic glint in her eyes.

"Justice?" My voice roared, raw and ragged. "Killing your daughter is justice?"

"Sometimes," she whispered, "the Devil wears the face of an angel. And the angel must fall."

"Is that what you tell yourself at night?" I demanded, every fiber of my being rejecting her twisted logic. "To sleep after snuffing out your own flesh and blood?"

"Sleep?" Her laugh was hollow, devoid of humor. "Who said I sleep?"

Joanne's face twisted, her lips curling into a sneer. "She trusted me," she said, her tone dripping with disdain. "When I picked her up as she walked to school. Like a lamb to the slaughter."

"Trusted..." The word was heavy and sour. I could feel my pulse thundering in my ears. "You betrayed her trust."

"Betrayal?" Joanne laughed sharply. "No, Detective Wilde. It was salvation."

"Salvation." I echoed, tasting the word's bitterness on my tongue. "You call this salvation?"

"From the evil she carried," Lucy retorted, her eyes wild with conviction. "From the darkness within her."

"Madison was a child!" I shot back, my hands clenched so tight my knuckles were white. "Your child!"

"Child or not, she needed to be stopped."

"Stopped. By killing her?" I asked, incredulous. "Your husband abused her, didn't he? And you found out. But it wasn't her fault. It was his. He is the adult. He is the one who is sick."

"No, you got it all wrong. She was the sick one. From the moment she was conceived. They all told me she was the Devil's spawn. I didn't believe them but when I caught them together, I finally saw the light. She needed to be stopped. She wanted this, and seduced him. I needed to stop her. By any means necessary," she replied, her gaze unflinching.

"Any means..." I shook my head, trying to comprehend the depths of her delusion. "You lost it while at the compound, didn't you? They drove you mad. You're sick."

"Am I?" She raised an eyebrow, a challenge etched into every line of her face. "Or am I the only one seeing clearly?"

"Seeing clearly?" I laughed, but there was no humor in it. "You see nothing but your own twisted reality."

"Twisted?" She leaned in closer, her breath foul with the stench of madness. "No, Detective. I've never seen more clearly."

"Clearly enough to murder your daughter?" I pushed out the accusation.

"Clearly enough to save her soul," she countered, a perverse righteousness radiating from her.

"Save her soul?" I felt sick, the room spinning with the gravity of her insanity. "By taking her life?"

"Life is fleeting," Joanne murmured, almost to herself. "Eternal peace is the true gift."

"Peace?" I scoffed. "You think you've given her peace?"

"Peace from this wretched world," she replied, her eyes distant, lost in her own twisted belief.

"Madison didn't deserve this," I stated flatly.

"Deserve?" Her lip twitched. "We don't always get what we deserve, do we, Detective?"

"Enough games, Lucy," I said, using her birth name to try and get through to her as I stepped closer. "What about the other girls? Kayla, and the mark you carved into her skin. That was just to make us look toward the cult, wasn't it? When I visited you, and we talked about the mark—but you were just sending me there, weren't you? I get that, but why Kayla and now Jenna? Why?"

"Love?" Joanne's mouth twisted into a grotesque smile. "You see, love is complex, Detective. Sometimes, it demands sacrifice."

"Sacrifice..." I whispered, the horror of her logic dawning on me. "You sacrificed your own daughter."

"Sometimes," she said, her voice barely above a whisper now, "that's what love requires."

"Love doesn't require murder, Lucy," I said, my voice rising. "It requires protection, care—"

"Care?" she cut in sharply. "I cared enough to end her suffering."

"End her suffering?" My fingers twitched, longing to shake sense into her. "What suffering?"

"The suffering of being who she was." There was a cold finality in her voice.

"You played God, Lucy."

"God?" A manic light flashed in her eyes. "No, Detective. I am the savior."

"Savior," I repeated, feeling a chill creep up my spine. "You saved no one."

"Saved..." Her eyes glazed over, her grip on reality slipping.

"I took her to the creek, and let her run, then hunted her down like the beast she was."

"She was still alive when you threw her in the water," I said. "The autopsy showed that. And Kayla? What did you do to her?"

"Oh, the same. I snatched her up on the way home from school, and took her to the creek, where I stabbed her first then let her try and run. Then I caught up with her and stabbed her again, before putting her in the water. To cleanse her. She too was seducing John."

I stared at her, the madness reeking from her face. "And Jenna? Was she one of John's victims too?"

"I found pictures," she hissed. "On his old iPad. I knew who she was, Kayla too. Lots of pictures. They needed to be punished for what they did."

I couldn't bear listening to anymore of this. But it made a twisted kind of sense as to why Joanne had seemed indifferent to what had been found on John's computer. "Put the knife down," I ordered. "Or we will have to shoot you. And believe me we want to."

I stepped closer, gun raised, my voice calm and steady. "Lucy, Joanne, I need you to drop the knife. We don't want any more bloodshed tonight."

"Too late for that, Detective." She smiled, her grip on the knife tightening. "I'm not afraid to die. I have done what I came for. They've all been washed clean of the mark of the beast."

I swallowed hard, trying to ignore the fear that was creeping up on me. "You're delusional. You're going to go to prison for this."

"No." She shook her head, her eyes gleaming with defiance. "I am not. They'll see it as a righteous act."

I signaled to my partner, Scott, to get ready. He nodded and slowly approached from behind, gun drawn. I knew the risk we were taking, but we had to protect everyone else. As he moved closer, Joanne's eyes locked onto him, and she looked ready to make her move.

In a sudden burst of movement, Scott fired two shots. Joanne collapsed to the ground, her twisted delusions and dark secrets finally coming to an end. I exhaled, feeling a mix of relief and despair. It was over, but the tragedy still lingered, like a heavy fog over us. I ran to Jenna and took her in my arms. She was weak but she was alive.

As we waited for the ambulance and medical examiner to arrive, I couldn't help but think about what we had just encountered. The darkness that Lucy had allowed to consume her had turned her into a monster, a sinister force that had taken the lives of innocent children. How had she become so twisted? How could anyone, even a mother, turn to such evil? It was a question that would haunt me for a long time.

EPILOGUE

One week later

I clutched the phone tighter, my breath hitching as I awaited the words that would unfold the next chapter of my life.

"Billie Ann," my lawyer's voice broke through with a clarity that seemed to pierce the room, "the judge granted your visitation rights. Every other weekend, starting this month."

"What? You're kidding me. What happened?"

"Apparently you have friends in higher places. Your boss, Chief Harold, wrote to the judge and vouched for you. Said you were her best employee and that the children would be safer with you than anywhere else. She added evidence on how you saved some girl's life recently, and stopped a terrorist organization. The judge agreed to give it a try. It's on a trial basis, so don't mess it up."

A wave of relief crashed over me, so potent it was nearly physical. My lips curved into a smile that felt like it might split my face—an uncharacteristic burst of emotion for someone who lived in the crosshairs of skepticism and control. "Thank you," I managed, more exhalation than speech.

"Thank your friend the Chief. And stay out of trouble," he reminded me, his tone half-joking but underlined with the weight of my past months. I responded with a laugh that didn't quite capture the gravity of his advice but expressed my elation, nonetheless.

"Will do," I said and ended the call.

I set the phone down gently, as if the news it had delivered was a delicate creature that might be startled away. A small, almost rebellious fist pump escaped me, a gesture reserved for moments alone like this—when the walls I built could momentarily crumble without witnesses.

Turning on my heel, I made my way to the kitchen, the familiar sound of my feet against hardwood grounding me. The kitchen counters gleamed under the muted light, a testament to my efforts at creating a semblance of order within the chaos that often surrounded me.

I reached for a bottle of wine nestled in the corner, its label a reminder of celebrations long deferred. The cork gave way with a satisfying pop, the sound marking the end of an arduous battle and the beginning of something new—hope, perhaps, or at least a step toward it.

I poured the crimson liquid, watching it cascade into the glass, the color deep and rich. Each glug promised a moment to revel in the victory, however small, against the backdrop of battles still to be fought. In that pour, there was anticipation—not just for the first sip, but for the weekends to come, for laughter and warmth and the chance to be Mom again, not just Detective Wilde.

The glass filled, a perfect measure of triumph and trepidation, the aroma rising to tease my senses. I brought the glass to my lips, the cool rim promising a balm for the weariness that clung stubbornly to my bones. This was good news worth savoring, a rare sweetness in a life that demanded relentless fortitude.

"Cheers," I whispered to the empty room, to the children

who were now a tangible part of my future once again, to the hope that seemed to grow with each passing second. "To new beginnings."

The first sip of wine was like a deep, calming breath. I set the glass down on the counter, my eyes losing focus as I sank into thought. This case, it was a winding labyrinth with so many turns it made my head spin just to consider all the angles.

I tapped a finger rhythmically against the countertop, the sound echoing in the silence of my apartment, a metronome to my contemplations. Each tap was another piece of the puzzle falling into place, another secret brought to light.

"Joanne," I mumbled under my breath. She was dead and gone, and so was Amelia. Both of them had been crazier than I thought humanly possible. And then there was John Harris. The thought of him sparked a flare of anger, his average face and cold demeanor a stark contrast to the dark currents that ran beneath. His arrest had been quiet, uneventful even, but the ripples it caused were anything but.

"Convenience store clerk by day, monster by night," I said to no one, my voice barely above a whisper. The walls of the kitchen seemed to close in as the reality of what we'd uncovered pressed down on me.

I reached for the wine again, needing the grounding effect it promised. Joanne's secrets, John's hidden life—it was all too much, too heavy. But it was progress, undeniable progress. Each revelation was a step closer to justice, a promise that we could keep others safe from the likes of him.

The finish line was in sight, however blurred it may have seemed. My parents had woken up, and I had gone to see them. They regretted what they had done, and told me it was over. When I told them everything, they finally came to their senses, and understood what Amelia had done to them and so many other people. If my parents were going to have health trouble later due to this, only time would tell, the doctor had said.

I drained the last of the wine and set the glass down with a soft clink, my mind segueing from the parents in their beds, recovering, to another kind of victim. Jenna. The hospital had been her temporary sanctuary, a place where she could heal from more than just physical wounds. There was talk she'd be discharged soon—good news that should've lightened the heaviness in my chest.

"Come on, kid," I whispered, envisioning Jenna's tentative steps out of that sterile room, "you can do this." A small smile crept onto my face at the thought of her recovery, mingled with a sigh for her ordeal.

The phone buzzed—a text from Jenna's mother, replying to my text earlier asking her how they were holding up:

> *We're doing okay. Taking it one day at a time. Thank you for everything, Billie Ann.*

> *Of course*

I thumbed back, the glow of my phone screen casting shadows across the kitchen tiles.

But Jenna's secrets—God, they were like acid on my conscience. She had spilled them to me in hushed tones, her eyes darting around as if the very walls might whisper them back to John Harris. How he had lured her and Kayla, how money exchanged hands on that desolate stretch of beach... money paying for their favors, and pictures that he would take. My fingers curled into a fist, nails biting into my palm.

The taste of bile was rising in my throat. The truth a vile thing sometimes, a revelation that made you wish ignorance wasn't just bliss, but an option.

The silence of my apartment pressed in on me, a stark reminder of the solitude that came with the badge, the sacrifice.

But there was no time for self-pity—Jenna needed justice, and I'd be damned if I didn't deliver it.

I stepped out onto the balcony, the evening air a balm for my troubled thoughts. The city's hum was a distant lullaby, the stars above indifferent witnesses to the chaos below. I leaned on the railing, letting the day's weight settle on my shoulders.

A glass of wine remained clutched in my hand, its contents forgotten as images of Jenna, frail and haunted in that hospital bed, flickered behind my eyes. The mother's face, lined with worry and exhaustion, haunted me just as much. Their gratitude was a heavy mantle; her hope for Jenna's continuing recovery, my silent prayer.

The doorbell's chime shattered the stillness, an unexpected intrusion. My head snapped up, heart hammering a sudden staccato rhythm. Curiosity pricked at me, mingled with an odd sense of anticipation. Who could it be at this hour?

"Coming," I called out, more to steady myself than to inform the visitor of my approach. I set the wine down with a careful precision that belied my inner turmoil.

Taking a deep breath, I unlocked the door and swung it open. There she stood—Danni. My chest tightened, a cocktail of emotions flooding my system.

"Hey," I managed, my voice a hoarse whisper.

"Billie Ann..." Her name for me always sounded like music, even now, when the night seemed filled with unsung melodies.

My smile broke free, unbidden and genuine, lighting up my face. Relief softened the lines around my eyes. The world outside faded away; in this moment, there was only her—Danni, the woman who understood my silence just as well as my words.

"Didn't expect to see you," I admitted, stepping aside to let her in.

"I thought I'd pop by," she said simply, and something warm

unfurled within me—a hope that maybe, just maybe, the timing was finally right.

"Come in," I said, stepping back to usher Danni inside. Her presence seemed to fill the room, pushing away the shadows that had settled in my corners. "I've got something to celebrate."

The apartment felt warmer with her there, as if she carried sunshine in her pockets. I fetched the bottle of wine from the counter, still uncorked, and filled two glasses. The ruby liquid glinted in the dim light, promising a shared moment of reprieve.

"Cheers," I said, handing her a glass, my grin broad and unguarded. "To good news."

"Billie Ann," she started, her voice trailing off, not mirroring my enthusiasm. She hadn't touched the wine, her hand frozen mid-air.

"What's wrong?" My heart, just recently aloft, plummeted at the sight of her downturned eyes.

"Mike... the kids..." Danni's words tumbled out in fits and starts, her usual fluency gone. "I can't do this anymore. I'm going back to him—for the twins. They need me."

The glass slipped from my fingers before I could think to stop it, shattering against the hardwood floor, red splashes staining the grains like blood. My pulse throbbed in my ears, a silent scream stuck in my throat. The man had cheated on her. They had been separated a year now. I had thought she was finally moving on. And now this?

"Danni, you can't mean that." My voice was barely a whisper, my lips numb.

"I have to think of what's best for them," she said, her eyes brimming with pain. "I'm so sorry, Billie Ann."

The air was suffocating, her words crushing me. My hands trembled, reaching for something, anything, to steady myself. But there was nothing—only the echo of our fractured future ringing hollow in the room.

I lurched forward, my hand outstretched, grazing the fabric of her sleeve. "Danni, please."

She sidestepped, a dance we never practiced. "I can't, Billie." Her voice was light, but it landed like a blow.

"Talk to me. We can figure this out." Desperation in every word, thick and tangible.

She shook her head, a gentle refusal, and backed toward the door. "There's nothing left to say."

"Damn it, Danni!" Anger flared, hot and quick, but it died as soon as I saw the finality in her steady gaze.

"Take care of yourself," she said, her term of endearment feeling more like a sentence.

Her lips pursed, blowing a kiss that would never land: an invisible marker of our parting.

The door closed with a soft click, sealing the warmth of our shared past. My fingers curled into a fist, nails biting into flesh, trying to hold onto something already gone.

Tears breached the dams of my eyes, unwelcome torrents carving tracks down my cheeks. The sobs came next, racking through me, an earthquake shaking the foundation of my resolve.

I found myself on the floor, knees drawn up, arms wrapped around them. Each breath was a shudder, each exhale a whimper. The taste of salt on my lips mixed with the metallic tinge of despair.

"God, Danni." The words were muffled against my knees. Alone. The emptiness echoed, a cavernous void where her laughter once lived.

The air grew thick, the silence of my apartment oppressive. I let out a ragged breath, in my heart the void was too immense to fill. Lifting my head, the room spun, a carousel of memories flashing—Danni's smile, her touch, our laughter now ghosts in these walls.

The detective in me craved control, but she was buried

deep beneath layers of pain. I pushed up, my body heavy, as if wading through wet concrete. My legs faltered, a stark reminder of my newfound fragility.

"Damn it." The curse was a puff of air, a futile attempt to rally. The wine bottle lay on its side, the last drops bleeding onto the counter—wasted. Like us.

My fingers traced the rim of her glass, still standing tall. It mocked me with its stability, its ability to remain upright when I couldn't. With a swipe, I sent it shattering against the wall, watching the fragments fall like the pieces of my composure.

"Billie Ann Wilde doesn't break," I said, trying to convince the reflection in the mirror. But the woman staring back, with red-rimmed eyes and slumped shoulders, had never looked so defeated.

"Doesn't she?" The question taunted. The badge on the table glinted, catching the light. A symbol of order, of strength. How could I uphold justice when my own life was in disarray?

"Tomorrow," I declared to the empty room. "Tomorrow, you get your act together."

But the night stretched ahead, hours of Danni's absence. I wrapped my arms around myself, a poor substitute for her embrace. Sleep would be a battle tonight, each tick of the clock a reminder of what I'd lost.

"Where do we go from here?" The whisper barely made it past my lips, the question directed at no one, at nothing. There were cases to close, leads to follow, lives to piece back together. But mine? The path forward was obscure, uncharted.

"Wherever it is," I breathed out, "you'll walk it alone, Billie Ann." And that truth, cold and unyielding, settled into my bones, promising no respite from the ache.

A LETTER FROM WILLOW

Dear reader,

Thank you for choosing to read *Find My Girl*. If you did enjoy it, and want to keep up to date with all my latest releases, just sign up at the following link. Your email address will never be shared, and you can unsubscribe at any time.

www.bookouture.com/willow-rose

I hope you loved the story, and if you did I would be very grateful if you could write a review. I'd love to hear what you think, and it makes such a difference helping new readers to discover one of my books for the first time.

The idea for this story came to me when I heard about the Madeleine Soto case. She was a young girl who disappeared here in Florida, close to where I live. Her stepdad was the first suspect, because he had dropped her off on her way to school, but said he didn't take her all the way there. The police found inappropriate content on his computer and arrested him for the murder of his stepdaughter. The other part of the story, the cult part has been with me for quite a while, and actually from before I began even writing this series. I knew Billie Ann's family were involved with a cult and that was why she wasn't talking to her brother. Now, the story of the cult and the police raiding the compound is actually taken from real life, which makes it even more crazy. And the real life story is even more insane than this one I just offered you. You can read about the fifty-one days of siege in Waco, Texas here:

https://www.history.com/topics/1990s/waco-siege

And a personal story from one of the survivors here:

https://www.rnz.co.nz/national/programmes/ninetonoon/audio/2018640102/waco-survivor-grace-adams-this-is-where-i-am-now

It's truly scary what religious leaders can make their followers believe and do, and I needed to write about that. I hope you enjoyed it.

I want to shout out a huge thank you to my editor Jennifer Hunt for helping me make this book come to life and for believing in me and this series.

Don't forget to leave a review if you can, it means the world to me,

Take care,

Willow

www.willow-rose.net

facebook.com/authoroleary

x.com/madamwillowrose

instagram.com/willowroseauthor

bookbub.com/authors/willow-rose

PUBLISHING TEAM

Turning a manuscript into a book requires the efforts of many people. The publishing team at Bookouture would like to acknowledge everyone who contributed to this publication.

Audio
Alba Proko
Sinead O'Connor
Melissa Tran

Commercial
Lauren Morrissette
Hannah Richmond
Imogen Allport

Cover design
The Brewster Project

Data and analysis
Mark Alder
Mohamed Bussuri

Editorial
Jennifer Hunt
Charlotte Hegley

Copyeditor
Janette Currie

Proofreader
Jon Appleton

Marketing
Alex Crow
Melanie Price
Occy Carr
Ciara Rosney
Martyna Młynarska

Operations and distribution
Marina Valles
Stephanie Straub
Joe Morris

Production
Hannah Snetsinger
Mandy Kullar
Jen Shannon
Ria Clare

Publicity
Kim Nash
Noelle Holten
Jess Readett
Sarah Hardy

Rights and contracts
Peta Nightingale
Richard King
Saidah Graham

Printed in Great Britain
by Amazon

60301118R00163